IRON MASTER

SHIFTERS UNBOUND, BOOK 12

JENNIFER ASHLEY

JA / AG PUBLISHING

ONE

"*S*tuart."

She was the only one who called him Stuart. The rest of the Shifters and the two humans he worked for called him *Reid*, except for Graham, the Lupine clan leader, who called him *That effed-up, weird, dark Fae shit*.

Peigi had only ever called him Stuart since the day he'd helped rescue her from a feral Shifter compound and traveled with her to the Las Vegas Shiftertown. She was still the only Shifter who didn't take a few steps back from Stuart when they smelled the taint of Faerie on him.

Peigi came up behind him as he stood in the darkness, gazing across the moonlit desert at the edge of Shiftertown.

"What is it?" she whispered.

Stuart didn't share the same sense of smell as the Shifters he lived among but he always recognized the faint orange and cinnamon, like a winter tea, that brushed Peigi's skin. She'd told him once, when he'd commented on it, that it was her shower gel, but for Reid, the scent meant *her*.

"I don't know." Reid studied the silent expanse of sky touched by the glow from Las Vegas's lights.

He should have known better than to believe he could slip out of the house in the middle of the night without Peigi noticing. She not only had Shifter hearing but looked after six orphaned cubs. She could hear a leaf fall.

"Something must have made you wander out at three in the morning," she said. "You hate getting up early."

"I thought I heard …" Reid broke off as he heard the whisper again, the one that had cut through his dreams.

Come to me …

It was like music, a song familiar but unremembered. Beckoning, calling, urgent, unrelenting.

"Shit," he whispered.

"What? What do you see?"

"It's not what I see. What I hear."

Peigi peered past him into the darkness. "Which is?"

She must not be touched by the silvery sound, the pull. *Come …*

"One of my people. Calling me."

"Your people …" She trailed off in worry.

Stuart nodded grimly. "The *ðokk alfar*, yes."

"How?" Peigi scanned the empty lots at the end of Shifter-town's row of houses, land left undeveloped because few humans wanted to live near a Shiftertown. Wind danced in the dry weeds, cold and sharp in the January night. Even Las Vegas grew cold in the winter, temperatures sometimes dropping to below freezing at night.

"I don't know how." Stuart heard his voice sharpen and softened it for her. "They shouldn't be able to talk to me."

Exile meant *exile*. Cut off entirely from his home, from the few people he knew who were still alive, even from his old enemies. The high Fae had locked him into the human world for many years now. Stuart had managed to go back only once, to rescue a Shifter woman and her human mate who'd believed in him when he'd given them no reason to.

After that the gates had closed again, permanently, and here

Stuart was. But exile wasn't so bad these days, not with the woman who stood behind him, Shifter-close, in the way Shifters did. Her warmth, her breath on the back of his neck, was the only thing at the moment keeping Reid from full-blown rage tinged with panic.

"Go back to bed," he advised.

Peigi's snort of derision ruffled his hair. "Sure. Leave you alone with someone Fae calling you through thin air? 'Cause that always ends well."

"They must have tapped the ley line."

"Which is closed. Graham and Eric made sure."

Reid wanted to turn to her, bathe in her strong beauty, the tall bear Shifter who made him wonder how he ever thought Shifters less than amazing. But he kept his eyes on the darkness in case anything charged at them out of the night, like a thousand angry high Fae with glittering swords. Peigi was right—dealings with Faerie never ended well.

"Graham and Eric aren't Fae," Stuart said. "They sealed the hole, but that doesn't mean the ley line went away."

He could still feel the magic of the line running under the houses built for Graham's nearly feral wolves who'd moved down from northern Nevada when his Shiftertown had been closed.

"We can ask them," Peigi said. "Tomorrow."

Reid scanned the air. The whisper had vanished, along with the tingle that prickled his skin through the cold of the night.

Had it been a *dokk alfar* calling to him? Or a trick of his dreams? The voice had gone, and it was difficult to be sure.

Reid took one last look around the dark lot, the blackness beyond complete. No more city after this point, just the bulk of mountains resting against the clear sky. "Yeah." He let out a breath. "Let's go back."

He felt Peigi relax behind him, and at last, he turned to her.

Her presence always smacked him like a physical blow. She was almost as tall as he was, as bears were in human form. She had very dark hair that waved back from an arresting face and eyes of deep blue that pulled at him.

He wasn't supposed to be attracted to Shifters. Feel sorry for them, sure, as they'd started as slaves to the Fae who'd fucked them up as much they had Reid's own people. Commiserate as fellow sufferers who'd kicked free.

Peigi was different. She had a strength that went beyond that of other Shifters, yet it hadn't made her hard. Compassionate and caring rather, and so very beautiful.

Reid wanted to kiss her, right here, right now. Feel her body against his, taste her lips, absorb her warmth. He slept in her house much of the time, but down the hall from her room, walls between them.

He pressed down the temptation with effort. Once Reid started kissing Peigi, he'd never want to stop.

A dark Fae and a Shifter. Could it happen?

Reid fought it, not because Shifters and Fae never mixed, but because one day, he might go home. He belonged in his own world, not this crazy one where humans ruled, Shifters lived in Shiftertowns, and people flocked to enjoy themselves in this city of games.

But Reid's world, filled with high Fae out to destroy all *dokk alfar* and enslave Shifters, was no place for Peigi and the cubs. So he fought his desires and let himself go slowly insane.

She studied him, as though knowing what went on behind his eyes. Peigi had a quietness that belied being captive for years to a crazy bear Shifter, forced to be his mate.

There was pain deep inside her, and much more besides, but on the surface, she was calm and watchful. Made Reid wonder what would happen if she ever cut loose.

"You all right?" she asked.

No. And he'd never be. "Sure," he said. "Come on. Before the cubs wake up."

She gave him a faint smile, knowing what he meant. They

were noisy, the cubs, and if they woke up too early, all the Shifters on this side of town would complain for days.

They turned and walked back together. Very close together, but their bodies never touched, no matter how much Reid wanted them to.

———

PEIGI OVERSLEPT IN THE MORNING AND BLINKED AWAKE TO bright if cold daylight.

She recalled the strange sense of wrongness that had pulled her out of the house last night to find Stuart on the edge of Shiftertown staring out into the desert, but everything seemed perfectly normal today. Her tiny room, the smallest in the house, her clothes neatly hung in the open closet, shoes lined up and waiting. Nothing out of place, and no warning inside her that all was not well.

The racket of voices down the hall told her the cubs were up. The deep rumble of Stuart's reply made her breathe out in relief.

He had been spending more and more nights in this house as time passed—he'd originally lived with the alpha bear family of this Shiftertown, but when Nell and Cormac had mated, Stuart had taken to sleeping at Peigi's to give them more room. *Not* finding Stuart in the kitchen in his DX Security shirt, making coffee and starting breakfast, had become unusual.

His room was the farthest from Peigi's, as though he needed to reassure her that he'd never come closer than she wanted, and also tell the world there was nothing going on between them.

Who knew a Fae would be shy? *Dokk alfar,* as Stuart quickly pointed out when the topic came up.

Peigi was willing, and lonely, and tired of everyone thinking she was completely broken. She was only *half* broken. Eric, the Shiftertown leader, had been wise letting her take charge of the cubs, because it had brought her back from the edge of despair and kept her alive.

Stuart was the other reason she stayed alive.

Peigi threw off the covers and slid out of bed, clad in a tank top and shorts. She was too large for the frilly nighties human women wore—bears were on the big side—but she didn't care. Tank top and shorts suited her better anyway. Easier to shift in, run, fight, or chase wayward cubs.

She pulled on sweatpants against the cold, thrust her feet into sneakers, and crept out of her bedroom, making her way to the kitchen. The first two bedroom doors she passed were open, the three girls and three boys who occupied each gone. All but one of the beds was made—Noelle usually rushed out after the others were gone, snatching sleep until the last possible minute.

At the end of the hall, closest to the kitchen and living room, lay Stuart's small bedroom. That door always remained firmly closed.

She found Stuart in the kitchen cooking up a mess of bacon, six cubs setting plates on the table. Donny, the oldest at eight, supervised, and the youngest boy, Kevin, who'd been a baby when the cubs had been rescued, had the job of carrying the stack of paper napkins. Donny watched him with the grave intensity of an alpha protecting his pack.

Peigi took a minute to study Stuart, as she did any chance she could. He was slim rather than bulky like a Shifter, but his muscles filled out his black T-shirt and his back view wasn't bad at all. His dark hair was cut short, barely touching his neck, which let her see the structure of his hard face. He was not drop-dead handsome on human terms, but his midnight eyes and intense strength lit fires inside her.

She opened her mouth to ask him if he was all right, but the cubs cut in.

"Morning, Peigi!" The greetings overlapped, filling the kitchen with high-pitched sound.

Three of the cubs were bears, though Hannah, the youngest girl, and Patrick, the middle boy, were gray-eyed wolves. Kevin hadn't shifted yet, so they had to speculate on what type of

Shifter he was. His mother had been human but died bearing him, and Peigi wasn't certain which of the feral Shifters had fathered him.

"You overslept!" Noelle, a grizzly cub, crowed in triumph. "*I* was up before you."

"Yes, sweetie, you were." Peigi moved past the crowd to Stuart at the stove. A bowl of eggs next to him waited to be broken and scrambled.

"Have you talked to Eric yet?" she asked in a low voice.

Stuart shook his head. "Graham. He's heading over."

Peigi's eyes widened in dismay. "*That's* all I need on an empty stomach."

Stuart sent her a grin. "Better eat something then."

Peigi made a face at him and grabbed a slice of bacon from the stack draining on paper towels. She didn't always like pork — she was a bear and preferred fish — but salmon was expensive. Bacon would have to do.

She helped the cubs take the rest of the food to the table — thawed berries from the freezer, a stack of toast from the eight-slice toaster, the bacon, and plenty of butter and jam. Stuart started scrambling the eggs.

The cubs had learned to wait until all the food was on the table and everyone served before they started eating. When they'd first moved in, meals had been a free-for-all, the cubs fighting for every crumb. The women confined at the compound with Peigi hadn't been much better, though they'd let Peigi, the alpha, have the first serving of any meal. They'd all lived like animals, the cubs starting to go as feral as the males who'd sequestered them.

Peigi set out the toast and bacon and allowed the cubs to dig in. They couldn't be expected to wait much longer. She was pleased to see they handed around the food politely, each taking no more than their share. Donny and Noelle made certain the younger ones had enough before they went for the rest. She warmed with pride watching them.

The scent of coffee—heavenly coffee—pulled at Peigi, and she turned back to grab a cup.

Stuart wasn't there. The eggs were sizzling, almost dry, the spatula sitting in the middle of the frying pan, but Stuart was gone.

"He teleported," Noelle informed her as Peigi stood staring in surprise. "I saw him."

Lucinda and Hannah nodded. They gazed at Peigi worriedly, waiting for her to tell them everything was all right.

She wished she could. Stuart had the ability to teleport his body to any place he wanted, provided he'd seen that place before. But he rarely used the ability, preferring to walk or jog— or drive. And he never jumped out without telling her. He could be anywhere, for any reason, and the strangeness last night made her tighten with fear.

Before she could decide what to say to the cubs, the back patio door darkened, and a bulk of a man appeared on the porch. An even bigger man stood behind him. One Lupine, one bear.

"Hey!" the Lupine yelled through the glass as he pounded on the door. "Open up. It's fucking cold out here."

TWO

Graham McNeil, the leader of the Lupine side of Shiftertown, cupped his hands to glare in the door.

This was all Peigi needed. Stuart had said he'd called Graham—but why vanish just when Graham was due to arrive?

Peigi went to the sliding door. The cubs remained at the table, round-eyed, but even a year ago, they would have run in terror, seeking a place to hide. They were getting stronger, braver, happier.

They relaxed completely when they saw the bear Shifter who'd accompanied Graham.

"Uncle Shane!" they chorused, and Shane gave them a grizzly grin.

"Hey, little ones." Shane, who bulked behind Graham, waved his big hand. "Let us in, Pegs. Graham's not wrong about the cold."

"Oh, please. This isn't cold." Peigi opened the door, letting in a wave of chill, and gestured them inside.

They'd never have entered without her permission, because this was Peigi's territory. While Peigi was nowhere near as high in dominance as Graham or Shane, they wouldn't dream of pushing their way in. First, they were respectful of territory, and second, Peigi was protected by Eric, the Shiftertown leader, and no one messed with Eric.

Plus, they knew Stuart guarded Peigi *un*officially. While Stuart didn't possess Shifter strength — as far as anyone knew — the Shifters were a little bit afraid of him. Everyone was, except Peigi and the cubs.

"Stuart isn't here," Peigi said as Graham gave the room a once-over, as though expecting to find Stuart in a corner.

Graham swung on her, his gray eyes hard. "What do you mean, he's not here? He called *me*."

"He teleported," Noelle offered.

"I thought he'd gone to see you," Peigi said to Graham.

"Obviously not. What the hell? He calls me to come see him at the crack of dawn, and he's gone? What's he doing — joy-tele-porting?"

A few of the cubs giggled, but Donny and Noelle watched in worry.

"Graham." Shane's rumble was as good-natured as always as he moved to stand at the Lupine's shoulder. "Why don't you and Peigi go talk about this? I'll hang out with the cubs. I smell fried eggs."

"Oh crap." Peigi rushed back to the stove and stirred the burning eggs, dumping them on a plate and leaving the blackest bits in the pan.

Shane's big hand was there to take the plate when she turned around. "Go. Talk."

His tawny eyes told her he knew something was very wrong, but he didn't want to upset the cubs with it.

Shane had come, Peigi knew, not so much to keep Graham under control — only Graham's mate could do that — but to reassure Peigi and her cubs. Shane was second in command to the alpha bear of this Shiftertown, his mother, Nell. Graham was in charge of the wolves, and Eric Warden was in charge of ... everyone.

Shifter hierarchy was more layered and complex than humans understood, but Shifters knew instinctively who was who, and who not to mess with.

Shane's mom was another Peigi-protector. Nell would guard her even against Eric, and so when Peigi had to deal with other Shifters, especially growly leaders like Graham, Nell made sure one of her sons was in place to help.

Peigi gave Shane a grateful nod. She walked past Graham, avoiding his stare, grabbed a jacket, and headed out the patio door. It was cold, yes, but not too bad with her sweatpants and coat. They couldn't talk anywhere in the house, because the cubs would hear, and Peigi didn't want them afraid while she figured out what was going on.

Graham understood, but he grumbled as they walked to the middle of the field that backed the houses on this street.

"Okay, let's talk. Make it fast. I'm freezing my balls off."

"It isn't that cold." Peigi faced him but let her eyes rest on his cheekbone. If a Shifter gazed directly at Graham he might take it as a challenge. "Alaska is cold. The Arctic is cold. This is the Mojave desert."

"And you're a bear with a thick hide. I'm a sensitive little wolf."

"Sure you are." Peigi let herself smile. "I bet it was chilly when you lived in Elko."

"Damned chilly." Graham folded his thick arms over his chest. "We've established the weather, so what do you want? And where is Reid?"

The best way to face Graham, Peigi had learned, was to answer back and ignore his abruptness. He was brusque and didn't soften himself for anyone but his mate and cubs, though Peigi understood that his fierceness had kept an entire Shifter-town of nearly wild Shifters in line in the middle of nowhere Nevada.

"I have no idea where he is. Let me tell you what happened."

Peigi described her midnight meeting with Stuart at the edge

of Shiftertown and her suggestion that they ask Graham and
Eric about the ley line.

"We buried it," Graham said quickly, a flicker of unease in
his gray eyes. "Blew the basements and buried the thing so no
more Fae could ride in and say howdy, not to mention
enslave us."

"I know, but Stuart says the ley line is still there. Whoever
was trying to talk to him last night must have used it, right?
Stuart might be with them, or somewhere along the line, or ..."

"Or on top of Mount Charleston." Graham scowled. "The
man can go anywhere. Maybe he's in Hawaii. It's nice there this
time of year."

Peigi balled her hands. "Please, can you—"

"Unbury the ley line?" Graham shuddered. "No can
do, Pegs."

"Well, do *something*. Stuart might be in trouble. I got a very
bad feeling last night, like the air itself was hostile."

At least Graham didn't dismiss her out of hand. Shifters had
terrific senses that went beyond the five—they could instinctively
tell when something was very wrong, and Peigi, with her trau-
matic history, had those instincts honed like razors.

"I get it." Graham softened his tone. "But I can't dig up
Shiftertown because Reid decided to pop out and grab more
bacon from the nearest convenience store. And let's face it, I
can't disrupt my Lupines at all for him, because ..." He coughed,
flushing. "He's not Shifter."

"Seriously?" Peigi's anger flared, bolstered by worry. "After
all he's done for you?"

"*I* know he has. But my wolves, Peigi ..." Graham shook his
head. "They are stubborn, superstitious shitheads. They don't
like Fae, any Fae, even kindhearted *dokk alfar* who hate the high
Fae as much as we do. I can't do it until I have more evidence
he's in trouble."

Peigi didn't need evidence. She *knew*.

Only one thing to do. "All right," she said.

Graham blinked at her, surprised she'd given in so fast. "Well, okay, then," he said uncertainly.

"I'll just have to go over your head."

His scowl returned. "Don't think so. I have free rein over my Lupines, and this is a problem for *my* Shifters. Eric doesn't have jurisdiction. Even he'll tell you that."

"I wasn't talking about Eric." Peigi made herself meet Graham's eyes, if only briefly. "I mean Misty."

Graham stilled, the look on his face priceless. If only Peigi had a camera—she'd be posting that photo on the Shifter network. *Hashtag, Graham shits himself.*

His flush deepened. "That's just playing dirty."

Misty was Graham's mate. She was human, cute, soft, adorable, and had Graham completely wrapped around her fingers. The big man had a warm heart deep, deep down inside him, and Misty knew exactly how to reach it.

"I'm worried about Stuart," Peigi said. "He didn't simply disappear for no reason. What if someone abducted him?"

"Teleported *him*, you mean? Does that work?"

"How should I know?" Peigi asked in exasperation. "But he mentioned the ley line as though it was key. So we need to find it."

Graham heaved a long and aggrieved sigh. "All right, all right." He held up his hands in surrender. "We'll have to talk to Eric about it, *and* my Shifters. That's how it has to be. But don't, *don't*, for the love of the Goddess run to Misty and spill your story. She'll be all up in my face, and damn, can she *yell* at me."

————

STUART DIDN'T LIKE DARKNESS. THE SHIFTERS THOUGHT HE did, since he was a "dark" Fae, but that was just a literal but not quite accurate translation of *dokk alfar*. He didn't like *this* kind of darkness anyway, one that sucked even the memory of light. A nice cave for a little spelunking was fine, but this place was dank and smelly and held the weight of ages.

"You couldn't talk to me at a coffee shop?" he called out. "Las Vegas has some good ones. I could be sucking down a triple espresso instead of standing in the dark."

We need you.

The disembodied voice was creepiest of all. Reid knew it was a struggle to communicate across the worlds, which distorted sound waves or thought waves, or whatever. The ley lines marked where the folds in reality were weakest, but the lines weren't open gates one could run through any time, thank the Goddess. One needed a talisman, or a spell, or a ritual that often involved blood and violence.

"What do you need me *for*?" Reid snapped. "I'm done saving your asses. It got me exiled into the human world and made me into a bad person. Now that I've got my head out of my butt and have a chance to be happy, you want me to come back? What the hell?"

They will destroy us all.

"The *hoch alfar*? Of course they will. What do you expect — they'll give us a party? They're always trying to kill off *dokk alfar*. It's why they get up in the morning."

Silence. Reid had no idea which *dokk alfar* sat on the other end of the ley line, trying to get his attention, and only knew he was *dokk alfar* because he spoke that language. No *hoch alfar* would soil his tongue with it.

Stuart didn't know where he was. One minute, he'd been cooking eggs for the cubs and Peigi, the next, he'd had the compulsion to teleport. *Here.*

He couldn't teleport into a place he hadn't checked out himself, so reason dictated he actually had been there before. His brain had to know where to go. Not a vague, *Let's go to Tahiti!* He'd have to buy a ticket and fly out to suss the place first — teleporting didn't necessarily save on airfare. Also, Reid couldn't go very far in one burst. Tahiti from Las Vegas was out.

The whisper sang again, the musical language of the *dokk alfar*. *We need the Iron Master. They have stolen the* karmsyern.

Reid stilled. *Karmsyern* was the *dokk alfar* word for, roughly translated, *iron guard*. It was a talisman, made of iron, that hung in a grove at the entrance to *dokk alfar* lands. The *hoch alfar* hated iron—it poisoned them—and the talisman kept them from invading.

Well, that was the theory. The *hoch alfar* still raided, harassed, and killed whatever *dokk alfar* they could find, but it was true the talisman prevented them doing anything large scale too far inside the *dokk alfar* territory. The talisman was also woven with powerful, ancient, and forgotten spells—it wasn't simply an iron doodad hanging from a tree.

"How did they steal it when they can't go near it?" Reid demanded.

Another silence, this one longer. *They have slaves. Perhaps the Battle Beasts they've taken back helped them.*

Reid sucked in a breath. In recent years, some Shifters had been daft enough to return to Faerie and actually work for the Fae. Those Shifters believed the Fae would help them achieve their freedom, even let Shifters overrun the human world and gain control of it.

Some idiots would believe anything.

If Shifters had stolen the *karmsyern* and taken it to the *hoch alfar*, that was a whole lot of shit getting layered on deeper and deeper.

"Are you sure?" he demanded.

The whisper grew annoyed. *Certain enough for a couple of us to twist ourselves inside out to contact you. Hope this pain is worth it.*

"I don't even know who you are."

The silence this time lasted so long, Reid thought the voice wouldn't return. In the end, it said, *Talk to the red wolf.*

Then it vanished. Reid waited. Nothing. He called out a few times, but the voice was gone. Either the guy on the other end was done talking or the break in the ley line had closed.

Reid was left alone in the dark with his troubled thoughts, not someplace he wanted to be. He pictured the sunny kitchen with the cubs good-natured and noisy, and Peigi's beautiful smile. He willed himself to *be* there, bracing for the abrupt drag of the teleport.

He didn't move.

Reid tried again, and again. Instead of the rubber-band stretching feeling and the bizarre juxtaposition of being in two places at once, he got a whole lot of nothing.

He was stuck underground in wherever, in pitch darkness, with no idea where he was or how to get out.

————

"IT'S THERE," ERIC SAID, POINTING TO THE GROUND.

As Peigi and Graham had moved through Shiftertown, following Eric toward the recently built houses, they'd picked up an entourage.

Graham had taken Peigi to Eric and told him Peigi's theories about the ley line, and Eric, interested, was all for digging up Shiftertown until they found it. Graham objected, of course, because it was his part of Shiftertown where the digging would occur. There was more debate—snarled curses on Graham's part —until Eric overruled Graham, as he could.

Eric had the appearance of an easygoing, calm guy, happy to sit in the sunshine with his mate and cub, but when he laid down the law, even Graham and his wolves shut up.

Eric led the search off right away. Eric's seconds—his sister, Cassidy, and Brody, Shane's brother—joined them. Shane had stayed behind at Peigi's to take care of the cubs. Iona, Eric's mate, came along. Diego Escobar, who was Reid's boss and Cassidy's mate, had been at Eric's eating breakfast, and he followed as well. The cubs in Eric's house were too little to stay alone without their parents, so Cassidy and Iona brought them along.

Nell banged out of her house as they passed, asking what was up. She was technically Peigi's clan leader, so she fell into step with Peigi, daring Graham to tell her to leave. The only people in Shiftertown who could keep Graham in line were Eric and Nell —not to mention Misty—and Graham didn't say a word.

Nell's mate, an easygoing bear called Cormac, walked with her. They picked up more of Graham's wolves as they went— Dougal, his nephew and his second, and a couple others. The rest of Shiftertown, who couldn't mind their own business if paid to, wandered out of houses asking each other loudly where Eric and Graham were going as they trailed behind.

Therefore a group of about thirty halted just shy of the small front yard of a house around the block and down the street from Peigi's.

The Lupine who lived there came charging out. "What the hell?"

The Shifters, and the few humans too, had stopped before setting foot in the Lupine's yard. This was the Lupine's territory, and even pack leaders, clan leaders, and Shiftertown leaders had to respect territory. On this patch of land, the half-awake Lupine in a muscle shirt and jeans, who glared at them over his mug of morning coffee, ruled.

"We need to dig down to the ley line," Graham announced. "Better if we have your permission, but if we don't, we'll start digging in the street and tunnel under. Hope your foundations hold up."

The Lupine, with messy brown hair and a dusting of dark beard, stared at Graham in disbelief. "What the fuck for?"

"To figure out what happened to the dark Fae."

More staring. "Hold it. You want to rip up my yard and tunnel under my house to find that creepy Fae shit? ... Oh sorry, Peigi. Didn't see you."

He went red and took a quick drink of coffee as though he wanted to swallow his words. Even a belligerent wolf would think twice about going after a female bear's mate.

Not that Stuart was Peigi's mate in truth, but everyone in Shiftertown had paired them up. Everyone, that is, except Peigi and Stuart. There wasn't a Shifter term for *It's complicated*.

"Okay then," Graham growled at the Lupine. "Diego, can you get us a backhoe?"

Diego raised his brows. "Sure, I keep them in my pocket. Where the hell am I going to get a backhoe at seven o'clock on a Wednesday morning?"

Graham gave him a look of mock surprise. "You come up with all other kinds of equipment at the drop of a hat. I just thought you knew someone."

"Yeah, but that takes time. Phone calls ..."

"We'll wait."

"I don't know." Brody, who was a slightly smaller version of Shane, rubbed his hands. "There's enough of us. We all go at it with shovels, we could make a pretty good dent."

Cormac stood next to him, studying the ground. "Might need a jackhammer for the street. Think the humans would freak out if we started breaking up the road?"

"Probably," Eric said in his quiet way. "Yard would be easier, but we can't force Kurt to let us tear up his landscaping."

As with most houses in Las Vegas, this one had a small patch of grass, kept alive by a watering system, surrounded by bushes like oleander, pyracantha, and lantana. A row of vincas, bright in the wintertime, lined the sidewalk.

Graham eyed Kurt, who lowered his cup in irritation. "Oh, *come on*. My mate's just planted these." He waved his coffee at the flowers. "Don't piss her off, Graham."

Graham studied him without bluster. Eric could easily override Kurt's objections, but he stood back and let Graham deal with it. No one was tense or angry, but Peigi had plenty of experience living with a mixed group of Shifters, and knew that this morning outing could become a bloodbath in a heartbeat.

"Normally, I'd say screw it, and send everyone home," Graham said. "But Reid is important. He has useful intel about the Fae, and I've seen him battle them like they were nothing. Plus he can do that teleportation thing. We need him, so we have to find him. For the good of Shiftertown. Peigi's worried, so that makes me worry. Eric too."

Eric made the shrugging motion that said he agreed but wasn't going to make a big deal out of it unless necessary.

Kurt surveyed the group spread out on the street and took another sip of coffee. Peigi saw shadows in the windows behind him—his mate and cubs. They were curious, but they wouldn't come out until Kurt indicated it was safe.

Kurt glanced heavenward and heaved a long sigh.

"You don't have to dig up the yard," he said heavily. "Or the street. I'll let you downstairs. Not *all* of you." He added this quickly as the bulk of Shifters surged forward. "Graham and Peigi only. Diego if it's necessary, but that's *it*."

THREE

"You heard him," Graham called to his Shifters in the street as Kurt banged his way into the house. "Keep off his turf. Come on, Peigi."

"If you need digging equipment, call me." Diego mimed holding a phone to his ear. "I'll keep out of the way until then."

Peigi gave Diego a grateful nod. Diego was human but understood how sacrosanct a Shifter's territory was, and how hard this would be for Kurt.

Shifters kept their deepest secrets in their cellars. They lived many more years than humans and so had acquired treasures or other valuables that had let them exist in the human world for centuries. A first edition of an eighteenth-century novel or a piece of art from Catherine the Great's collection kept their worth longer than paper currency or stocks, if preserved well. Though Shifters did invest in stocks from time to time, through humans who could keep quiet about it.

A Shifter's hoard was passed down through the pride, pack, or clan, and no outsider was allowed to see it or know what that Shifter family possessed. Therefore, Kurt only reluctantly led them to a concealed door in his back hallway and unlocked it for them. His mate hovered nearby, watchfulness in her wolf's eyes, but she didn't argue.

Peigi had no such stash under her house. She'd lost touch with her clan long ago, even before they'd been rounded up and put into Shiftertowns. She'd spent most of the past twenty-five years with a group of feral Shifters led by a bear called Miguel. His name wasn't really Miguel—he changed it depending on where they lived, trying to blend in with the locals, as though he ever could.

Peigi's folly in believing in him had left her clanless and nearly homeless. She had a place to live these days, but she'd had to start from scratch, no treasure stashed in her basement. Stuart insisted on paying rent for staying in her spare bedroom, and used much of the paycheck he earned from DX Security to buy food for the cubs.

She owed Stuart, big time.

Kurt led them down a flight of stairs, Graham right behind him, Peigi bringing up the rear. The hall that opened from the foot of the staircase was plain and empty, the doors on either side closed. Kurt's family's secrets would be safe from their eyes, but Peigi scented Kurt's nervousness.

Kurt halted at the end of the hall in front of a door little different from the others, except this one was held closed by a metal strap with a padlock. Kurt took a key from the ring he carried and unlocked it.

"Cubs were playing down here a couple months ago and found the pocket in the ley line," Kurt explained to Peigi. "My mate and I filled it in and built this door in front of it. Haven't felt anything since, so we figured the line was dormant."

And might still be. There was nothing to say they'd find Stuart or where he'd gone behind that door, or discover who the voice that had called to him belonged to.

Kurt opened the door. He had to wrench it—the hinges were stiff.

Beyond was a room with a brick wall in the middle of it.

Except the wall sported a gaping hole, like the entrance to a cave. Bricks were scattered across the floor of the small room and lay inside the hole.

"What the hell?" Kurt took a hasty step back, snarls in his throat. "We sealed this up."

Graham likewise growled, and Peigi's fight-or-flight instinct rose high.

"Well, someone tore it down." Graham stated the obvious. "Maybe your cubs?"

"No way in hell. They know it's off limits. They don't even like to come this far down the hall."

Kurt was sweating, his face gray. Peigi kept silent, but she didn't blame him for his reaction. She wanted to run, run. The vibe she got from the opening was unnerving — fear and the smell of something rotten, combined with a push of magic she really didn't want to understand.

But if Stuart was in there …

"We should check it out," she heard herself say.

Kurt looked ill. Graham glowered at Peigi, but he squared his shoulders. "Kurt, stand guard. Run for Eric and Diego if anything goes wrong."

Kurt stepped back, both relieved and chagrined. He was terrified but ashamed Peigi volunteered to go when he couldn't. But Kurt didn't have a lot of dominance, and Graham, a good leader, wouldn't force him into a situation he couldn't handle.

Peigi started forward. Graham rumbled in irritation and got ahead of her. He was leader, so damn it, he'd lead.

As worried as she was about Stuart, Peigi did *not* want to go inside that hole. Since her captivity in a cellar of an abandoned warehouse, dank basements didn't thrill her. She'd been fine in Kurt's well-lit, dry, tiled and painted hallway, which could have been in any part of the house, but this tunnel was different. It meant confinement, no air, nowhere to run.

"I hope Stuart appreciates this," she muttered as she ducked inside after Graham.

Graham's laugh came back to her. "I'll make sure he does."

The tingle of magic grew stronger, raising the hairs on the back of Peigi's neck. Her bear snarled and cursed. Bears were supposed to like caves, and Peigi used to. Another thing Miguel had taken from her.

White mist began to swirl around them, clinging and damp. The overall scent was of acrid smoke with a touch of mint.

"I hate the Fae," Graham muttered. "Hate, hate, hate."

Peigi was right there with him.

They took another two steps, three, and the mists engulfed them.

"We need to get the hell out of here," Graham said, but at that moment, Peigi saw a dark shape in all the white.

"Stuart!"

She darted toward him. Graham grabbed at her to pull her back, but Peigi jerked from him and dashed to the tall, motionless man.

Stuart gazed into the mist, staring at nothing, arms at his sides, his body still. He didn't turn when Peigi ran to him, didn't acknowledge her.

"Stuart!"

"What's wrong with him?" Graham manifested from the mists. "Wake him up. Let's go."

Peigi put her hand on his strong shoulder, finding him cold beneath his shirt. "It's me. You okay?"

Stuart didn't move. His dark eyes were wide, fixed, as though he saw something she couldn't. He was breathing, alive, but eerily motionless. Fear wound through Peigi's heart. She couldn't lose him. Couldn't.

"Screw this," Graham said. "I'm carrying him out."

"No, let me." Peigi started pulling off her shirt, kicking out of her shoes, ready to shift.

She folded her clothes out of habit—she'd taught the cubs that they shouldn't simply scatter their things but gather them neatly, so they could redress when they were done playing in their animal form.

Peigi handed the folded pile to a nonplussed Graham.

"Anyone ever tell you you're a neat-nik?" he demanded as he took it.

"Yep." Peigi turned from him, and became bear.

It felt good to be in her bear form, something she'd wanted to do all morning. She stretched her strong limbs, shaking out her fur, a full growl issuing from her throat.

Peigi could scent so much better in this form. Graham smelled wolf-y and nervous—he didn't like this any more than she did. But he'd never let on. Not Graham the ferocious alpha wolf.

Stuart's scent melded with the mists—he was a being of Faerie, so he carried a hint of smoke as well, but nothing like the bright sharpness of the high Fae. He was more like sandalwood and darker spice, strength and silence.

His body remained rigid, eyes empty. Stuart was trapped— how, Peigi didn't understand and didn't much care. She just wanted him out of there.

Peigi circled Stuart, took a long breath, and barreled straight into him.

Stuart was tall, and he toppled like a tree. Graham caught Stuart as he went down, suddenly loose-limbed, and draped him over Peigi's back. Stuart didn't wake. Graham held him steady as Peigi started back out the way they'd come.

At least, she hoped it was the way they'd come. The mists were confusing, sounds absent. She had scent, but with the over-whelming stench of the ley line, she couldn't be certain where Kurt's basement lay.

From Graham's wolf snarls, he didn't know where it was either. "We need Reid to wake up and magic us home. I *hate* when he does that." Graham shuddered. "But damn, it's handy."

Peigi growled warningly at him. Graham needed to leave

Stuart alone—he could be hurt, dying, damaged by whatever spell held him, who knew?

Graham subsided. Even he didn't want to mess with Peigi when she became protective of Stuart.

They walked another five or so minutes, but Peigi couldn't spy the outline of Kurt's basement door, only thicker mists.

"Shit," Graham muttered. "I don't want to be stuck in Faerie. Been there, done that, burned the fucking T-shirt."

Peigi didn't want to be stuck in Faerie either. A Shifter bear and a dominant wolf would be great prizes to a Fae warrior, who'd either try to enslave them or make them into hearth rugs. Graham was a good fighter, and Peigi as bear was strong, but the two of them and an inert *dokk alfar* against a multitude of Fae?

The high Fae would tear Stuart apart. Probably torture him for a long time before he died. She refused to let that happen.

"I think we're screwed," Graham said after another ten minutes. "We have to wake him up, Peigi. I bet he's the only one who can—"

"Uncle Graham!"

Two small boys hurtled out of the dark mist and slammed straight into Graham's legs. They began shifting as soon as they smacked into him, becoming wolf cubs with huge feet and long ears. High-pitched yipping pierced the air.

"What the hell are you doing here?" Graham roared. "Why aren't you with Misty?"

One of the cubs, Kyle, or maybe Matt—they were twins—shifted back to his seven-year-old boy form. "We came to get you out. Follow us. Follow us. Follow *us*!"

He shifted again to wolf, and the cubs started running in a sideways lope, tails going ninety miles an hour.

Graham started after them, keeping up a diatribe about cubs who needed to learn to do what they were told. Peigi, with Stuart, quickly followed.

As the cubs dashed through the mists, the fog began to thin. Cooler air surrounded Peigi, and in a few more minutes, she saw the artificial yellow light filling the square of Kurt's basement door.

The cubs charged through, Graham on their heels. Peigi increased her speed and burst through the door after them, heaving a sigh of relief as she hit the tile floor.

Kurt, who'd been waiting, his eyes wild, quickly shut the door and padlocked it. "He all right?" he asked anxiously.

Peigi lowered herself to her belly, and Graham and Kurt helped slide Stuart gently to the floor. Stuart didn't wake. He lay limply, eyes closed, his black hair damp from the mists.

Peigi nuzzled him. *Wake up. Please. I can't do this without you.*

The cubs came tearing back to them. Graham leaned against the wall, his breath ragged. "Will you two *settle down*?"

At his roar, Matt and Kyle stopped running. Instead of cowering before Graham, they trotted to Stuart and began busily licking his face.

Peigi remained bear, not wanting to shift back in front of Kurt, with Graham holding her clothes in his balled fists. He was wrinkling the hell out of her shirt.

The cubs continued to lick, tails waving, and under their ministrations, Stuart jerked. The cubs kept at it as Stuart blinked, eyes opening in confusion.

Peigi saw awareness returning to his black-dark eyes, and then the realization that a pair of wolf cubs were smearing their tongues all over his face.

"I'm awake, guys. You can stop." Stuart pressed the wriggling little bodies away from him with gentleness, then he sat up and wiped his cheeks. "Anyone have a towel?"

———

REID DECIDED TO PROVE TO GRAHAM HE WAS FUNCTIONING normally by teleporting Matt and Kyle home. He landed on Graham's front porch and handed the cubs to Misty, who'd jerked open the door when he appeared.

"You all right?" Misty asked worriedly. She was a sweet human woman who'd managed to turn Graham from belligerent asshole to a more reasonable Shifter who took care of his new cub, his nephew, and Matt and Kyle with surprising compassion.

"I think so." Reid wasn't certain how he'd become stuck in the patch of mist, or how Peigi had come in to get him out, but he was alive and breathing, which for him was enough. "Thanks to your paramedics."

Both cubs, still wolves, hung in Misty's arms, tails waving. Matt began licking her chin.

"I sent them to find you," Misty said. "I remembered they were called Guards, or at least descended from them. When Dougal came and told me he was scared Graham was stuck in Faerie, I told him to take the cubs over and see if they could sniff you out."

"Good thinking." Reid scratched both cubs behind the ears, his already considerable respect for Misty rising.

They'd been told that the two cubs had been called Guards, Shifters bred by the Fae to be larger, stronger, faster, smarter, et cetera, et cetera than other Shifters. They'd guarded the Fae generals and high leaders, until the Shifter-Fae war, when most of the Guards had died fighting for Shifter freedom. Like the white tigers, who'd been bred for the indulgence of Fae princes, the Guards had turned on the Fae and helped Shifters escape to the human world.

Matt and Kyle, barely seven years old, were the only Guards left in existence—that any knew of.

"Thanks for bringing them home," Misty said.

"Thank *them* for rescuing me. Give them extra ice cream tonight. I'll buy."

The cubs went into paroxysms of joy. They loved ice cream, straight from the carton.

Misty smiled. "Glad to see you're all right."

Reid gave her a nod, embarrassed he'd had to be rescued at all. Also not happy he'd gotten himself stuck, unable to teleport.

He only lost that ability when he was inside Faerie, and he hadn't been there entirely, just a pocket in between. Right? Did that mean both his abilities—teleportation and mastery over iron, disappeared in the between place? Not something comfortable to think about.

Stuart said good-bye to Misty and the wriggling cubs and walked home. He knew he could teleport there, but walking in the cold winter mid-morning felt good.

The Shifters were dispersing, the crisis over. Brody high-fived Stuart as he and Cormac approached. "Glad to see you in one piece, Reid."

Stuart never had understood the high five, or the fist bumps, or the variations he'd seen over the years in the human world, but he'd learned to return the gesture. It meant friendship, acceptance—things, ironically, Stuart hadn't found until he'd moved to Shiftertown.

"You all right?" Cormac peered at him, concern in his tawny eyes.

"Fine." Reid realized he sounded abrupt and softened his voice. "Yeah. Thanks."

Cormac laid his giant hand on Reid's shoulder. "You know if there's a rescue mission, we all have to be in on it, right? Have to brag later that we were key."

"In other words, Shifters can't mind their own business." Brody chuckled, waved at Reid, and walked on.

"You need anything, you ask." Cormac regarded him seriously. A relative newcomer to this Shiftertown himself, Nell's mate knew about being an outsider.

"Thanks," Stuart repeated. "Is Peigi all right?"

Cormac gave him a nod of understanding. "She'll be fine. She was worried as hell about you, but she's a strong lady."

"I know she is."

Cormac's expression warmed. "She is. Take care of yourself."

He gave Reid another pat on the shoulder and moved on, calling to Brody to wait for him.

Other Shifters waved, wished him well, or simply walked off. Not all of them were comfortable with Stuart, though he'd lived in this Shiftertown for a couple of years. Eric sanctioned him, and Nell and Graham stood up for him, but even so. If those three ever withdrew their support, Reid had the feeling that a few of the Shifters would try to throw him out, if they didn't attempt to kill him outright.

For now, there was a truce. Reid had proved useful, and so the Shifters let him stay, even if most of Shiftertown watched him from the corners of their eyes.

By the time Stuart made it back to Peigi's small house at the end of the road, the Shifters had gone back to their own lives. Even Eric and Graham had departed to take care of more Shifter business. Their jobs never ceased.

Reid's heart lightened as he viewed the small rectangular house where he slept most nights. The miasma of the Fae place he'd been stuck in and the uneasiness the *dokk alfar's* words had caused dissolved as he approached the front door and reached for the knob.

The door was ripped open from the other side, Peigi behind it. Before Reid could speak, she yanked him inside the house and into her arms, enclosing him in a hard embrace.

FOUR

S tuart had never understood why Shifters found touch
healing until he'd met Peigi. As she snuggled into his shoulder, her arms firmly around him, Stuart surrendered to it.

He gathered her to him, loving the cinnamon scent of her
warm hair, the length of her body against his. Shifter women
were tall, bears even more so, and Peigi could rest her head fully
on his shoulder.

The embrace tightened, Peigi shaking. Reid stroked her
back, wanting to soothe her and absorb her strength at the
same time.

Several cannonballs bashed into his legs, more arms coming
around him, the cubs joining in. Donny had shifted to bear, and
he circled the hugging ball, nuzzling Reid whenever he could get
his nose in.

Peigi lifted her head, wiping her cheeks. "They were scared
you weren't coming back."

Stuart gazed into eyes of rich blue, framed with lashes of
deepest black. He brushed back a lock of her sable hair. "You
know I'll always come back."

In all this time, this was the closest Stuart had come to a

declaration. He and Peigi never spoke about what was between them, as though they feared its shimmering bubble would break into unresolvable shards.

Her mouth was so close, her breath touching his lips. Stuart could easily lean to her, brush a kiss to her mouth, taste her. Her chest lifted with her breath, longing flickering in her eyes. She wanted it too, a kiss that would seal whatever it was they had and maybe lead to something more.

Stuart had learned to embrace his exile because of this woman. Peigi had beauty like no other, and she too was exiled, alone, making a family from those no one else wanted.

This morning he'd been called by someone beyond the divide who needed his help, who told him of peril. Stuart knew he was a selfish bastard, because at this moment, with Peigi before him, their breaths mingling, he could think of nothing but staying with her, forever.

Two small fists smashed the back of his legs. "I'm hungry!" Kevin, who rarely spoke, declared in a loud voice. "We had to wait so long for you and Peigi to get home. Can we have pancakes now?"

"ARE YOU GOING TO TELL ME ABOUT IT?"

After the cubs had been fed their second breakfast—Shane had given them the eggs from the first—Peigi sat in the sunshine on the back porch on an Adirondack chair, soaking up warmth. As typical in Las Vegas, the bone-chillingly cold morning had given way to a pleasant seventy-five degrees, a nice change from the brutal heat of summer. In this climate, winter was greeted with relief.

Stuart, in spite of his ordeal, had helped make the pancakes and supervised the cleanup afterward. The cubs had then attacked their daily chores with minimum fuss and then headed out to play, meeting cubs in the middle of backyards for whatever game they had going. Shifter adults lounged on porches, keeping an eye on the little ones.

"I'm not sure what to tell." Stuart reposed on the low porch's one step, long legs in jeans stretched out to the gravel beyond. "It was a weird experience. I'm not even certain what happened."

"You told me you couldn't teleport out of there," Peigi said. He'd related at least that much. "Which was why I had to go into that terrifying hole in the ground and pull you out."

"Which I am truly thankful for." Stuart sent Peigi a glance that warmed her blood. "I'll have to give you something to show you how grateful I am. That jeweler Diego and I helped last month with his theft problem has some beautiful things in his store. Want to go pick something out?"

"What would I do with a diamond necklace?" Peigi asked, eyes wide. "Wear it to the prom?"

Stuart's grin grew broader. "Wherever the hell you wanted. Doesn't matter. I'll get you something. Maybe new patio furniture."

Peigi settled more deeply into the wooden chair. "More practical, but the cubs will tear it up. Solid and old is better."

"You are hard to please, woman."

Peigi shrugged, pretending his voice, smile, and very presence didn't make her rejoice. "I'm just glad you're all right. The cubs are a handful."

"They're good kids." His gaze went to their six running around and screaming with the other cubs in Shiftertown.

Noelle, a grizzly cub, would likely be an alpha if given the chance. She could rally the younger cubs of Shiftertown to her side and hold her own against the older ones. Donny seemed to be fairly carefree, not as easily frightened as he used to be. Maybe he wouldn't be an alpha but certainly not too far down in the hierarchy. Peigi was a bit more concerned about Hannah and Kevin, the youngest two, who were uncertain about their place.

"They want me to come back," Stuart said.

Peigi snapped her gaze to him. "They? Who's they?"

"The *dokk alfar*." Before she could ask what he meant, he gave her the full story of his encounter in the pocket of un-reality and what the dark Fae voice had said.

When he finished, Peigi shivered, the ramifications hitting her. "They're afraid of invasion?"

"A full-scale attack hasn't happened for a long time, but the high Fae are always searching for ways to edge out the *dokk alfar*, to get rid of the iron that weakens them. Iron is why they haven't been able to eradicate us completely, but if they use Shifters to help them ..."

"Are you sure he meant Shifters?" Peigi asked.

"He said *Horkalan*, which is the *dokk alfar* word for Shifter. More correctly, *Battle Beast*, which is what the high Fae have always called you."

A cloud eased over the sun, making the warm day suddenly cool. "I've heard rumors about Shifters joining the Fae, but ..."

"But you didn't want to believe them?" Stuart said. "I'm not privy to all the reports Eric receives, but he shares a lot with me. There was a Shifter in New Orleans recruiting Shifters to work for the Fae again. Convincing them Fae are better allies than humans, a better chance to get free."

"That's insane." Peigi drew her feet up and wrapped her arms around her knees. "What Shifters are fool enough to believe that?"

"Unfortunately, plenty. In fact, the voice told me I needed to 'talk to the red wolf.' I'm pretty sure he means Dimitri Kashnikov, who helped break the recruiting ring in New Orleans. Dimitri went into Faerie and saw what was going on."

"Does this mean you're going to New Orleans?" Peigi tried to keep the catch from her voice but couldn't quite manage it.

"I don't know yet. I'll make some calls, see if Dimitri can come to me."

Peigi tried to make herself be reasonable. "It's risky for a Shifter to travel. You should go to him."

"I'd only do that if ..." Stuart broke off, his gaze going to their cubs who were running, shifting, playing, yelling.

"If what?" Peigi prompted. "If Diego doesn't want you to solve another jewel heist?"

"If you came with me." His words were quiet, almost inaudible, but Peigi heard them just fine. "But you're right. Too risky for Shifters to travel —"

"Yes," Peigi cut through his words.

Stuart glanced over his shoulder. "Yes, what?"

"Yes, I'll go with you."

Stuart turned to study her, his sin-dark eyes pulling her in.

Peigi had no idea why she was attracted to a Fae. At first, she'd thought herself so traumatized by male Shifters she would chase anything *not* Shifter, but she soon realized this wasn't the reason.

Stuart had a way of looking at her — at *her* — not the pathetic rescue the other Shifters treated gently, as though she'd go feral if they made too many loud noises around her. He treated her like a person, not a therapy case.

And, all right, she was attracted because Stuart Reid was seriously hot. There wasn't a part of him not solid muscle, and his night-dark eyes held secrets Peigi wanted to touch.

"What about the cubs?" Stuart asked after the silence had stretched.

Leaving the cubs, who'd relied on her since Cassidy had led them out of that basement, wouldn't be ideal. Peigi didn't like the emptiness she felt when she thought about not being with them, but then again, she didn't want Stuart running off on his own where anyone could kill him.

He'd have to seek Dimitri at Kendrick's compound, where Shifters lived in secret without Collars and human restrictions. They had no love for anything Fae, and who knew what they would do when they saw Stuart among them? Better Peigi was with him.

"I'll ask Nell to come. She and Cormac love the cubs. Shane

and Brody are great babysitters too. No one will mess with them with Nell's family around."

"No argument there." Stuart watched the cubs again. "They're dependent on you, though."

"You too." Peigi met his gaze as Stuart turned to her in surprise. "Don't look at me like that. They need us both. So like hell I'm sending you off in Marlo's plane alone to deal with an enclave of un-Collared Shifters who are all paranoid about the Fae. I want you back in one piece."

Stuart had the gall to let his lips twitch. "So, what—you'll be my bodyguard?"

"Damn straight. No one messes with a she-bear."

The twitch became a full smile—no, a grin. "You're right about that." He stood up and she did too. He drew closer to her, his body heat awakening her every need. Then his beautiful smile faded, and his somberness returned. "I'll set it up with Eric."

Peigi assumed he'd say something more, but Stuart stared down at her, his eyes with worlds inside intent on her. Wouldn't she love to see him look at her like this while he hung over her in the night?

She stopped herself leaning into him, or grabbing on with both hands, begging him to be with her. Stuart studied her a few moments longer then turned away without a word.

It was always like this between them—they'd almost reach the point of no return, and then one of them would back down and walk off. The *not quite* never turned into *yes, now*.

One day, Peigi thought as she watched him walk down the yards, his stride long, head up, *it will be* now. *And then I won't ever let go.*

———

REID WAS NEVER COMFORTABLE ON MARLO'S PLANE, NO matter how many times he'd flown with the man.

This plane they were on was a new one, as the former had gone down—thankfully without hurting Marlo or his lone passenger too badly.

The ageless, bony man was one hell of a pilot, and after Marlo had recovered from his injuries, he'd cheerfully bought another old plane, fixed it up, and was soon aloft. He was nuts.

Marlo had flown Peigi away from her captivity a couple years ago and to the Las Vegas Shiftertown. Reid had been on that trip, his heart burning as he'd witnessed the pain Peigi was going through.

Most of the Shifter females the feral bear Miguel had sequestered had eventually gone home to their families—Eric located them—but Peigi hadn't had anywhere to go. Eric had mate claimed all the females for expediency, to keep them safe, then he'd released them from the claim once they were clear of danger.

Peigi had asked to stay in the Las Vegas Shiftertown. The bear leader, Nell, supported her choice. The orphaned cubs had been left with Peigi, as she'd already formed a bond with them in Miguel's compound.

Reid remembered how terrified Peigi had been on the flight to the airstrip outside Las Vegas and how relieved at the same time. She hadn't quite known what to do with her freedom, and even at first behaved as though she didn't deserve it.

As a one-time captive of the Fae, and then being exiled by them, Reid understood. But he'd known that talking it through wouldn't help Peigi. Having her feel safe and capable of finding happiness would.

On this flight, Peigi sat in the co-pilot's seat and gazed interestedly out the window at the passing desert below. She asked Marlo on-point questions about the plane and navigation, and laughed at his jokes.

Reid occupied the seat behind them and simply watched sunlight dance on Peigi's hair, which she'd drawn into a ponytail for the journey. When she laughed, her face warmed and her eyes sparkled.

The trauma of her life hadn't hardened her, hadn't ingrained itself as lines on her face or a permanent frown. Peigi regarded the world with interest, as though she wanted to embrace it and explore what she'd missed.

Whatever the hell Stuart ended up doing, nothing would be worth it if he had to leave this woman behind. She was tough, far more than she gave herself credit for. The cubs loved her. Nell loved her. Brody ... might have his eye on Peigi, Stuart sensed, but he was backing off because of Reid.

If Reid returned to Faerie for good, Brody would likely step in and court her. Peigi would do well with Brody, who was one of Eric's trackers and from a powerful clan. Logical that Peigi should end up with him.

Reid heard the growl in his throat, worthy of any Shifter. He suddenly wanted to teleport the affable Brody to the other side of the world and tell the bear to find his own way home.

Peigi laughed at Marlo, her silver voice filling Reid's ears over the roar of the plane. Damn the Fae for kicking him to this world and endangering his heart. When he'd been a general of his *dokk alfar* clan, he'd prided himself on being a leader first, last, and always. These days his emotions were a messy tangle that wouldn't smooth out any time soon.

Marlo landed them on a deserted airstrip, a long way from anywhere. The South Texas field was flat and empty, and Reid had spied cattle grazing a few miles away.

The plane bumped and rolled to a stop, the engine dying into blissful silence.

"I love this part of the country." Marlo exhaled in satisfaction as he unbuckled himself from the seat. "Vast. Peaceful."

Not enough cover, Reid thought. Still a soldier at heart, he felt exposed and vulnerable in this plane, a target. He chafed with impatience as Marlo shut everything down and wrestled with the catch on the door. Finally the door creaked back, falling heavily against the fuselage.

"Stairs don't always work." Marlo stomped on the arm that kept the steps up, to no avail.

"I don't care." Peigi pushed past Reid, dropped her overnight bag on the dirt and dried grass, and leapt gracefully down after it. "Need some exercise after the long ride anyway."

Marlo quickly climbed down and took her arm, steadying her on the uneven ground. Stuart tried not to kill him as he jumped out and landed next to the two.

Peigi shaded her eyes and scanned the horizon. "I hope they don't expect us to walk all the way. I don't want *that* much exercise."

Marlo chuckled. "Kendrick said he was coming, and he will. Tell everyone I said hi."

"You're leaving?" Panic edged Peigi's question.

"Can't sit out here for long without someone investigating," Marlo said. "You call me when you need a ride. I won't go far."

Reid stepped closer to Peigi, gripping the handle of his small duffel bag. "I do this all the time. Kendrick, or one of his seconds, will show."

"Easy for you," Peigi said. "You can just teleport."

"Don't say *easy* and *teleport* in the same breath." Reid kept his tone light. "Means you have no idea how exhausting it is. Tell you what, if Kendrick leaves us too long, I'll take us to a B&B that isn't far—you'll like it."

"Sure, because the owners won't freak out if we just pop in."

"I'll find a rental car place, and we can drive the last part of the way."

Peigi's eyes danced. "Then we have to worry about the rental car agent falling over when you suddenly appear in his office."

"I planned to be a little more subtle." Reid was pleased to see her relaxing. Peigi didn't like to feel trapped, and being stranded was a close second. She never had to be trapped again, he wanted to tell her.

"Shouldn't have to worry." Marlo jerked his chin at a line of dust rising into the pale blue sky. "Someone's coming."

Reid came alert. Could be Kendrick, could be highway patrol. Peigi caught his tension, but she calmed before he did, sniffing the air. "Shifters," she announced.

FIVE

Peigi had met Dimitri and Jaycee before, at Shifter gatherings, but she didn't know the two well. They'd had their mating ceremony not long ago, and Jaycee was carrying her first cub.

Jaycee was curvy and didn't hide those curves in her form-fitting jacket, leather pants, and motorcycle boots. Her body didn't show her pregnancy much yet, but to Peigi, it was obvious —her scent was different, as was the sparkle in her eyes, and the careful way she moved, though she retained the litheness of her leopard.

Behind her came Dimitri in jeans and a sweatshirt with a beer logo on it. He had red hair, a graceful athleticism, and wore a wide grin.

"Reid. How's life t-treating you?" Dimitri came at Stuart, arms open, ready for a Shifter hug of greeting.

Stuart hesitated, then Peigi saw him decide to allow it. Dimitri, at the last minute, lowered his arms abruptly, laughed, and reached out a hand instead.

"Just kidding." Dimitri and Stuart clasped forearms, another form of Shifter greeting. "I know you aren't a touchy-f-feely kind of dude. But Peigi is. Except for being a dude."

Dimitri let go of Stuart and went to Peigi, open-armed once more. Dimitri could hug almost as well as bears did, lifting Peigi and spinning her around.

Dimitri released Peigi, and before she could catch her breath, Jaycee came in for a hug of her own. Jaycee's warm, lush body enfolded her, and Peigi again scented the cub inside her, the life she and Dimitri had created.

Behind them, Marlo shouted both a greeting and good-bye and started up the plane. The roar of the engines precluded further discussion.

Dimitri beckoned them to the pickup resting in the dried grass, opened the doors, and ushered them inside. Stuart went first, Shifter style, and helped Peigi into the back seat. Jaycee jumped into the front in a single bound while Dimitri took the driver's seat.

"A bear, a Feline, a Lupine, and a Fae got into a pickup." Dimitri started the truck and bumped it around toward the dirt road. "How will this joke end?"

"You tell me," Stuart said. "A *dokk alfar* instructed me to talk to you."

"Yeah?" Dimitri's eyes sharpened as he glanced at Stuart in the rearview mirror. "Kendrick didn't mention this—he said you needed some help only Jaycee and I could give. I figured it was because we were bad-ass. What *dokk alfar*?"

"I was pulled partway into Faerie so one of my people could communicate with me. When I asked the *dokk alfar* who he was, he told me to speak to you," Stuart explained calmly, far too calmly, in Peigi's opinion, for the frightening event.

"Ah." Dimitri slowed the truck as the dirt road ended at the highway, waited for a couple of passing vehicles, then pulled onto the asphalt. "I wonder if that was Cian. Huh. Nice to be remembered."

"Cian?" Stuart's brows went up. "I don't think I know him."

"He was my cell mate when I did time in a high Fae prison." Dimitri's words were light, but Peigi saw pain flicker in his eyes. His experience could not have been good. Jaycee, watching him, put a comforting hand on his thigh.

To give Dimitri time to recover, Peigi asked Stuart, "How would you know that you don't know this particular Cian—out of all the Cians who might be out there in Faerie?"

"Because *dokk alfar* don't duplicate names," Stuart answered. "They're unique. They can be passed from generation to generation but only if the bearer of the name of the previous generation has died."

"Humans should do that," Jaycee said. "Imagine doing research on a guy called John."

"Or Thomas," Dimitri said. "Shifters should do one name per generation too. There are a lot of Dimitris."

"Are there?" Jaycee started. "Well, crap. More of you to put up with."

"James—that name comes up a lot," Dimitri continued, pretending to ignore her. "William. Jack. A lot of Jasons."

"I heard that one of the most popular names these days is Aiden," Jaycee said.

Traffic thickened and Dimitri pulled into the passing lane. "I don't know about that. How about Trevor?"

"Are you asking if it's popular or if we should name our cub that?"

Dimitri shrugged, grinning. Peigi cleared her throat. "So there is only one Cian?" she gently steered the conversation back to where it had begun. "And only one Stuart Reid?"

"Stuart Reid isn't my true name," he said. Peigi had known this—he had a fairly long name in his own language, which he'd told her meant he was high in his clan. "Cian won't be his entire name, but what he goes by."

Dimitri nodded. "Yeah, Cian has a long-ass name, like …"

"Cian Tadhg Cailean an Mac Diarmud," Jaycee said. She sent Dimitri a sweet smile. "Lady Aisling told me."

"Because she's your best friend. Can you believe my mate is friends with a Tuil Erdannan?" Dimitri asked the back seat. "Translation: scary as shit woman who can terrify the high Fae." He shuddered. "That doesn't worry me *at all.*"

"*Anyway,*" Peigi broke in. "Tell us about Cian."

"A good guy." Dimitri returned to business with ease. "I don't know much about him, because I don't speak *dokk alfar* and he didn't speak English or Russian. He got himself captured, and I think he's a tracker, like me. Some kind of scout to see what the Fae were up to. That's the impression I got, anyway. He helped me escape—and I helped him. Once we were free, he saluted us and took off. I'm glad to hear he's alive and well."

"Hmm." Stuart's brows came together, his expression thoughtful.

Jaycee, as impatient as Peigi, turned in her seat to face Dimitri. "You could have told Eric that on the phone, instead of dragging Peigi and Reid across two and a half states in Marlo's plane."

Stuart sat forward. "I don't think so. There must be something Cian wants me to know. If you tell me everything, Dimitri, the whole story, every detail, I might figure it out. Better than a quick phone conversation."

"You mean putting up our feet, breaking out the beer, and shooting the breeze." Dimitri nodded. "Sounds good to me."

Jaycee rolled her eyes. "Anything to get out of, you know, actual work."

"Hey, this is work. I'm a tracker. I'm tracking. Doesn't mean I can't enjoy a beer at the same time."

"Whatever helps you sleep at night, sweetie."

Peigi hid a smile as Dimitri drove on, speeding up to get around the traffic. Jaycee and Dimitri were so easy with each other, good friends, and obviously deeply in love. True partners.

Would Peigi ever achieve that with Stuart? Or might this journey bring them to the end of whatever it was they had?

Stuart would never turn his back on his people if they were

in true danger, Peigi knew, and she wouldn't let him. No matter how much his departure might hurt her, she could never force him to make that choice.

————

KENDRICK'S RANCH LAY IN A FOLD OF DRY LAND THAT HID IT from all roads. Dimitri turned in at a white gate that lined the highway and drove slowly over a low hill.

The hill's crest showed Reid a sprawling single-story ranch house at the bottom of another hill and a scattering of smaller houses behind it, culminating in a barn at the top of the next rise. Cubs, in both human and animal form, ran between the large house and the smaller ones, or up to the barn, outside of which a horse patiently grazed.

Contentment, Reid decided. *It looks like this.*

Kendrick had established a safe place for his un-Collared Shifters, and they were thriving. They had to hide out, true, which meant the cubs were home schooled, and venturing far was dangerous. But within Kendrick's territory, the Shifters were safe and happy, free to live their lives.

Dimitri drove around the big house, waving at Shifters and cubs in passing. He maneuvered the truck to a halt in front of what Reid knew was these days called a "tiny house"—a compact but clean-lined home with a door and a window on the ground floor, and a window above suggesting a loft or small second floor.

A loft, Reid saw as he ushered Peigi inside, following Dimitri and Jaycee. While the interior was incredibly small, it had been filled with comfortable chairs, a table under the window, and a niche kitchen. An open door behind the kitchen revealed a minute bathroom. A ladder-stair in the corner led to the loft, likely the bedroom.

The interior was painted a soft white, making the space airy, with brightly upholstered chairs, pillows, and throws plus gleaming appliances in the kitchen lending color.

"This is lovely," Peigi said in delight.

Jaycee flushed, modest, but pleased at the same time. "Had to do something with Dimitri's bachelor pad. He didn't even have sheets when I moved in."

"Now it's a department store," Dimitri growled, but Reid could see he didn't mind very much.

"When the cub comes, we're building on," Jaycee said firmly. "The house is cute, but we constantly run into each other."

"Not that it's a b-bad thing." Dimitri winked at her.

"Cubs need a lot of room," Peigi said, her tone feeling. "Trust me on this."

"I do," Jaycee said. "It's an ongoing debate between Dimitri and me. Again, he just doesn't want to do the work."

Dimitri's spirits wouldn't dampen. "Red wolves were made to laze in the sun. Speaking of—let's have that brew and chat, Reid. We'll go outside so the ladies can t-talk about us behind our backs."

He moved to the refrigerator and drew out two long-neck bottles, motioning Reid to follow him out the back door. Reid glanced at Peigi, who was busy admiring the little house, her expression longing.

Maybe Reid could convince Eric to let him build on to the house in Las Vegas—Reid would offer the funds. He knew Peigi didn't have the hidden riches other Shifters did, DX Security did well, and Reid's salary wasn't bad. Getting around regulations about Shifter houses wasn't easy, but Eric could manage it—his mate's family owned a home construction company.

Stuart left Peigi with reluctance, but the two women were already chattering about kitchen towels, for some reason. Peigi returned Stuart's glance and smiled. He wrapped the smile around him and followed Dimitri outside.

The afternoon was warm. While South Texas could have cold snaps, it lay on a latitude that let the temperatures stay in the 70s and even 80s in the dead of winter, the sunshine nice. Dimitri led

Reid to a pair of lawn chairs set up in a sunny patch of grass, dropped into one, and popped open his beer.

"Just out of Shifter hearing range from my neighbors," Dimitri said, handing Reid the second bottle.

Reid twisted off the cap and sipped the beer he'd learned to like as he lived in the human world, and contemplated the spread of land. The Shiftertown in Las Vegas was crowded, the houses close together. In turn, that Shiftertown was surrounded by city, which encroached into the desert a little farther every year. This ranch allowed plenty of space between the small homes, acres in which Shifters could run without restraint.

"Nice place." Reid took another sip. Human beer tasted a little like *dokk alfar* ale, giving him a nostalgic feeling.

"It's home." Dimitri lounged back in his chair, the man able to relax anywhere.

"As long as Shifter Bureau doesn't find you all."

"Exactly." Dimitri lifted his beer in a toast. "Here's to Shifter Bureau stumbling over its own shoelaces."

Reid clicked his bottle to Dimitri's. In theory, Reid didn't have to worry about Shifter Bureau, because humans weren't much aware of Fae, and they assumed Reid was another human. He was watched because of his close ties with Peigi and Shifter-town, but mostly left alone apart from that.

"Tell me everything you can about Cian," Reid said after they'd drunk in companionable silence a few minutes.

"Don't know much. The Fae general who captured me tried to make me kill Cian, but Cian and I decided to join forces and fight our way out instead. That idea did not work at all." He grimaced, and Reid saw the memory of pain his eyes. Dimitri had a pale scar on his throat, where a Collar had briefly scorched him.

Reid had heard some of the story. "You were put into a cell, but you helped each other escape."

"Cian did most of the helping." Dimitri took another pull of beer. "He knew how to bandage ribs—I wondered if he was a doctor."

"Could be. *Dokk alfar* make good healers. Have to, to survive against the *hoch alfar*."

Dimitri nodded in sympathy. "And then Cian did this weird thing—he dug his fingers right into the rock and started pulling a hole in the ceiling, around the grate. Craziest shit I've ever seen."

Reid's heart beat faster. He hadn't heard *this* part of the story. "A *ghandeltraum*," he whispered. "Bloody hell."

Dimitri blinked. "A what now?"

"There isn't an equivalent word in English, as far as I know. A *ghandeltraum* can move through solid substances—rock, metal —anything not living."

"Sort of like you can teleport?"

"It's a different gift but similar. I can't teleport when I'm inside Faerie, but there, I can make iron do whatever I want."

"Yeah? Must be handy when you need to fix a hinge."

"It is. It also scares the crap out of the *hoch alfar*, which is truly satisfying."

Dimitri chuckled. "I'll bet. I take it this *ghan*—whatever thing is—is rare?"

"They are," Reid answered. "I've never met one before. They're even more rare than iron masters."

"Which is what you are."

"Yep."

They fell silent. Wind danced across the grasses and whispered through the large tree that lent shade to Dimitri's house from the harsh summer heat.

A *ghandeltraum*. Reid digested that. Cian had to be more than just a tracker or a scout—the *ghandeltraum* ability was passed down through the great families of ancient lineage. His interest in Cian rose.

"So," Dimitri said after a moment. "Guess we need to contact Cian and see if we can k-kick some *czul* ass."

Reid nodded with appreciation. Dimitri used the word the

∂okk alfar reserved specially for the *hoch alfar*, roughly translated as *bastard*, but with deeper and more enraged connotations.

Laughter drifted from inside the house. Peigi leaned back on an open windowsill, amused at something Jaycee was saying. Dimitri, whose hearing ability beat Reid's, listened, his eyes going soft.

"My mate is an amazing woman," he said. "She goes out of her way to make my life hell. I am one lucky Shifter."

Reid studied the lines of Peigi's back, her sloppy tail of dark hair dancing as she laughed. She kept herself calm and reasonable most of the time, but with Jaycee, was letting herself unwind.

Dimitri raised his bottle of beer to Reid, a knowing glint in his eyes. "You have it bad, my friend. Take my advice." His infectious grin spread across his face. "Surrender. Don't even fight the fall. The landing is hell-a worth it."

———

PEIGI SLID FROM THE WINDOWSILL AS JAYCEE HANDED HER A bulbous glass of red wine. Jaycee had served herself water in deference to her pregnancy, but had readily poured the wine for Peigi, saying she wanted to see it enjoyed. Peigi knew little about wine, but Jaycee was reputed to be an expert, and Peigi agreed when the smooth liquid rolled over her tongue.

"Nice, isn't it?" Jaycee asked, watching Peigi's expression. "So, what about you and Reid? You shagging yet?"

Peigi coughed. She sucked in a ragged breath then took a larger gulp of wine. "No."

"She says with regret. What's stopping him? Or is it you?"

Peigi sighed. "Me, probably. Or maybe him. I don't know. Stuart isn't pushy. Gives me plenty of space."

"He knows you went through a lot of bad shit. Seriously bad shit you don't just get over. But maybe if you hint that hitting the sheets with him will help ..."

"We also live in a houseful of cubs." Peigi glanced pointedly at Jaycee's abdomen. "They tend to have crises during intimate moments. You and Dimitri will have to get used to that."

"True, but the kids in your house are Shifter cubs. They know adults do it to produce more cubs, and they leave you to get on with it. Sex isn't a terrible, scary thing."

"Mmm-hmm. Hold on to that thought when you and Dimitri are getting hot and heavy, and your cub bursts in with some interesting fact they've discovered about frogs. Bringing one with them for demonstration."

Jaycee stared at her, then her peals of laughter rang out. "Did one of yours ...?"

"Noelle, yes. She has no sense of timing—or maybe she does, because she manages to get plenty of attention. But no, Stuart and I weren't, as you say, hitting the sheets. Just taking a moment."

"A moment with a frog."

Peigi remembered Noelle's joy in showing them the frog she'd caught—the desert was full of them—when Stuart and Peigi had been standing close together in the hall, Stuart just starting to touch Peigi's face. He'd come out of his room as Peigi headed for hers, and they'd stopped.

As they'd gazed at each other in silence, Peigi's heart had banged as though it would break through her chest. She'd hoped, prayed, that Stuart would take her by the hand and lead her to her bedroom.

Noelle had run in from outside, bubbling over with excitement, Donny and Kevin behind her. The cubs always came first, so Stuart and Peigi had broken apart, Stuart explaining that the frog needed its freedom and should be put back where they found him. He'd gone with Noelle to do that, leaving Peigi restless and frustrated.

Jaycee listened in sympathy. "What you do is set up a babysitter, and then you and Stuart find someplace far away and private. Dimitri and I look after Addie and Kendrick's cubs so they can steal away together. Kendrick doesn't get a lot of down time, and from what you're saying, you and Stuart don't either."

"But we aren't together," Peigi said quickly. "Hard to justify asking Shane to babysit so I can run off to a cabin with Stuart."

"*Aren't* you together?" Jaycee's tawny were eyes full of insight.

"No. Like I said." Peigi started to set down the glass, then changed her mind and took another swig of the fine wine. "He's worried about what's going on with his people, as he should be."

"I know. It sucks being with someone important. Dimitri and I are two of Kendrick's top trackers and sometimes we have to be caretakers instead of enjoying our lives. Still…." She lowered her voice conspiratorially. "Tell you what you do. Once Reid has figured out what Cian wants, and you two are back in Shifter-town, take him aside and tell him you want to jump his bones. Or just jump them without informing him. That man is hot for you — I see it. If you need cub watchers, call me. Dimitri and I will house- and cub-sit for you while you two get it out of your system."

"*If* Stuart wants to go back to Shiftertown after this." Peigi's exuberance vanished. "He's been stuck on this side of the gates for decades. If he has the chance to go back home, to become what he was — why wouldn't he want to stay in Faerie?"

Jaycee wrinkled her nose. "I wouldn't worry about that too much. I've been to Faerie, and I've been in Shiftertowns, and I'd pick a Shiftertown, even with their restrictions, any day. Reid isn't Shifter anyway — he has plenty of freedom in the human world, can go anywhere and do anything he wants. Faerie seemed sparse with regard to restaurants, nightclubs, great kitchen stores …"

"You're Shifter," Peigi pointed out. "So am I. Stuart's going to regard Faerie differently. To him, it's home, the place he can be what we was meant to be, with the people he loves."

Jaycee's expression held sympathy. "I think you might be wrong about where the people he loves are."

"I'm not—"

Peigi broke off as the porch vibrated with Dimitri and Stuart returning. Dimitri leaned in the open back window, resting his arms on the windowsill.

"Reid and I d-decided we'd drive to New Orleans and see if we can find the doorway through the haunted house. Want to come?"

SIX

R eid knew Peigi was skeptical about the trip to New Orleans, but instead of arguing, she began to help Jaycee pack an overnight bag and snacks for the road.

Dimitri said he had to run the idea past Kendrick and get his okay, and he dashed out with wolf swiftness to the main house, leaving Reid at a loose end while the two women packed what seemed like a lot of food and clothing for a short trip.

Reid stepped off the porch and made phone calls. First to Eric to let him know what was going on, then to Diego, explaining he'd need a little more time off from work. Then Nell, who told him he worried too much—she and Cormac, with Brody and Shane to assist, could take care of the cubs just fine. He heard the cubs making a hell of a racket in the background, and he resisted asking what they were up to. Probably better not to know.

Last he called the current caretaker of the New Orleans house, leaving a voice mail when he didn't answer.

By the time his calls were done, Dimitri had returned. "Kendrick says we're to lend you whatever you need, including more backup if necessary." He gave Reid a look of respect. "Which means you've made a big impression on him."

"Or on Dylan," Peigi pointed out. "Dylan regards Stuart as a secret weapon, and Shifter leaders take their cue from Dylan."

She sounded disapproving. Reid knew she didn't like how he often had to drop everything and teleport off to help Dylan, or Dylan's sons, or Eric, or whatever Shiftertown leader in any part of the country, with their problems.

Reid readily assisted, because he owed Shifters—they and Diego had saved his life. Ironic, because the death of a Shifter was supposed to have been inevitable in Reid's quest to return home. One Shifter had died, though not by Reid's hand, and he still felt horrible about it. Assisting Eric, and through him, Dylan and others, was the least he could do to make up for it.

"Can I ask the obvious?" Jaycee said. "There's a ley line in the Austin Shiftertown, with a Fae sympathetic to Shifters guarding it. Why not just go there?"

She meant Fionn Cillian, a Fae warrior who had fathered the mate of Sean Morrissey, Andrea, who was half Shifter, half Fae. Fionn camped just inside the ley line so he could see Andrea and his grandson whenever he liked as well as to keep other Fae from pouring through and killing Shifters.

"Dimitri already asked me the same question," Reid answered. "And I said no. It's one thing for Fionn to help Shifters, but *dokk alfar* are another matter. Fionn might be the most angelic *hoch alfar* ever born, but I can't trust him with *dokk alfar* secrets. Or that Cian wouldn't try to kill Fionn on sight. Safer if I meet Cian alone."

Jaycee nodded, conceding. "I see your point."

Reid noticed Peigi sag relief. It was still hard for her to be among large groups of Shifters she didn't know. Better for them to do this with only Dimitri and Jaycee.

Dimitri studied the group stuffed into the small house, Jaycee with bags packed and ready to go, Peigi with two large coolers and her own bag.

"Think we're taking enough?" Dimitri asked. "Want to shove in the stove, or maybe the kitchen sink?"

Jaycee hoisted one of the duffel bags. "When you're yelling, *why the hell didn't I bring a change of underwear*? You'll thank me."

Dimitri flushed. "It was only the one time."

"Which is why I started packing for you. Can we do this?"

Reid watched Peigi smother a smile as Dimitri sighed and ushered them out the front door. He didn't lock up behind them, because no Shifter would invade his territory, as small as it was.

Dimitri led them out past his pickup to the barn and a black semi-truck cab that rested behind it, out of sight.

Peigi eyed the semi doubtfully as they approached it. "You can drive that?" she asked Dimitri.

"Sure. Can't you?"

"Ignore him," Jaycee said as she opened the passenger door. "He's very proud."

She and Dimitri tossed in bags, which he and Jaycee arranged under seats and the storage area behind the curtain in the back. That area also contained a bed, Reid saw as Dimitri stuffed the luggage back there.

When he finished Peigi climbed in and settled on the back bench seat and Reid hoisted himself up beside her. His instinct was to slide close to her where he could touch her, but he suppressed this and made sure there was a foot of space between them. No need to tempt fate.

"Sweet," Dimitri said as he leapt into the driver's seat and slammed the door. "Road trip!"

"We always take road trips." Jaycee had already closed her door and buckled up. "It's the only way we can get anywhere."

"Fair point." Dimitri revved the engine. "But I s-still like to yell it."

"I know you do, sweetie."

Dimitri winked at Peigi through the mirror. "She loves me."

Peigi smiled back as Dimitri rolled the truck down the rise and to the dirt road they'd driven in on. Shifters waved as they passed, and Kendrick's cubs ran after the truck, shrieking an ear-piercing farewell.

Reid sensed Peigi's excitement as Dimitri steered them onto the paved road and stepped on the gas. She might not be sanguine about the trip to New Orleans, but she gazed around with eager eyes, drinking everything in.

"It's nice to get out," she said when she saw Reid watching her.

"There's a whole lotta n-nothing out here," Dimitri said. "But I know what you mean. Makes me want to howl like the crazy wolf I am."

Jaycee covered her ears. "Please don't."

Dimitri shook his head. "Man, it's hell living with a Feline. So delicate."

"Elegant," Jaycee countered, lowering her hands. "Unlike mangy Lupines."

"Hey, I've never had mange in my life. *You* screech when you get a tangle in your hair. She's constantly licking her paws too," he informed the back seat. "Middle of the night, I wake up to a leopard on the end of our bed. Lick, lick, lick. I always think we have a leak somewhere."

"I'm trying to drown out your snoring," Jaycee said in a honeyed voice. "Anyway, cats are nocturnal. We nap during the day and guard at night. Lupines sleep *all* the time."

Peigi burst out laughing. She had a musical laugh, as beautiful as the rest of her.

"I have to side with Dimitri on the last thing," she said. "Bears like to sleep too."

And yet, when any of the cubs so much as twitched, Peigi was right there, soothing them, reassuring them, loving them. She had a large heart that hadn't been destroyed by that asshole, no matter how much he'd tried to break her.

Stuart had watched Peigi slowly heal in the last couple of years, seen the light return to her eyes. She'd kept from despair by taking care of the cubs, determined not to abandon them.

He'd witnessed her move from barely standing upright to eagerly rising in the morning, ready to face another day. Goddess bless the cubs for that.

As she laughed at Dimitri and Jaycee and their banter, he enjoyed the beauty of her, and rejoiced that she'd returned to life.

———

PEIGI DOZED OFF AND ON AS THE SUN SANK AND DIMITRI drove into the night. It was nice to relax, close her eyes, leave the responsibility to someone else. She loved the cubs and enjoyed being with them, but she rarely had any alone time. One of the cubs always had some sort of drama going on—there was no such thing as all of them quiet and peaceful at once.

Stuart gazed out of the window as though he could see into the blank darkness of the night. He'd said little since they'd pulled away from Kendrick's ranch, and Peigi sensed the tension in him.

He wanted answers. He chafed to dive back into Faerie and find out what was going on—that fact screamed itself to Peigi's Shifter senses.

Stuart sat too far away from her. Peigi felt his warmth through the space between them, but she craved his touch.

Jaycee, cross-legged on her seat, scanned through radio stations. Occasionally, one would come through clearly, and she'd lean back, humming or singing along. Dimitri would join in, the two of them easy with each other, happy.

Peigi surreptitiously slid closer to Stuart. He didn't seem to register this until her thigh bumped his.

Instantly Stuart turned his head and looked at her, his dark gaze cutting through the night.

His eyes were like pieces of midnight, deep with secrets. Peigi had learned a little how to read what was inside Stuart, but much of him remained enigmatic. Tonight his tension cut like a diamond.

Peigi said nothing. She didn't move her leg either. She daringly lifted her hand and closed it over his where it rested on his lap.

Stuart's chest rose sharply. Peigi longed to touch his face, cup it while she kissed his lips.

She settled for squeezing his hand. Peigi expected him to withdraw, to move away and leave her full of restive need. Instead Stuart threaded his fingers through hers, thumb brushing fire across the top of her hand.

Peigi's heart sped as she scooted even closer to Stuart, and she boldly rested her head on his shoulder. She felt his abrupt intake of breath, and then the breath released slowly, as though Stuart instructed himself to remain still.

Peigi closed her eyes. The truck moved with the road, music trickling through the cool air, and she drifted to comfortable slumber, Stuart warm against her.

She jumped awake a long time later when the truck abruptly halted. Peigi snapped upright, ready for danger, but all was quiet, the radio off, dawn light seeping through the windows.

"We made it, kids," Dimitri announced.

Peigi ran her hand through her mussed hair, feeling strangely empty, and realized Stuart was no longer at her side. He was already climbing out of the truck, springing down to the ground in front of a rambling and beautiful house.

Rose vines, devoid of blossoms at the moment, climbed over trellises and up the walls and draped over the porch. The porch itself was wide and inviting, with seats and a porch swing for lazing on a summer afternoon. Even in the winter, it would be a nice place to lounge in the sunshine.

Peigi had heard about this house. It was sentient, built on a ley line, for what purpose no one knew. Maybe the house hadn't been sentient when built but had absorbed the magic streaming beneath it for so long it had become magical itself.

"Hey there." Dimitri approached the porch steps. "Remember us?"

"Of course it remembers us." Jaycee skipped up the steps, patted the porch railing fondly, and knocked on the solid front door. "Is Ben here?"

"He hasn't answered my calls," Stuart said, his deep voice cutting over Jaycee's. "Don't see his motorcycle either."

Dimitri shrugged. "Ben comes and goes. As long as he left the refrigerator stocked ..."

The front door suddenly opened without sound. No frightening noises—the door simply swung inward as though the latch had been jarred loose.

"It used to creak like a bad movie," Dimitri said. "I guess it didn't want to scare us today."

Peigi's bear hackles rose as she sensed the house's aura, but Jaycee tripped inside without fear, calling out a greeting. Dimitri growled and hurried after her—female Shifters were supposed to let males go into a new place first, checking it for danger. Peigi had the feeling Jaycee only followed that rule when it suited her.

Peigi hung back, Stuart next to her. "Think it's safe?" she murmured.

"No." Stuart regarded the house warily. "We know it likes Shifters and Ben, but what about *dokk alfar*?"

"One way to find out."

"I like your courage," Stuart told her. "We might get answers if nothing else." Peigi started forward, but Stuart clasped her elbow, tugging her close. "I'm glad you're with me," he said softly.

Peigi heated as his breath brushed her ear, her pulse banging sloppily. She fumbled for words in answer and came out with, "So I can protect you from the house?"

Stuart chuckled, his laugh tickling inside her ear. "Partly."

He remained near, his lips parted as though he'd say more, then he closed his mouth, released her, and gestured them forward.

"Males are supposed to go first," Peigi said lightly.

"Yes, so the males will be eaten first, and the wise females can run away."

"That's the idea."

Stuart took her arm again. "How about we go in together?"

"If the door is wide enough," Peigi said. "Bears are big."

Stuart slid his dark gaze over her, taking his time. "I think you're just right."

If he kept on like this, Peigi would never be able to stand up, let alone walk through the door. Her knees were watery, and she pressed closer to him so she could stay upright. "Let's do this."

The front door remained open, welcoming. Or gaping like a mouth? Peigi drew a breath, exchanged a glance with Stuart, and then the two of them plunged through together.

They fit just fine, the old-fashioned doorway made to admit ladies with giant skirts without tearing delicate fabric.

Once inside, Stuart released her arm, to Peigi's disappointment. She stepped away from him, pretending indifference, and took in the airy hall, the paneling and throw rugs, the slender-legged tables with silver knick-knacks. Elegant without being stuffy.

Behind them the front door swung slowly shut, settling into place with a quiet click.

"Not creepy or anything," Stuart murmured.

"You're a dark Fae," Peigi said, trying to hide her nervousness. "Some people's definition of creepy."

"Some *Shifters'* definition you mean." Stuart moved past her and gazed up the massive staircase that wound through the center of the house. "Okay, and some *hoch alfars'*. We have a lot of enemies."

Peigi joined him. An iron chandelier hung down from the top of the house, fitting perfectly inside the curve of the staircase. "Well, you *are* scary on a dark night."

Stuart gave her a look of pretended dismay. "I hope I'm scary *all* the time. What happened to our friends?"

"Up here," Jaycee's voice floated down to them. "Kitchen."

The kitchen was on the second floor—Jaycee had explained during the trip that the living quarters were upstairs, while the lower level of the house was kept in its eighteenth-century decor for tourists.

"Ben takes the tourists through," Jaycee had finished. "I bet that's fun."

The mysterious Ben, who sometimes called himself Gil, had been alive for centuries and probably had known people from this house's heyday. Peigi hadn't answered, but reflected she'd love to take a tour of this house he conducted.

There was no sign of Ben, however, as Peigi and Stuart ascended the stairs and made their way down the hall to the large sunny kitchen. Dimitri was digging through a pantry that, judging from the armloads of provisions he dragged out, was stocked enough to satisfy him.

He moved to the counter and began breaking eggs into a bowl. Stuart watched him for about ten seconds before he waded in and started pancakes.

"Let him," Peigi said when Jaycee tried to protest that Peigi and Stuart were guests. "He's Pancake Expert. Stuart doesn't just make ordinary pancakes—he does lemon and ricotta cheese, or chocolate chip, or orange and spice, banana with walnuts ..."

Jaycee considered. "Okay. I'll take one of each of those."

Dimitri went back to his eggs—Stuart stole a handful of them from the carton. Jaycee started on coffee and toast, making it clear she didn't expect Peigi to do any of the work.

Restless, Peigi decided to scope out the house. On this floor she found fairly modern rooms, not only this kitchen with the latest appliances but also a couple well-appointed bathrooms, with giant tubs for soaking off stress.

Each bedroom held furniture from a different period of history—Peigi wasn't familiar with all of them, but she could distinguish between the sleek forms of the Colonial years and the heavily carved, massive pieces from the Victorian age.

She continued downstairs, running her hand lightly on the

polished staircase railing. On the ground floor, the house was like a stage set, containing beautiful furniture, drapes, and paintings, waiting for the family of long-ago to receive callers, dine, or host a ball.

The slave quarters had also been restored, Jaycee had told Peigi, another snapshot of history, but the darker side. Peigi walked out the back door—which opened itself for her—across a wide veranda, and down steps to the path that led to the line of outbuildings.

The sun was rising, the clear sky flushing pink. The place was beautiful, serene. Peigi drew in a cleansing breath. She could get used to this.

Or maybe not. She already missed the cubs' constant noise, their energy. She should call Nell and see how they were getting on, or she could resist the urge and not wake them up too early. She had to remember there was a two-hour time difference between Louisiana and Nevada—Nell wouldn't thank her for calling while it was still dark.

Peigi paused beside a stumpy, gnarled tree devoid of leaves. An old one, she surmised, though still solid. It had a presence, anchoring one end of the path, probably why it hadn't been cut down.

She let out a sigh—she'd been keeping her frustration in check, but it boiled up inside her. She wished the *dokk alfar* had left Stuart the hell alone. She and Stuart could be waking up in their little house in Las Vegas, planning a day together, tearing their hair out trying to keep the six cubs whole and out of trouble.

From what Stuart had explained, this Cian guy and probably all of Stuart's people, needed his help. He was right to find a way to keep them safe from the high Fae, and Peigi agreed. On the other hand, she wanted Faerie to disappear forever and Stuart to stay with her and never leave.

"I'm a selfish bitch," she said out loud. "I know he needs to go, but damn it, *I* need him too. So do the cubs."

A ripple of wind stirred the short branches of the ancient tree. The sound was comforting, almost as though the tree exuded sympathy. But why not? This was a haunted house, why not a haunted tree to go with it?

"I guess every soldier's wife feels like this," she confided to the tree. "She's proud he runs off to fight for what he believes in and to help others stay alive, but at the same time, she wants to hold on to him and pray he isn't taken from her."

Another rustle, and then the wind died, bringing silence.

"And I'm talking to a tree." Peigi rubbed her hair. "I am *so* sleep deprived. And seriously need caffeine."

She hurried up the path and into the house, exhaling in relief when she burst inside to the strong scent of coffee wafting down from upstairs.

AFTER A BREAKFAST OF THREE DIFFERENT KINDS OF PANCAKES, tasty omelets from Dimitri, a platter of toast courtesy of Jaycee, and several cups of rich coffee, Peigi felt much better. Shifters could put away food, so the pantry's stores were depleted by the time they finished.

Once they'd cleaned up the breakfast detritus, Dimitri led them downstairs to a small parlor and pointed to a wall. "*Here* is where the door was."

Peigi stared at the nicely paneled and papered wall, no doors in sight. A breeze rustled outside the open window, the rose vines creaking.

Stuart ran his fingers over the wall where a door frame would have been. He leaned to the paneling and put his ear to it.

"Hear anything?" Dimitri asked.

"Just you." Stuart closed his eyes, pressing his cheek to the paneling. He touched the wall with gentle but strong fingers.

Peigi held her breath, watching Stuart absently stroke the paneling, all his concentration on what might lie behind it. She couldn't stop herself imagining how she'd feel with Stuart's strong fingers on *her*, she the subject of that intense attention.

Another breeze drifted through, making her shiver.

"Who opened the windows?" Peigi whispered. "It's cold."

Dimitri and Jaycee started. From their expressions, they thought *she'd* opened them.

Having a house do what it wanted could be inconvenient, Peigi decided, though she admitted the distraction had stopped her from gazing at Stuart and drooling. She moved to the long window and closed it, shutting out the wind. The gnarled tree was visible from this room, standing guard over the end of the path.

Stuart opened his eyes and straightened up. "The house probably likes to open and close its own windows. Maybe it needs to breathe."

"You do like escalating the creep factor," Peigi said. "Can you tell if there's a door there? Or a gate, or whatever?"

Stuart touched the paneling. "If there was a way through, it's gone."

"It closed up and vanished after a Fae tried to get in and kill us," Jaycee said. "Or maybe Lady Aisling shut it down. I don't really know."

"We weren't paying much attention at the time." Dimitri slid his arm around Jaycee and slanted her a knowing look.

"You had mating on your mind, yes." Jaycee leaned into him. "All right, I admit, I was pretty far gone on mating frenzy at the time too." Her smile held satisfaction and not one bit of embarrassment. "I wonder if Lady Aisling could help get Stuart through? If she closed the door, she might be able to open it. There's an old sundial on the other side …"

"Lady Aisling told you to summon her only in time of dire emergency, remember," Dimitri said. "Would she consider this a dire emergency?"

Stuart leaned on the paneling again, touching it with light fingers. "The Tuil Erdannan deemed the Shifter-Fae war a ten-minute distraction, like watching ants battle over a leaf. I doubt this Lady Aisling would lift a finger to keep the *hoch alfar* away from the *dokk alfar*. They never have before." The grim note in his voice reminded Peigi that his clan had been wiped out by the high Fae, with no one charging in to help them.

"Ben told us the Tuil Erdannan created the *dokk alfar*," Jaycee said. "Or at least that was a rumor. Did they?"

Stuart shrugged. "No idea. It's not one of our creation stories. But we were first in Faerie, long before the *hoch alfar* appeared. That's historic record."

"We need Ben's take on this," Jaycee said. "He's been living in the house a while. I bet he's figured out a lot of its secrets."

"But where the hell is he?" Dimitri growled. "I've been trying to call him."

"So have I," Stuart said. "I keep getting voice mail."

Peigi had turned to the window while they debated, taking in the bright mid-morning. More wind sprang up, fluttering the dried branches on the old tree, as though the tree itself were moving.

Peigi's jaw went slack. The tree *was* moving. Its bole flexed and two branches rose and fell, exactly like a person might stretch when he woke in the morning.

The bark of the old tree rippled. Peigi gawped, too transfixed to call out to the others, who went on discussing the door, the house, the Tuil Erdannan, and Ben.

The tree's branches thickened until they resembled arms hanging from broad shoulders. The roots came out of the ground, as though the tree had bent a knee and flexed its toes.

As the tree walked forward, the bark flowed together to become skin—tough and leathery. The large round knot on the front of the trunk could be its face, the remaining leaves and branches on top its hair.

The creature became less and less treelike as it approached the house, though it retained the characteristics of the tree in its barrel shape and solid strength. By the time it reached the porch steps it had clothes—jeans, sweatshirt, and motorcycle boots. The knot had indeed become a face, with a broad forehead, wide nose, and very dark eyes that held the wisdom of ancients.

The man sprang up onto the porch outside the parlor and rapped on the window.

"Hey," he said to Peigi. "Can you let me in? I think I dropped my key."

"Ben!" Jaycee cried behind her. "There you are. About time."

SEVEN

Ben sauntered in past Peigi and gave her a sly wink, which made Reid's annoyance flare. Peigi continued to gape at Ben in shock.

"Sorry I wasn't around to welcome you," Ben said. "Things to take care of."

Peigi drew a breath as though to throw questions at him, then she snapped her mouth shut and bathed him in a frown. Ben only grinned at her, as though they shared a secret, which made Reid simmer all the more.

Dimitri waved Ben to the wall and tapped it. "Can you bring back the door? Reid is trying to get through."

"So I heard." Ben slid his cell phone from his pocket and thumbed through his screen. "On, what, eight messages?" He clicked the phone dark and replaced it in his pocket. "I have to apologize again—you've wasted the trip. The door doesn't come to my calling. Jazz said she never saw it before, and I haven't seen it since I moved in to take care of the place."

"Damn," Jaycee said softly. "Like the swimming pool." To Reid's raised brows, she said, "Swimming pool appeared when I needed to cool off. Jazz told me later she didn't have one."

Peigi cleared her throat. "Maybe if we ask the house nicely?"

Ben grunted a laugh. "Maybe. But if the house thinks it's too dangerous for us, it won't comply. The only reason the door appeared before was to give Jaycee a way to rescue Dimitri." Dimitri nodded at this, unoffended.

"So you can't help us." Peigi scowled at Ben, angry at him for some reason.

"I didn't say that." Ben returned her gaze neutrally. "This house is on a ley line. That might be some use."

Jaycee studied the blank wall. "Ben, I heard that you can find your way into sort-of pockets between this world and Faerie. So said Bowman from North Carolina when he had a meet-up with Kendrick. How about doing that?"

"I *can*," Ben said hesitantly. "But it might not do Reid any good. He could get stuck in that pocket, or find his way to someplace that was neither Faerie nor here. Do you know anything about the multiverse theory of quantum physics? The idea is that there are infinite numbers of worlds out there—and they aren't kidding."

Jaycee flinched. "That's unsettling."

"Most of the time we don't notice, or care, in our everyday lives," Ben went on. "But every once in a while, enough energy from one coalesces, and a gate opens. Usually on a ley line. Faerie has a strong enough connection with our world that we get there the easiest, but we could go other places by accident."

"Like I said, unsettling," Jaycee repeated.

Reid nodded agreement. "Even if we do get through a gate to Faerie, there's no way of knowing where I'd land there. It's a big place."

"I know," Jaycee said glumly. "I saw a map of it once. That's why I suggested Lady Aisling. She would know the way and have transportation."

"*If* she was interested," Reid said, his impatience growing.

"Hang on a sec," Ben broke in. "I met Lady Aisling. She's one frightening lady. You do *not* want to piss her off. You talk about her like she's a friend, Jaycee, but she's a *Tuil Erdannan*."

"Ben's scared of her," Jaycee said in amusement.

"Because I'm sane. She can kill all of us with her pinky."

"Aw, I thought she liked you," Jaycee said. "That's what Zander told me."

"She was *interested* in me," Ben said. "I am not going to test that."

"None of this is helping Stuart." Peigi stepped forward, and everyone but Stuart blinked, as though they'd forgotten her presence. Jaycee and Dimitri were more dominant than she was, but when Peigi decided it was time to make a point, she let dominance go to hell. "If Stuart can't go through to Faerie with this route, then where can he? Not the Austin ley line. I agree with him about that."

Ben rubbed his chin. "Have to think about it. There's a ley line in Las Vegas, you know. Runs right under your Shiftertown."

"Which I got stuck in," Reid said. "I don't think it's open all the way anymore."

"Is there a map of ley lines?" Peigi asked. "With helpful pointers to where working gates exist?"

"Huh," Ben said. "Would be handy. I know Andrea had one she mapped herself, but she turned all that research over to Sean for the Guardian database. Guardians, I hear, have a way to know, through the database, when a gate opens and closes. We could ask one of them."

"One I can trust?" Reid sent Ben a quizzical look. "Most Shifter leaders like me where they can find me. Would they let a Guardian help me? Trust that I'd go back to Faerie and not cause a shitload of trouble? And come back out again?"

"Zander's mate, Rae, is a Guardian," Jaycee said. "And trustworthy."

"She's a relatively new Guardian," Ben said. "She's still learning about the Guardian secrets and their knowledge pool. I was thinking more of the Guardian of the North Carolina Shiftertown, a Feline called Pierce Daniels. He's smart and sort of trusts me. We could talk to him."

"Hell of a d-drive," Dimitri said. "Why not your own Guardian? What's his name — Neal?"

Peigi broke in. "Because Eric might stop him. Stuart is an asset." She said the last word in disapprobation. She didn't like that Eric used Reid anytime he needed him.

"That's why I thought of Pierce," Ben said. "His Shiftertown leader — Bowman — does his own thing. Bowman wouldn't give a shit if Eric didn't want Reid leaving. And Pierce might not bother telling Bowman he was helping us. The Shifters out there are seriously independent. I guess that comes from living in the middle of the woods."

Reid considered the suggestion. "All right, contact him. Anything Pierce knows about finding gates would be helpful. Doesn't mean I can get through, but it's worth a shot."

"Don't you need a Fae artifact to help?" Jaycee asked. "Or a chant or something? Dimitri got pulled through by a spell and stinky incense."

"Depends." Ben tapped his fingertips together. "Humans and Shifters, yes, need some magic to help open a gate. For a Fae, I don't know. They seem to be able to move back and forth at will."

"I've gone through gates before," Reid said impatiently. "But I won't find out if I can until I get *to* a gate. If the house won't open the door ..." He glanced at the wall, which remained stubbornly solid. "Jaycee, Dimitri, Ben, Peigi — sorry I wasted your time."

"Not a w-waste," Dimitri said. "You needed me to tell you about Cian."

"I still think I should talk to Lady Aisling," Jaycee said. "Ask her opinion if not for her help."

Ben stopped tapping and laced his fingers together. "The way you say that, like you'll simply call her for a chat, is seriously terrifying. Be careful, Jaycee. Being casual with the Tuil Erdannan is like playing around with an antitank missile."

"It sounds like everyone has a plan." Peigi's voice was calm, but her anger cut at Reid. "Why don't you pursue it, and Stuart and I will go home and take care of our cubs."

Again, the others broke off and turned to her in surprise. Peigi was good at staying quiet while everyone argued, but when she did speak, she made people listen. She didn't just blather to fill space.

Dimitri sent her a big smile. "Yeah, we're kinda useless. But you're in this big house, and it's a long journey home. Rest, chill out, and we'll start back in the morning. Ben and I will make calls, Jaycee and I will argue about her contacting Lady Aisling, and you and Stuart can take a little vacation. There's lots of food, beer, TV, online games, whatever you want. This place is like a resort for Shifters."

Peigi relaxed a smidge. "Probably won't hurt for us to rest a while. But please tell Marlo to meet us as close by as he possibly can."

"Or we can go into New Orleans and p-party," Dimitri said. "We know a Shifter club ..."

"If you mean the one where I got thrown off a balcony, then no thanks," Ben said, shaking his head. "I'll hang out here, cook burgers, stay safe."

"I've never been to a Shifter club," Peigi said.

That earned her more startled expressions. "Never?" Jaycee asked in amazement. "I thought there was a great one in Vegas."

"There is, but I don't go." Peigi sounded wistful. "Cubs to take care of. Plus I haven't felt up to it until lately."

"New plan then." Dimitri laced one arm around Jaycee and drew Peigi lightly into the embrace with his other. Nothing sexually charged, just friendly. "We make our calls, take some naps, freshen up, and hit the club tonight."

"Are you sure it will be safe?" Peigi asked nervously. "What if we're carded? Shifters aren't supposed to travel out of their states."

"I'll call the guy I know who lets people in and out," Dimitri said. "He's a friend. No one has to know."

Dimitri spoke with the confidence of one who knew how to get away with anything, but Reid wasn't happy with this plan.

He started to say firmly that, no, they'd stay put until time to go home, but he didn't miss the eagerness on Peigi's face. She truly hadn't had a chance to have the fun that Shifters took for granted. She was slowly coming out of her shell, tentatively trying new experiences, but of course taking care of cubs took precedence. While the Shifters in Las Vegas piled into cars to head to Coolers, the Shifter bar, Peigi fed cubs macaroni and cheese and read them bedtime stories.

"All right," Reid said, deciding. "We can spend a few hours at the club and enjoy ourselves. But that's it. I need to focus."

"You don't have to go at all," Peigi said quickly. "I know hanging out with a ton of Shifters isn't your thing."

"What are you talking about?" he asked in feigned astonishment. "I hang out with a ton of Shifters every day, in our house. If I can handle the cubs, I can handle a club full of drunk Shifters. And like hell you're going out without me."

Peigi's eyes went starry, and her smile warmed everything inside him. Reid was so focused on her it was a moment before he noticed the other three were highly amused about something, Dimitri nudging Jaycee.

He realized he'd said *our house* and *our cubs*, without thinking about it. As though he and Peigi were mates, in Shifter terms, sharing their lives.

Well, they were. Reid returned his friends' gazes without wavering, and didn't take the words back. He'd said what he said, and he believed it in his heart.

———

BEN TRIED TO RUN FROM PEIGI WHEN SHE DESCENDED FROM her long nap and shower to find him alone downstairs. The sky had darkened with night, and Ben tried to fade into the shadows of the back hall.

Peigi, who'd learned long ago how to keep track of cubs who could hide *anywhere*, quickened her steps and went after him. Ben slid out the back door, but Peigi caught up to him on the veranda. He tried to blend in with the darkness there, but Peigi'd had to be too watchful in her life to fall for that trick.

She stopped right in front of him, arms folded, and Ben looked sheepish.

"Was that your true shape, or were you just eavesdropping?" Peigi demanded.

"How could I be eavesdropping?" Ben had to tilt his head to peer up at her. "You came right up to me and started talking."

"And you're not going to repeat a word of it." She bent a stern eye on him. "My private thoughts are just that, all right?"

"Hey, don't worry. I can keep a secret. I'll pretend I was your confessor or something."

Peigi relented, but only a little. She didn't know Ben well enough to decide whether to trust him.

"But seriously, you're a *tree*?"

"What?" Ben said, outraged. "No. I'm a goblin. We can take various forms, whatever we want—well, within certain parameters. But I'm *not* a tree. No photosynthesis here."

He was definitely man-shaped, complete with hard muscles, tatts, black hair, and vibrant dark eyes. He looked a *little* like the tree-thing she'd seen, mostly in height and strength.

"I get it," Peigi said. "Same way a stick insect resembles a twig but isn't even close. Or a praying mantis resembles leaf. Right?"

Ben huffed, offended. "Sort of. I guess. Don't even think about calling me a stick insect."

"I didn't. I'm trying to understand."

Ben deflated. "Yeah, well, there's a lot of shit I don't understand either. Do me a favor, though, take care of Jaycee tonight. She has faith in her friendship with Lady Aisling, but Lady Aisling is dangerous. I met her, and I was impressed, but I'm still aware of her power. To her, Jaycee is a dust mote. Lady Aisling might be interested in the dust mote at the moment, but as soon as she's done ..." Ben made a flicking gesture with his finger and thumb.

"I know." Peigi's voice softened in understanding. "Powerful people will always throw around their power. They don't know how not to."

"That's what I like about you, Pegs. You don't say much, but you have a wise head on your shoulders."

"That's how I survive. I listen and learn, and keep my mouth shut."

"Is that you telling me you'll keep my secrets?" Ben asked.

"If you keep mine."

"Deal." Ben held out his hand.

Peigi took it. "Deal."

Ben's grip was tight, a strong man in a compact body. On impulse, Peigi tugged him closer and enfolded him in a Shifter hug.

"Oh, this is good." Ben's voice quieted, and he returned the embrace with a tight one of his own.

A brush of wind touched Peigi, and suddenly Stuart was next to them. "When you're done," he growled at Ben.

Ben opened his arms and hastily stepped back. "Only being friendly. Shifter-style. No groping, nothing hands-y."

"I hugged *him*," Peigi said to Stuart, her face heating. "For being nice."

"Nice. Yeah, that's me. Mr. Nice Guy. Who is going away now ..."

Ben's voice faded with him, leaving Peigi facing Stuart. "I really was thanking him."

Stuart gave her a nod meant to be nonchalant, but Peigi scented his rigidity. "You sure you want to go tonight?" he asked.

"Yes, I do. It's a rare night I'm not looking after cubs." Peigi thought a moment. "All right, this is the *only* night I haven't been looking after cubs since I can remember."

Stuart's rigidity evaporated. "You should have said. Any time you want, I'll talk Shane into babysitting, and take you out. We can go as human—they have swank clubs in Las Vegas. I know —I used to raid them when I was on the force."

Peigi let out a laugh. "That's your club experience? Knocking down the door, weapons drawn?"

"We didn't knock down doors. We cornered the manager and told everyone to leave. Lot of drug dealing in back rooms."

Peigi's amusement continued. "Well, if that doesn't make me want to go dancing, I don't know what will."

"Not what I meant. I mean—I know some nice places if you want ..."

Peigi touched her fingers to his lips. "I'm teasing you. I do that. Let's go out *tonight*. It's New Orleans. I might never be able to visit again, and I don't want to miss out."

Stuart had gone completely still. His mouth was quiet under her touch, lips smooth and warm.

They stood alone on the porch, Ben having banged into the house, Dimitri and Jaycee laughing about something upstairs.

Peigi moved her fingers away, and before she could stop herself, she leaned into Stuart and kissed him on the mouth.

EIGHT

Reid froze as Peigi's lips touched his, her breath warming everything cold inside him.

Her mouth was soft, hot, strong. She stepped closer, her tall body against his, Peigi nearly matching him for height.

The world stopped. Reid's heart halted between one beat and the next, and then he ceased caring whether it started again. He let out a muffled groan and caught Peigi in his arms.

Reid expected her to pull away, to turn in embarrassment and go. Instead, she deepened the kiss, flowing against him. His hands found her sleek hair, the satin skin of her neck, the supple curve of her waist.

Mouths moved, Reid tasting her, his body as incandescent as the brush of her tongue. His blood was on fire, need suppressed far too long roaring forth.

Fae and Shifter were supposed to be completely different, so boasted the Fae, the Shifters animals far inferior to the perfection of the Fae.

Bullshit. Peigi was a beautiful woman, Reid a man, didn't matter which side of the genetic coin they came from. They fit together, they felt, they *needed* exactly the same. As Reid needed her now.

She was everything to him, a balm to his soul. Reid had gone from lonely guilt to being at ease with himself for the first time in decades, all because of this woman.

Peigi made a noise in her throat. She slid her hands down his back, and his thoughts fled. Sensation took over—her fingers at his waistband, her breasts against his chest, her spectacular kiss he hoped would never end ...

Wanting gouged him, the longing that woke him in the night. He'd be hard, the enraging frustration that she was just down the hall, quietly sleeping, destroying him. She'd make a soft sound, as though enjoying her dreams, her skin scented with the winter tea fragrance.

Stuart imbibed her fragrance now as he kissed her, their mouths fitting exactly as he drank her in ...

"Oops." Dimitri's good-natured voice broke through the fire. "I'll j-just ... wait inside."

Reid heard Dimitri's footsteps retreat. Again, Peigi didn't jump away, or gasp, or act ashamed. She pulled back a tad and brushed her fingers across Reid's cheek, her eyes shining.

"I guess we'd better go," she whispered.

Shit. Reid reluctantly released her, and Peigi turned away without awkwardness, as though they'd merely been chatting. Reid caught her hand. Peigi glanced back, inquiring.

"Later." Reid coughed, his voice hoarse. "We're going to talk."

"Of course." Her smile blossomed. "We'll have a nice discussion."

He couldn't tell if she teased or was serious. Peigi surprised him with her humor but it sometimes left Reid baffled. *Dokk alfar* could be wild partiers, but Shifters infused everything with teasing that bewildered him.

Peigi's fingers drifted from his and she walked into the house, her body swaying in her natural gait. When the door closed,

Reid turned to the railing and leaned heavily on it, dragging in breath after breath. His cock was rock hard and not about to go down anytime soon.

"Son of a *bitch*," he whispered, a growl of frustration escaping.

Wind chimes rang and the rose vines vibrated, Reid could swear in sympathy.

———

PEIGI HADN'T PACKED PARTY CLOTHES, NOT THAT SHE OWNED any, but it didn't seem to matter at this Shifter club. Her jeans and sweatshirt weren't out of place, she saw as they walked in.

Most Shifters dressed casually, though a few Shifter women wore slinky dresses or skin-tight pants. The only people who truly dressed up were the groupies, in their fake ears, painted on whiskers, and clothes that bared skin. A few had tied on tails, though they had to hold them up to dance on the crowded floors.

Dimitri had driven them to New Orleans in the semi, which they'd parked several blocks away, approaching the club on foot. The four had decided, after a confab, that if Shifter Bureau or police lurked, they'd quietly go back to the house, but if not, the three Shifters would put on their fake Collars and blend in with the others.

No official-looking guys were hanging around, so on went the Collars. Other Shifters would know they were Shifter without any problem, and not having Collars would attract attention. Peigi wanted to have fun tonight, not be noticed.

A large Lupine Shifter guarded the door. "Angus, my old friend," Dimitri called out as they approached.

Angus, who wore a scowl over wolf-gray eyes, unbent a little and greeted Dimitri with a Shifter hug, Jaycee likewise. On their way from the house, Jaycee had told Peigi and Reid the entire tale of how Angus had helped her rescue Dimitri last year.

Angus had a mate, she'd related, a fox Shifter. Peigi hadn't known fox Shifters existed, but obviously they did, though they were extremely rare. She was there tonight, the red-haired young woman emerging from the darkness inside the door, greeting Jaycee with a warm smile and a delighted hello.

They embraced, the smaller woman nearly engulfed by Jaycee. The woman emerged without harm and hugged Dimitri, then turned an interested face to Peigi.

"Angus told me you were coming," she said to Peigi as she led them deeper into the club, Angus returning to his door duty. "Well, Angus said maybe three words about it, which is all I had time to pry out of him. I'm Tamsin, by the way. Angus's mate."

She said the words proudly. Tamsin had a pointed face and tawny eyes a similar color to Jaycee's, but those eyes held a quick dart that spoke loudly of fox. Tamsin grinned at Peigi, as though understanding her curiosity.

"We both have histories," she said, slipping her arm through Peigi's. "And I'd love to get to know you, and your *dokk alfar* friend, but first, we're gonna dance the night away."

She pronounced *dokk alfar* exactly right, earning a startled glance from Stuart. Tamsin didn't seem aware she'd done anything unusual, and herded them toward the dance floor.

The club rose three stories, balconies ringing each floor. Each level was full of dancers and tables, waitresses hurrying up and down the iron staircase with trays of drinks.

The human groupies stared with interest at Peigi, very obviously a bear, and Dimitri, with his red hair and gray wolf's eyes. Jaycee earned a lot of attention from the men, and everyone's gaze went to Stuart, trying to work out what he was. Stuart was the only one not in a Collar, and Peigi watched the humans conclude that he must be human too.

The Shifters, on the other hand, scented Fae. They came alert, rising stiff-limbed, menace in their eyes.

Tamsin kept hold of Peigi and slid her other arm through Stuart's. "Don't worry about them," she said loudly over the music. "You're under Angus's protection."

Shifters heard her loud and clear. They subsided, if not happily. Angus must be widely respected.

"And mine." A tall black man broke from the crowd, a bottle of beer in his hand. "I'm Reg. Welcome." He nodded at Peigi and then Reid, and turned to enfold Jaycee and then Dimitri in a Shifter hug.

"See?" Tamsin said. "Reg is Angus's best friend and the second of his Shiftertown. We're one big, happy family. Well, it's neutral ground anyway. Dance and have fun."

Tamsin released them with a grin then walked off with Reg, talking at him a mile a minute.

"She's interesting," Peigi said to Stuart.

"And smart," Stuart said. "I watched her note the position of every single Shifter and their proximity to us before she made her announcement that we were friends of Angus. She knows how to plan. I'd like to have a conversation with her about it." He sounded admiring.

"How about we dance instead?"

"Ah." Stuart glanced at Dimitri and Jaycee, who had already waded into the crowd. They began dancing very close to each other, moving to the thumping beat. "I don't dance."

"No?" Peigi swayed to the music, unable to help herself. The bass vibrated her body, urging her to join it. "Is it a *dokk alfar* thing?"

"It's a Stuart Reid thing. When *dokk alfar* dance, it's a performance, not personal. And then it's pretty crazy. Sometimes nude."

Peigi laughed in surprise. "I dare you."

Stuart shook his head swiftly. "No way in hell."

"I so need to see that."

"Uh-uh. Not tonight."

Peigi took his hands. "I get it. You're shy. Okay, no nude crazy dancing. How about I dance, and you stand with me. Just shuffle your feet every now and then so people think you're catching the groove."

Stuart got that expression on his face when he wasn't sure she was joking. Peigi loved to mess with him—he brought out her sense of humor like no one else.

The music swept her up, and Peigi danced.

The release was incredible. Peigi's body remembered moves from long ago, when she'd been young, happy, certain her life would work out. Just past their Transitions, she and her friends would go to clubs and concerts and let themselves go. This was before Shifters were outed, and she could party to her heart's content.

Peigi whooped as her cares fell away, the years of worry, restraint, and downright terror. She'd lived in constant fear that one of Miguel's un-Collared Shifters might decide to kill one of the women, the cubs, or her.

She remembered the day she'd been rescued, Miguel fleeing, the warehouse where she'd been confined blown to smithereens. Reid had stood firmly as the warehouse went up in flames, his strong body silhouetted against the chaos. He'd escorted her to the plane when she could barely move, making sure no one was left behind.

Because of this man, Peigi could rest easily and dance like she didn't have a care. Because of a Fae, who understood her.

Peigi danced close to Stuart and rested her hands on his hips, swaying against him. In spite of claiming he couldn't dance, Stuart too caught the rhythm, keeping it slow, moving with Peigi in a circle that was all their own.

His scent was of the earth and fresh wind, which never failed to make her blood tingle. While other Shifters smelled Fae when he came near them, Peigi was only aware of *Stuart*. The thought that other Shifter females in this bar might wake up to the fact that he was desirable made her growl.

Stuart moved smoothly, his body melding with hers, the music rendering the two one. Peigi rested her head on his shoulder and breathed out, touching him with her warmth.

Stuart gathered her close, unaware of what she did. Peigi

would explain later, but the Shifters around them would know he was under her protection. *Mine.*

The other Shifters got the message. By the time the song segued into another, the Shifter women around them were alert, but backing off.

Peigi expected Stuart to want to sit the next song out, maybe have a drink. She smiled as he pulled her close again, and they continued their slow dance in the middle of the tumult.

———

WHEN THEY FINALLY LEFT THE CLUB, WHICH KICKED SHIFTERS out before their curfew so they could get back to their Shifter-towns on time, Dimitri and Jaycee were giving Reid strange looks.

Jaycee started to speak, but Peigi shook her head imperceptibly, and Jaycee closed her mouth. Dimitri appeared to be suppressing laughter with effort.

Reid had no idea what Shifter thing they were discussing with their body language, but he'd have to ask Peigi later, when they reached the house and before she bedded down for the night ... Or maybe they'd take a walk under the stars. They could talk, he could ask, and they could kiss, finishing what Dimitri had interrupted.

"How about we ditch these and go to another club?" Dimitri tapped his Collar as they reached the semi, dark and alone on a side street. "Bars stay open for a while longer."

Reid had no intention of spending his time with Peigi trying to shout to her over extreme music while people around them got drunker and drunker. He'd seen enough of what alcohol and late nights did to people when he'd been a cop, and didn't want Peigi around that.

"Mind if we head back to the house?" Reid asked, as though he didn't care what any of them did, really. "Peigi and I want to get an early start to head back to the cubs."

Dimitri pulled keys from his jacket pocket. "Can you drive a rig?"

"I can, in fact." Reid had driven as a trucker undercover once. He'd enjoyed it so much he'd toyed with the idea of giving up the police and hitting the road. Too bad his obsession with finding his way back to Faerie had stopped him.

"All right then." Dimitri tossed him the keys. "Jase and I will find another club. She can't get enough of the dancing."

"Don't have much opportunity," Jaycee said, leaning into Dimitri. "And once this cub comes, we'll be home all the time."

"Yeah, that will suck." Dimitri's smug expression betrayed the lie.

"How will you get back if we take the truck?" Peigi asked in concern.

"Let us worry about that. We have a lot of friends." Dimitri pulled Jaycee to him and they began to walk away, Jaycee waving her farewells. Soft clinking sounds told Reid they were pulling off their Collars.

Watching them, Reid wondered what it would be like to kick back and have friends and family, a simple existence. To hell with missions, obsessions, and high Fae *czul* who ruined his life over and over again.

For the joy of it, he drew Peigi to him and kissed her.

She softened in his arms, rising on tiptoe to kiss him back. Her warmth surrounded him, soothed him, spread contentment through him he'd never felt in his life.

Reid parted her lips, letting the kiss turn deep. Peigi quietly laced her arms around his neck, relaxing against him. The New Orleans street grew quiet, Jaycee and Dimitri long gone, the tourists seeking other parts of town. Peigi and Reid were alone in the night, a moment for the two of them to kiss, touch, explore each other and the needs they'd bottled up for so long.

Peigi's mouth warmed him in the night, her hands roving his back. Reid slid his hand up her waist and cupped her breast, feeling its weight through her jacket and sweatshirt. Peigi made a noise in her throat and the kiss turned a little bit wild.

Reid's only warning was the smell. A foul odor assaulted him, and he pulled away from Peigi in time to see her eyes fill with terrible fear.

Shifters melted from the shadows to surround them, most in human form, but some as animals — wolves, a slinking shadow that might be a leopard, two bears. No Collars glinted on their necks.

One of the bears morphed into a huge man with mottled brown hair. One side of his face was scarred with old burns, and Stuart instantly recognized him.

Shifters grabbed Reid before the bear-man seized Peigi by the hair, yanking her head back.

"Hey, Peigi," he growled and then smiled, showing pointed teeth. "Remember me? Your old mate?"

NINE

R eid fought with fury, but the Shifters were strong and numerous. And they seriously stank.

"You're not my mate," Peigi shouted. She wrenched herself from the bear's grip, tears glittering on her face. "My friends blew your compound all to hell. I considered that a break-up."

"That's not how it works, baby."

Peigi balled her fists. "We never had the sun and moon, Miguel." She punctuated her next words with competent punches at the bear-man. "I. Am. *Not*. Your. Mate."

He deflected her blows with some difficulty. "Name's not Miguel anymore. It's Michael."

She stopped. "Right, you changed it in Mexico, to blend in, you said. Because you're an idiot."

Reid continued to battle. The Shifters were strong but Stuart knew how to fight dirty. The leopard went flying, yowling as it struck a brick wall. Reid got a kick into the wolf's gut, and both elbows into the Shifters in human shape. Some were clothed, some naked, but Reid didn't soften his blows for an opponent with bare skin. They'd just have to suck it up.

Miguel—or Michael—had his arm around Peigi's neck. She

fought him hard, kicking and punching, her vehemence obviously surprising Michael. He must have expected the weak and willing mate he assumed her to be, not the kick-ass woman who pummeled him with all her bear strength.

Reid fought his way to them. He'd break Michael's neck, then he and Peigi would jump in the semi and blast their way out of here.

He briefly toyed with the idea of teleporting Michael away, possibly releasing him off the edge of a cliff, but that would leave Peigi to fight the other ... ten? ... Shifters on her own. Reid didn't hear Dimitri or Jaycee running back to help—Michael must have waited until the two were out of range to spring his trap.

Reid could teleport Peigi to safety, but only if he could get his hands on her. That would leave Dimitri's truck abandoned, but Peigi was far more important.

Reid kicked and punched, backhanded and kicked again, trying to throw off the horde to reach her. Peigi shouted at Michael, spewing him with plenty of foul words as she punched him again and again.

Out of the corner of his eye, Reid saw the flash of a huge black wolf running down the deserted street toward them, and the brighter smudge of a smaller animal behind him. Nice of them to try to help.

Almost there. Reid kicked the leopard again, dislodging its claws from his flesh. The leopard bounced back, as leopards did, but it didn't matter. Reid only needed an opening.

He threw himself through the gap the tumbling leopard had left and launched himself at Peigi. He wrapped his mind over the first place he could think of, closed arms around Peigi, and willed himself there.

Michael's giant hands grabbed Reid's shoulders at the same time, and he felt the drag of the man's weight through the ley line and *un*-space, all the way to the haunted house.

————

PEIGI TRIED TO SCREAM AS DARKNESS AND NOTHING SQUEEZED her, but no air would come. She felt Reid's protective arms around her, but she also smelled the stench of Miguel-Michael, and knew he was along for the ride.

The haunted house loomed before them. Before Peigi could register it, they were inside, flying through the hall to the parlor as though they were insubstantial, coasting on a blast of wind.

The house shook, shutters banging, the furniture jostling, the vines outside rattling so hard they almost drowned out the wind shrieking under the eaves.

Peigi heard Michael say, *What the fuck?* the words filled with fear.

A door appeared in the paneled wall, growing and forming before her eyes. She and Stuart and Michael zoomed toward it, passing a startled Ben, the three of them still incorporeal, like the ghosts people believed inhabited this house. The door banged open, revealing a blackness deeper than the most moonless night.

Stuart's muscles bunched, as though he tried to stop their mad flight, but to no avail. The three of them tumbled into the doorway, an icy chill freezing Peigi to the bone.

Peigi landed on something hard. The pure darkness vanished, dissolving into gray daylight and thick mist. She found herself lying on ground covered with dead leaves and pine needles, Stuart and Miguel more or less on top of her.

The door behind them, hovering in midair, closed with a snap. Its outline quivered, and then it disappeared entirely. The wind died, and all was silence.

Michael's weight left Peigi as he gained his feet. "What the total *fuck?*"

Stuart climbed to his feet more slowly and reached down to help Peigi stand.

"You all right?" he asked her.

"Sure." She was bruised and shaken, but whole, as far as she could tell. She moved her arms and fingers, bent over and touched her legs, wriggled her toes in her sensible sneakers. "Nothing broken."

Michael looked around wildly then fixed his glare on Stuart. "What happened? Where are we? What is this place—" He broke off, dragging in scent. "Holy *shit*. This is Faerie. Isn't it? You've brought us to Faerie, you slime-eating, fucking bastard."

He came at Stuart, fingers sprouting claws, going for his throat.

Peigi stepped between them. It was a very frightening place to be, in front of Michael, who was crazy, but smart enough to hone his craziness to his advantage. And strong, powerful, and very dominant.

"Stop it!" she yelled at Michael. "Don't be stupid. He's the only one who can get us out of here."

"Why the hell am I here in the first place?"

"Because you wouldn't let me go." Peigi got in his face, something she'd never, ever dreamed of doing when she was his prisoner. But that was then, this was now, and she was furious. "You grabbed us. I bet the house knew you were effing dangerous, because it slid us right through. You were following us in New Orleans, weren't you? If so, it's your own fault you're here, so *back off*."

Michael stared at her in amazement, then to her surprise took a step away, claws receding.

"No, I couldn't let you go. You're my *mate*, Peigi. I came to find you."

"Not anymore," Peigi said heatedly. "I rejected that mate claim a long time ago."

"Did you? Huh. I don't remember hearing it."

"Then hear it now." Peigi drew herself up. "Michael-Miguel of the changing name, in front of witnesses, *I reject your mate claim*!"

Her words rang through the trees, and the wind-touched leaves shimmered in response.

"He's not a witness." Michael pointed at Stuart in derision. "He's *Fae*. And one of the dickwads who blew up my place. Yeah, I remember you."

Stuart, who had been scanning the area during this exchange as though Michael didn't exist, abruptly focused on him with the intensity only Stuart could.

"Your broken-down warehouse where you kept women and cubs imprisoned, you mean," he said. "Plus captured and hurt my friends. I'd blow it up again if I could. I'm only sorry you weren't caught in the blast."

Peigi was pleased to see Michael regard Stuart with some wariness. She'd missed much of the fight above ground when Diego and Shane had stormed the compound, but she'd heard the story over and over. Xavier, Diego's brother, especially loved to tell it. Stuart had saved Xavier's life and had achieved the status of legend.

"Them's the breaks." Michael growled and fixed Stuart with a hard glare, as though trying to intimidate him. Then he broke off, eyes going wide. "Holy fucking crap—you *scent-marked* him."

Stuart blinked, puzzled, but Peigi lifted her chin. "I did. Which means he's under my protection."

To her consternation, Michael only grinned. "That was a mistake, sweetheart. Because you know I can Challenge."

"Not if he didn't make a mate claim," Peigi said quickly. "And he didn't. I marked him to protect him from the Shifters in New Orleans."

"And to stake your own claim," Michael said, gaze knowing. "Shit, Peigi. I never knew you were into Fae." He turned back to Stuart. "Okay, Fae dickhead, let us out of here."

"I didn't bring us in here." Stuart studied their surroundings calmly. He could be cool in the face of screaming danger, assessing what needed to be done before he acted. That action was usually decisive and precise, taking out the danger in one swoop.

"But you're Fae. So open the door or whatever. This place is a shithole."

He was afraid, was Michael. He didn't want to admit it, but Peigi could scent his growing anxiousness.

"I agree," Stuart said. "But I didn't make the door, so I don't know where it is. Or where we are." He scanned the trees surrounding them, straight and tall in the mist, lines of dark boles without much break.

"Jaycee said something about a sundial," Peigi remembered. Conflicting feelings of rage and fear about Michael were coming at her in waves, but she had to put them aside to concentrate on getting herself and Stuart to safety.

"Sundial?" Michael gazed swiftly around. "What good is a sundial in the middle of the woods?"

"I don't know." Peigi felt brittle. "She said it pointed the way." She closed her mouth before she mentioned the mysterious Lady Aisling Jaycee had talked about. Michael didn't need to know about powerful Tuil Erdannan who might help them. Or not help them, as Ben had pointed out.

Stuart lightly sniffed the air. Peigi sniffed too, smelling cold and more cold.

"Snow's coming." Stuart gestured at the gray sky above the trees.

"And you without a heavy coat," Peigi said. Stuart did have a jacket, but it was made for mild climates of the Southwest, and she wasn't certain it would protect him from freezing.

Stuart sent her the ghost of a grin. "I'll survive. I agree we need to figure out where we are. Anyone have a pin?"

"What the fuck for?" Michael demanded.

"I want to make a compass. It would be a start. I'll also need a magnet."

"There's probably an app on your smart-ass phone," Michael growled.

Stuart gave him a patient look. "I doubt the Fae have sent up any satellites in the past thousand years or so."

A sound caught Peigi's attention. She trained her Shifter hearing on it, never as good when she was in human form. Michael lifted his head, alert.

"Someone's coming," he growled. "Probably this one's Fae friends."

"Can you tell how many?" Stuart directed the question at Peigi.

"Let me shift." Peigi turned around, toeing off her sneakers and sliding her jacket down her arms. "I can scent and hear better as bear."

Michael was already stripping without embarrassment. He'd often gone without clothes for long stretches of time, believing Shifters didn't need to bother with them. Of course, they'd been living in a warm place then, and Peigi had decided that Michael just liked to show off his body.

Peigi moved behind a set of close-growing trees to disrobe, not wanting Michael gawping at her. She folded her clothes carefully and set them and her shoes inside her coat, tying everything into a neat bundle.

Then she let her bear come.

The world grew brighter as more light entered her eyes, and sounds and scents flowed to her. She shook out her fur, fears falling away as her strength surged.

She returned to Stuart in a slow saunter, carrying her bundle of clothes in her mouth. She dropped the bundle at Stuart's feet and rose on her back legs to scan the area. Michael, who'd already shifted to his huge brown bear, did the same.

Peigi lowered herself and became her between-beast, more bear than human. She didn't like Stuart to see that part of her, but she could at least speak to him this way.

"Small party. One horse, others on foot."

"What kind of Fae?" Stuart asked her.

Peigi sniffed again. "I can't tell, but they don't smell like you." She wrinkled her nose, emitting a sudden growl, and Michael snarled beside her. "One is Shifter."

Stuart's brows rose, but he said nothing. Michael continued to snarl, rage overcoming his fear.

Peigi returned to her bear form and circled Stuart, halting protectively before him. Any Shifter, Fae, or weapon would have to go through her to get to him.

Stuart shucked his jacket, his eyes taking on a feral gleam. "Anyone have any iron?"

Michael glared at him, his dark eyes as mean as ever. He rose into his between-beast. "Your belt buckle."

Stuart touched it. "I think it's nickel."

Michael's frown turned his bear face fearsome. "Mine's stainless steel."

"Might work." Stuart walked without worry to Michael's pile of clothes and pulled the belt from his jeans. He studied the buckle then with a sudden wrench, tore it free of the leather. "Close enough."

Michael started at Stuart's burst of strength, but he pretended to be unconcerned. "What are you going to do with it? Make your compass?"

Stuart didn't bother to answer.

In the space of one breath and the next, Peigi sensed Stuart change from appendage dark Fae in a community of Shifters who didn't really want him there to a warrior more powerful than Michael would ever understand. Stuart's appearance didn't alter in the slightest, but his stance grew stronger, more alert, Stuart poised to fight.

And he would enjoy it. The glint in his eyes as he wove his fingers through the belt buckle made Michael retreat a few paces.

Whatever came, Stuart's expression said, he'd be ready to battle it into whimpering submission.

Peigi tried to stay in front of Reid as the brush

beneath the trees parted and a Fae on a large horse, flanked by a black-maned lion, trotted through. Michael tried to get in front of him as well, not so much to protect Reid as to form a fighting stance with Peigi.

The horse clearly was not comfortable with the lion running by its side, shying to put distance between them. The lion, a Shifter, just as clearly knew that Reid, Peigi, and Michael had invaded his territory.

Behind the horse and rider were men on foot in various kinds of armor, from leather studded with silver rings to full chain mail, which would be silver or some kind of alloy. They carried bows and spears, knives on belts.

The rider wore a gleaming silver helmet and white cloak that sparkled in the mist, the fabric picking up and reflecting whatever light trickled through the trees. Reid's lip curled in disgust.

The Fae was a prince or lordling—the kind who never soldiered but rode out hunting without bothering with camouflage. A true warrior wouldn't have announced his presence until he was right on top of Reid and the bears.

The Fae circled his horse, pulling up in a sweep for effect. "Is this what you smelled?" he called down to the Shifter. "Two scruffy bears and a *dokk alfar*?" The Fae sneered at Reid, though Reid saw the worry in his eyes behind his silver helm. One never knew what a crazy *dokk alfar* would do.

He also obviously thought Reid an ordinary *dokk alfar*. Well, it sucked to be a Fae prince today.

Peigi and Michael hadn't moved. The Fae spoke in the common Fae language, which neither would know. Reid found it interesting that the lion Shifter understood it. Meant he'd been in Faerie a while.

Reid called up to the prince. "Who's your pet Battle Beast?"

The Fae skimmed a haughty gaze over Reid then Peigi and lingered on Michael. "Seems I've acquired two more Battle Beasts. And one *dokk alfar* that will be skinned and hanged."

"The bears might have something to say about that," Reid said calmly.

The Fae rose in his stirrups. "No. You say *nothing*." He made an imperious gesture at his entourage. "Take them."

The men around him, hunters not soldiers, weren't thrilled that their master expected them to bring down two Shifters with their hunting knives. They weren't as concerned about Reid, but that was their problem.

The hunters approached, obeying orders, some shucking their cumbersome bows to draw bronze or obsidian knives. Peigi and Michael drew together, not because Peigi liked or trusted Michael, but because the two of them would make a dense wall of bear. They must have done this sort of thing before, the thought flicked in the back of Reid's mind, working as a team.

Reid's only weapons were a belt buckle and his own fists. All he needed.

He vaulted across Peigi's back and slammed the buckle into the jaw of the Fae unlucky enough to reach him first. The man screamed and recoiled, trying to grab at his face as though it burned him.

"Iron," the next in line yelled in horror. "He's got iron."

Reid slammed his elbow into him. Reid's energy, nearly spent from fighting the Shifters in New Orleans and accidentally tele-porting himself, Peigi, and Michael into Faerie, came roaring back, as though the freezing air refreshed him. He spun and hit, driving the buckle into another's face.

More screaming. The prince shouted in annoyance. "Kill him, damn you. *You*." He pointed at his Shifter. "Take the bears."

The lion went into a crouch, but hesitated, as any Shifter would when faced with two giant bears, one with his face half ravaged and growling ferociously. Felines possessed great agility, which made them a match for bears, but the odds were long against two of them. Reid left the lion to his fate and went straight for the prince.

Fae princes were the high Fae most hated by the *dokk alfar*. A general like Fionn Cillian had reasonable goals, skills, and an ability of command that elicited some respect. The princes, on the other hand, were spoiled, pampered beings, relatives of the *hoch alfar* emperor. They did nothing with their lives but hunt, have parties, debauch women, and kill whatever took their fancy. Even other *hoch alfar* didn't like them.

The prince saw Reid coming. He drew a short sword, expertly turning his horse to meet the attack. Princes were spoiled, but also went through a lot of battle training in their loads of free time.

Reid didn't bother fending off the sword. He tossed the buckle into the air and said a single word.

The buckle morphed and twisted, re-melding to become a narrow, sharp spear. It dove at the prince, who watched it come, mouth open. At the very last minute, the prince screamed and wrenched himself away from the projectile, falling out of the saddle.

Reid stopped the spear before it drove through the horse, which was an ordinary animal. Like an ordinary horse, as soon as the sharp object flashed close, it bolted.

Men scattered before the panicked horse, which streaked into the woods, scarlet draperies under the saddle flying. At that moment, the lion attacked.

It chose Peigi. Whether the lion sensed she was less dominant than Michael or chose at random, Reid didn't know. Peigi rose to meet his charge without hesitation, and the two met in a snarling tangle.

TEN

The Feline fought hard and dirty. The lion wasn't formidable like Dylan or his sons, but he was full grown, with a thick mane and ferocity in his golden eyes.

He'd attacked Peigi because he knew she was female and below Michael in hierarchy, the weaker of the pair. Or so he thought.

Peigi had been training with Nell for the past three years, and there wasn't a thing that mama bear didn't know about fighting. Sparring with an alpha grizzly on an almost daily basis had given Peigi skills she'd never dreamed she could acquire.

She brought her two giant bear paws together, slamming them into the lion's head. The lion snarled and tried to jerk away from her grip, but Peigi held him fast.

Michael was fighting off the hunters, who'd decided to attack him en masse once the lion engaged with Peigi. And Stuart?

He laughed, his voice deep, as a weapon gleamed in his hand. He threw the pointed thing up in the air and shouted a command. The Fae rider, already running, turned as the spear left Stuart's hand, terror on his face.

Peigi couldn't see what happened after that, because the lion finally wrenched himself out of her hold and smacked her with Feline swiftness. Peigi rolled with his punch, grabbing the lion to pull him down with her.

A bear's disadvantage was size, Nell had taught her, which made rapid movement difficult—Felines could match fast movements and turn the tables. A bear's advantage, on the other hand, was their size. *Yep, same thing. So use it as hard as you can.*

Peigi poured her weight onto the Feline, knowing he could slash her open with his claws, but not if she pinned him firmly enough. A brown bear didn't have the size of a Kodiak, but the species were related. Peigi drew on her inner Kodiak and willed the lion to stay *down*.

Michael fought the rest of the hunters alone. One hung back, still screaming with pain from Stuart's strike, but the rest went at Michael with mad intensity.

Under her, the lion went limp. Peigi didn't trust him an inch. She wrapped her paw around his body and rolled him hard into the dirt and then stepped on him.

Don't move. She snarled it as a bear, and couldn't know whether the lion understood, but she didn't care. He was Shifter —he'd get it. The lion was panting, blinking in pain. He shuddered and went still.

Peigi swung away and ran after Stuart, who'd sprinted into the woods following the lead Fae.

Michael roared behind her. Peigi glanced back to see the hunters converging on him. They'd kill him.

Peigi remembered all the times Michael had terrified her, and that was before his decision to lock her and the rest of the females and the cubs away. *For their own safety,* he'd said. He'd doubtless been right that they were safer away from the unstable feral Shifters in his makeshift group, but the days and nights in that fusty hole had never left her.

Michael deserved every smack he got, but that didn't mean she wanted to see a Shifter go down under the bronze knives of ten Fae. They'd either make him a bearskin rug or enslave him as they had the lion.

Too bad I'm so nice.

She let out a bellow of frustration and charged the group.

The hunters who saw her coming decided that being anywhere but in front of a ton or so of bear was a good idea and ran. The others didn't realize until too late, and were flung aside from her impact.

The lion decided that this was a great time to come out of his feigned surrender and go for Michael. The two Shifters met with a roar of mutual loathing, teeth and claws savaging. The lion got in a few good blows on Michael before Peigi grabbed him by the scruff.

A lion's mane was meant to protect him from another male lion trying to break his neck. But it couldn't protect him from an enraged bear compassionate enough to save a total asshole from too-great odds.

The lion roared and tried to fight, but Peigi shook him savagely, then let go, the momentum sending him tumbling across the forest floor. The lion hit a tree—hard—and collapsed.

Michael struggled to his feet, his dark eyes meeting Peigi's with a gleam of triumph. Peigi humphed her disdain and turned to lope after Stuart.

No. Michael growled behind her. *Leave the Fae. He's abandoned us. You and me, Peigi. Like always.*

Fuck that, Peigi answered loud and clear in bear, and continued on her way.

Stuart hadn't abandoned them at all, she knew. As she ran after him, a dozen tiny balls of steel whooshed past her the other way, heading for the remaining hunters.

She looked back to see the balls reach the Fae and dive at them. The hunters yelled, swatting and flailing as though at stinging bees. Then they quit the fight, and fled.

The tiny balls rose and flew past Peigi again, returning obedi-

ently to Stuart ahead of her. She put on a burst of speed and
caught up to him where he stood silhouetted against the fog.

Stuart lifted his hand. The balls melted into each other and
became one hunk of metal, which dropped neatly into his palm.

Peigi rose into her bear-human beast, trying to catch her
breath. "Where's the Fae?"

Stuart gestured off into the trees. "Gone. Maybe he'll catch
up to his horse before it reaches home." He shrugged, giving her
a half smile. "Or maybe not."

Peigi shifted all the way to her human form, the cold
touching her. "What if he brings back reinforcements?"

He rubbed his shoulder, loosening it. "I'm willing to bet he's
even now bragging that he single-handedly fought off two
Shifters and a *dokk alfar* and lived to tell the tale. Even if he does
decide to come after his Shifter, we won't be around for him
to find."

"How do you figure that? You know a way back home?"

Stuart released his shoulder, shaking out his throwing arm. "I
have an idea."

He kept his eyes on her face, politely averted from her naked
body. Like most Shifters, when Peigi first shifted from animal to
human, she paid no attention to her nudity. But Stuart standing
so close made her aware, especially when his eyes softened.

"You are truly beautiful, you know," he said.

Peigi's breath, which she'd just regained, deserted her again.
"I've been in a fight. I must look like hell."

"You're strong and have more courage than anyone I know."

New heat flashed through her, making air further elude her.
She coughed. "Maybe we should see if the Feline has recovered
enough to attack Michael again."

Stuart put a hand on her shoulder, fingers warm. "You don't
owe Michael anything. He once put out a hit on Shane,
remember?"

"He did a lot of things just as bad, and even worse." Peigi met
Stuart's eyes, loving how dark they were. Darkness could be

comforting after painful brightness. "I'm more worried about saving the Feline. He might know the way out."

Stuart's smile always made everything better. "Let's go make sure he stays alive then."

Peigi shifted to bear, and they walked together to Michael and the Feline, Stuart with his hand on Peigi's back.

When the Feline saw them coming, he struggled up, snarling and ready to attack again. Peigi and Michael started for him, but Stuart got quickly around them both. The steel he held formed itself into a sharp blade that he pressed to the Feline's throat.

"Stop."

Stuart spoke in English, and the Feline, with one last snarl, went still.

The scent he gave off was one of surrender—pissed-off surrender, but Peigi didn't believe he'd fight again. Michael, whether he sensed this or not, raised one large paw to finish him off.

Peigi caught his paw with her own. *No. We need him.*

Let go of me. Obey me! The unspoken command came through Shifter body language, and Peigi felt the old pull, the fear, and the anger of her younger self.

Peigi had soon figured out that Michael was a bully who used others and reigned by coercion and terror, but she'd struggled with the equal fear that without him, she wouldn't survive. Peigi's choice was staying with Michael, no matter how much he used and belittled her, or taking her chances on her own.

Being alone meant fighting for survival or getting rounded up by Shifter Bureau agents. Shifter Bureau would shove her into a Shiftertown at best, or at worst, execute her for being un-Collared and a rogue.

Peigi had stayed with Michael for lack of options. Michael was a powerful alpha, and she felt the tug.

Three years without him, Nell's tutelage on female independence, and most of all, being with Stuart, who'd taught her that strength and intimidation were two different things, made Michael's impact on her a lot less, but it still existed.

Peigi greatly feared she'd succumb to him again. Not because she believed obeying him was right, but because her brain might fall into its old habits. Do what Michael said, because the alternative was so much worse.

She made herself retain her snarl, the *I'm-sick-of-putting-up-with-your-shit* one Nell had taught her. *He might know how to get us home.*

Michael continued to growl, then he slowly shifted into his human form. "Why didn't you say so? Hey." He smacked the Feline across the jaw with his fist. "Shift and talk to us."

With reluctance, the Feline morphed into a hard-bodied man with dark hair and blue eyes. As he unfolded himself to his feet, Peigi was struck by how much he resembled Dylan Morrissey.

Michael must have noticed it too, because he recoiled a moment before he stopped and eyed the man more closely.

The Feline wasn't Dylan—that was apparent. He had the same coloring, and he was a black-maned lion, but he was younger and his face was softer and less square. But he had the defiance of Dylan, which Dylan had tamed into immense strength of will.

The Feline took in Stuart, Michael, and Peigi as she shifted back to her human form, and scowled. "Who the hell are you?"

"Who are *you*?" Peigi countered.

"None of your damned business," the Feline snarled.

Michael grabbed the man by the neck and shook him. "Shifter fucking traitor. I should cut your balls off."

Stuart regarded them both with his usual coolness, his steel blade held loosely. "He has a point. Give us your name, *Horkalan.*"

The Feline winced at the Fae word, and also at Michael shaking his head back and forth. "All right. All right. It's Crispin."

"Let him go," Stuart told Michael firmly. When Michael

glared at him, Stuart continued. "He gave us what we asked, so he gets a reward."

Michael growled but released the Feline, if reluctantly.

"What clan are you from?" Peigi asked him.

Crispin sneered. "None of your damned business."

"Guardian Network will have that info," Stuart said. "Do you know the way to the closest gate?" He gestured to the trees behind them, which all appeared the same to Peigi. "Over there somewhere? Why was your master hunting in this area today?"

Crispin's face screwed up even more. "He's not my master."

"No? He's a Fae prince, right? Or a duke, or whatever they call themselves."

"Prince. He's a son of Walther le Madhug, who is in direct line to become the emperor."

"I'm sure his mother is proud," Stuart said. "They love their *Horkalan*, Fae princes do. Used to be white tigers only. I guess he had to settle for a lion, because the Fae pretty much wiped out the white tigers. All tigers."

"Tough shit for them." Crispin folded his arms but kept a careful eye on Peigi and Michael.

"That means he's your master," Stuart went on. "You're running at his side, obeying his every command."

"Like I keep saying, none of your damned business what I do. He might think he's master, but that's his problem."

Michael lost patience. "Where's the gate, asshole?"

"Why the hell do you think I'll tell you?"

"Because if you don't, the guy with the knife really *will* cut off your balls, and I'll bounce you on your head all the way to the ley line. I can't wait to get you back to Shifters on the other side and tell them what a traitor you are."

Michael's rage rolled off him in waves. The fact that Dylan and others were searching for Michael back home with intent to kill him didn't seem to worry him at the moment.

"Do you know where the gate is or not?" Peigi asked.

Stuart nimbly twirled the knife in his fingers. "Think about the fact that this knowledge is keeping you alive," he said. "If you refuse to take us, the bear is correct, you are a traitor Shifter. I don't like your chances against the two of them."

Crispin wrinkled his forehead in worry, but kept up his belligerence. "You're one of those *dokk alfar*, aren't you?" he asked. "Dangerous bastards."

"That's right." Stuart's voice was smooth. "So if the bears decide to be nice to you, doesn't mean I—"

He never got to finish. Peigi came alert a split second before the shadows spilled forth a dozen or so Fae warriors to surround them. Each held a wicked-looking sword, and the men—and several women—had black-dark hair and eyes like midnight.

They were *dokk alfar*, but instead of greeting Stuart like a long-lost brother, they held their swords lengthwise, in a circle of steel, and advanced on the four in the middle.

ELEVEN

R eid spun in place, his knife poised, but he knew he'd never outfight a dozen *dokk alfar* warriors by himself. Didn't matter that he had three Shifters who might—or might not— back him up.

He didn't recognize any of the warriors, but he'd been gone from Faerie a long time. *Dokk alfar* wouldn't simply embrace him because he was one of them—they had plenty of clan wars and territory disputes amongst themselves, and they couldn't be certain where his allegiance lay.

Reid *could* use his iron master powers to turn their swords into melting piles of goo, but that wouldn't help if they pulled obsidian knives and came at him. Ruining a warrior's sword just made him or her that much more pissed off.

The soldiers wore leather and furs, and plenty of metal. The women had braided beads into their hair, which they wore fairly short. If any opponent figured the women would be the weaker fighters, the best place to attack, they'd be wrong.

Stuart did the only thing he could do. He raised his hands and let his blade point straight down.

"Peace," he said in *dokk alfar*.

One of the women stepped forward. "You Stu Aire de Kennan de Reed?"

"Yes." Stuart hadn't heard that version of his name in forever. It pulled at hidden spaces inside him. His formal name was longer, but this was what a stranger would use to address him. "What do you want?"

The woman didn't lower her sword. "I was told to find a *dokk alfar* who dressed in the weirdest clothes I could imagine."

"Find me for whom?"

For answer the woman let out a shrill whistle. The fog in the shadows parted once more for a man, another *dokk alfar*, to slide through.

He had the loose but strong limbs common to the *dokk alfar*, dark hair in many braids that fell past his shoulders, and eyes of intense black. Unlike his followers who wore leather vests or studded leather armor, he had a linen shirt, leather pants, and a cloak that brushed the tops of his boots. He approached Reid cautiously but with confidence, a man who knew he was in charge.

He glanced at the three unclothed Shifters, who retained human form but were ready to shift and attack if they decided to.

The *dokk alfar* halted a respectful distance away, meaning Reid couldn't reach him with his knife. "Did you speak to the red wolf?" he asked.

"Are you Cian Tadhg Cailean an Mac Diarmud?" Reid returned.

The man smiled, not a thing you'd want to see in a dark alley. "He recalled my entire name?"

"More or less." Reid decided not to mention Dimitri's mate or the Tuil Erdannan in front of all his soldiers. "Was that you whispering at me through a ley line?"

Cian gave him a nod. "It is an old spell, but a powerful one."

"One I'm guessing not many can do."

Again a nod, no false modesty. "It was necessary."

Reid rubbed the back of his head. He'd cut his hair short a

long time ago, when he'd found himself stranded in the human world, and had grown used to it. He'd decided cropped hair was better for fighting, but the circle of warriors brought back the touch of braids on his arms, cool leather on his skin, and the weight of an iron sword in his hand.

"Are we going to talk about this in the middle of the woods?" Stuart asked, as though unworried. "Hunting grounds of a Fae prince?"

"There is a place we can discuss things." Cian cast another glance at the Shifters, who wouldn't understand a word of what he was saying.

"Send my friends back through the gate, and I'll go with you," Reid said.

Cian shook his head. Reid hadn't thought Cian would agree, but it had been worth a shot.

"They will accompany us. But I'll need your word that they will not shift into their beast forms."

"And if they do?"

Reid let the question hang, but he had a pretty good idea what would happen. His word would make him a hostage for their behavior. If the Shifters shifted or attacked, or both, Reid would be the first to die under a *dokk alfar* blade.

Again the smile. "I have to ask those terms or my people won't back me. And we need you."

"Give me a moment to explain it to them," Reid said.

Cian frowned as though considering, but Reid knew he'd decided every word of this conversation before it had begun. "Go ahead." He gestured to Peigi and the two males. Again the movement was casual, but Reid sensed that this man did nothing without calculating twenty moves ahead.

Reid turned to Peigi and repeated in English what Cian had said. "Agree?" he asked.

Peigi's eyes narrowed. "They'll kill you if we decide to shift?"

"That's how it works."

Michael growled. "Why should we take orders from Fae shits?"

"Because they hate the high Fae more than you do," Reid said. "Trust me on that. And he has twelve trained warriors with very sharp swords who will do whatever he commands."

Crispin sent Reid a hard stare. "You want me to betray the people I work for?"

Reid returned the stare with a flinty one of his own. "You work for me now."

"Yeah? How do you figure?"

"Because if you don't, you'll be the first to go down. If they come for me, I'll make sure I gut you first."

Reid didn't have to speak very loudly or even forcefully to make his point. He'd learned a lot about dominance living among Shifters. Eric, the Shiftertown leader, rarely yelled at anyone and yet his Shifters fell all over themselves for him whenever he opened his mouth.

Reid didn't know Crispin's place in the overall hierarchy, but suspected he fell under Michael at the least, and probably Peigi as well. It would be difficult for Crispin to go against their combined wishes.

Michael let out a gravelly laugh. "I'm starting to like you, dark Fae."

"We won't shift," Peigi said, directing her words at Michael and Crispin. "But I want my clothes."

Dokk alfar didn't have the modesty rules humans did, but Reid understood, and it was cold. "Get them," he said to Michael.

Michael drew a breath as though to argue then abruptly walked off to retrieve the clothes they'd dropped before the fight with the Fae prince and his men.

Crispin would have to make do with his own skin. From his expression, he didn't care, which made Reid wonder how long he'd been in Faerie. He wasn't quite feral, Reid didn't think, but he was likely close.

Michael came back with the clothes and thrust Peigi's carefully tied bundle at her. "There you go, baby."

Peigi wrinkled her nose as she snatched the clothes from him. "You put your scent on them."

Michael only gave her a gleeful look. Peigi snarled softly then stepped behind Reid, turned her back, and began to dress.

Michael pulled on his clothes without hurry. "Want a T-shirt?" he asked Crispin.

"I'll be fine," Crispin said.

The *dokk alfar* soldiers wouldn't care if Crispin remained naked. Like the high Fae, they tended to regard Shifters as animals. They were far more compassionate toward those animals than the *hoch alfar* were, but they still regarded Shifters as inferior beings. *Dokk alfar* had as much arrogance as anyone else.

Once Peigi had pulled on her jeans, shirt, and sneakers, Reid drew her close. "Can you keep watch on those two?" he asked into her ear.

"Yes." Peigi's glare at Michael and Crispin didn't bode well for them.

"Sure you're all right?"

Peigi understood what he meant. "A couple years ago, I wouldn't have been. Now?" She slid her gaze to Michael. "I'm fine."

Reid heard the slight tremor in her voice, but Peigi held her head high, and he wanted to smile. Michael had no idea what he was up against.

The *dokk alfar* moved restlessly. Michael barely had his pants done — minus his belt buckle, when Cian waved at them to march out. Cian moved to Reid and stayed close to him as the party headed off into the woods.

PEIGI KEPT A SHARP EYE ON WHERE THEY WENT AS THEY

walked through the trackless forest. She could follow a scent trail better than any kind of sight trail, and she took mental notes accordingly. She saw Crispin and Michael sniffing the air, knowing they did the same.

Crispin was difficult to read. He must have learned to keep himself closed off while working for a Fae prince—correction, being a Shifter toy of a Fae prince.

She wondered why any Shifter would choose to abandon his life and throw in with the Fae, especially Fae royalty, who were known for their cruelty. The story of the first Sword of the Guardian was full of that cruelty.

Peigi felt sorry for Crispin, but then again, she didn't. He'd made his choice. If he'd been a captive of the Fae prince, he'd have told them that once he was free, instead of professing loyalty to him.

Cian also puzzled her. His scent told her he was sincere about whatever he'd said to Stuart, but she wished Stuart had taught her a little more of the *dokk alfar* language than the basics. She could say hello and good-bye, yes and no, and a few curse words, but that was about it. She couldn't even ask where the bathroom was.

Cian walked quietly beside Stuart, unworried, as though out for a stroll on a winter afternoon. Only an observant person, or a Shifter, would sense his tension. He wore thin-soled leather boots, good for feeling his way in the woods but strong enough to keep out thorns and rocks.

She absently wondered if the *dokk alfar* had cattle, or what sort of animal the leather came from. It gave off an odd scent, another tidbit of information she filed away for later use.

They walked for an hour or more. During that time she saw and heard no other Fae, the only sounds the scurrying of small animals in the underbrush or birds flashing from tree to tree.

Cian paused and the *dokk alfar* halted. Peigi quickly caught up to Reid, then growled in her throat.

The mists before them shimmered. Peigi did not like the smell of that air, like sulfur and burning charcoal. Michael and Crispin also halted, noses wrinkling.

The female *dokk alfar* soldier who'd first spoken to Stuart gave a command. The warriors formed up behind her, walked through the shimmering mist, and disappeared. Cian started to follow, noticed the others hanging back, and gave Stuart a pointed glance.

"It's all right," Stuart said to Peigi, though his undertone wasn't reassuring. "It's a link to deeper *dokk alfar* territory, and a barrier to keep the *hoch alfar* out. Similar to a scent-marked boundary."

Michael huffed. "A magic-marked one. Doesn't fill me with joy."

"It's more like camouflage," Stuart said. "It won't hurt you, unless you have *hoch alfar* blood." He gave Michael and Crispin a keen stare. "Anyone?"

"Like I'd be a half-blood," Michael sneered. Crispin screwed up his face in disgust.

"Now that we have that settled." Stuart took Peigi's hand. "We'd better go before they decide to come back and drag us through."

The warmth of Stuart's grip moved up Peigi's arm to twine her heart. It changed her, that touch, made her believe she could do anything. As long as Stuart was with her, all would be well.

She gave him a smile, clasped his hand tightly, and walked with him through the barrier.

The mists were cold, but the tingle of magic quickly fell away. Noise, color, and odors assailed Peigi as the rush and roar of a busy town surrounded them. The change from silent woods to a teeming square made her suck in a breath.

Dokk alfar were everywhere, men and women, children, dogs, horses, wagons, carts. The square and roads that led out of it were paved with cobbles, rounded and worn from centuries of use. The air had warmed, as though they'd traveled enough distance for a change in climate.

Shops lined the square, open-air places that sold produce, cloth, spices, dishes, candles—all sorts of goods, including what appeared to be musical instruments. A man pedaled a potters' wheel, his hands wet with the clay that formed under his touch.

Men wore the leather and metal studs Cian's people did, but also trousers and cloaks. Women too wore trousers and cloaks, and some men and women sported long robes that swirled in the constant breeze.

Cian didn't take the lead but let his entourage guide them across the square to a larger open-fronted building.

Peigi had been in enough bars in her lifetime to recognize this as one. A counter ran across the back of the room, behind which were shelves of colorful bottles. Tables and benches covered the floor space. A window to another room in the back slammed open, and a pair of hands shoved a tray of steaming plates onto the sill. A waitress grabbed the tray and sailed through the crowd to deposit the food in front of four *dokk alfar*, who greeted it with joy.

A stage rose about a foot from the floor on one side of the room. Three men and two women sat on this, making a rollicking noise with hand drums. They drowned out the chatter, almost as loud as any band in human clubs, but without electricity.

No one stopped and turned when Cian and his warriors walked in with Shifters. They didn't gape, gasp, draw weapons, or cease drumming. A few glanced at the nearly naked Crispin, who had condescended to put on a cloak one of Cian's men had handed him, but mostly, the Shifters and Stuart were ignored.

Cian led them to a table in the back, which was miraculously empty in this apparently popular tavern. Cian's people dispersed, except for the woman who'd first addressed Stuart, to shove themselves onto barstools or greet people who were obviously friends.

Cian, Stuart, the woman, and the Shifters gathered around the table, and the woman signaled to the barmaid. *"Gularain,"* she ordered.

Peigi squeezed in next to Stuart. Cian took a place at the head of the table and the two Shifter males perched on stools across from Peigi and Stuart.

The barmaid promptly brought six ceramic handleless cups on a tray and set it down in the middle of the table. Hands reached for the cups, which had been chilled. Good thing, Peigi thought. Anything to keep the liquid inside from combusting.

Stuart had once made a batch of home-brewed *dokk alfar* whisky and invited their Shifter neighbors to try it. The Shifters had taken one drink and then cursed hard and accused Stuart of attempting to murder them from the inside out. It was the closest Peigi had come to witnessing Stuart laugh his ass off.

He'd advised Peigi to try the drink cautiously, and had helped her work her way up from one sip to a whole glass over the course of about six months.

She lifted her cup, as Cian watched her closely, and inhaled the aroma as she would a fine wine. Cian's eyes narrowed as she sipped, nodded her approval, and set the cup down without a word.

Cian said nothing but Peigi noted his amusement. Cian threw his drink back, draining the entire contents at once. Stuart and the *dokk alfar* woman did the same.

None of them exploded. Cian let out an *ah* of satisfaction and thumped his hand to the table. Encouraged, Crispin and Michael seized their cups.

"I'd go easy on that if I were you," Peigi warned them.

She figured they wouldn't listen, and they didn't. Crispin took a tentative sip, probably more cautious from living in Faerie, but Michael decided to down his in one go. He swallowed.

Michael did nothing for the first second, and the second. In the third second, his eyes widened until the whites threatened to overwhelm his irises, the scarred side of his face pulling. He dropped the cup and gasped for breath, pawing at his throat. Fierce yowls leaked from his mouth, and he started to shift.

"No!" Peigi yelled at him.

The woman solider put her hand on her knife. Michael stopped himself before his claws sprouted, but his eyes became fully bear—large and brown with pools of black in the middle.

"Holy fuck." His voice barely emerged, hoarse and breathy. "What the total ..." He coughed, half rising from his stool and holding his stomach. "Shit, shit, shit."

Peigi took another demure sip. "*Gularain* can be a little strong."

"*Dokk alfar* whisky," Crispin said, his voice also hoarse. "Rumor has it they put old boots in it. And gravel. And iron."

"Exaggeration," Stuart said calmly. "It's a grain, sort of like barley in your world, and a little sugar. That's all. But distilled until it's pure. The aged stuff is a little more mellow."

"You mean mellow battery acid?" Michael demanded. He continued to cough. "Goddess, it's burning a hole right through my gut. I've been stabbed in the stomach before. This is worse."

"You have to get used to it." Peigi tortured him by taking another sip. Crispin, she noticed, had pushed his cup aside. "Are we safe talking in this place?" she asked Stuart.

"Probably as safe as anywhere." He turned to Cian and asked him a question in their language. Cian, still amused, shook his head. "He thinks so, but doesn't plan on divulging secrets. This is a stop to rest and refresh us."

"Refresh?" Michael growled. "I'm dying."

"That's very sad," Peigi told him. "Want me to burn an offering for you?"

Michael only sneered at her, but that triggered more coughing. He held his belly and looked miserable.

A small vengeance, Peigi thought as she took another small sip of the strong liquor. But a satisfying one.

———

"Peigi has a point." Stuart resumed his conversation with Cian. "Are we all right in here?"

Cian signaled the barmaid to bring another round. "Most are my clan or friends of the clan. They are loyal. They are also making a lot of noise."

The drummers had increased their tempo, hands flying as they kept up with one another. An older man with strings of bead dangling from his white hair hopped up on the stage. He drew in a breath and began singing a ribald song Reid hadn't heard in decades.

It was loud and long, with many verses, about a couple who tried everything to escape friends and family and catch a little alone time, which never worked. Their wagon would break, the horse ran away, the kids would chase them, *hoch alfar* would attack, and on and on. Whoever sang the song was allowed to add his or her own made-up verses.

Soon the room was singing along and roaring with laughter. Peigi listened in curiosity—Reid would have to sing it for her later. Even if it meant singing, which wasn't a good idea for him. Maybe he could just recite the verses.

Another man and then the woman with Cian got up to join in, but instead of singing, they used their voices like instruments to wail the melody without words. Two more women and a man got up to dance.

"I see what you mean," Peigi shouted over the noise. "About the dancing."

The best dancers Reid had ever seen in the human world couldn't compare. The footwork, the spinning, the high kicks, and acrobatics had the room on its feet, cheering along.

Cian leaned in to Reid. "How is Dimitri?"

"Good." Reid accepted another *gularain* from the barmaid and sipped this one to enjoy it slowly. It was like drinking nostalgia. "He and his mate will soon have a cub."

"He was a Shifter very much in love when I saw him. With a strong mate."

"Jaycee is very strong, yes," Reid agreed. One didn't argue with her if one couldn't back up the argument with martial arts.

"So is your bear." Cian's gaze darted to Peigi. "Are you …?"

"I don't know." Reid said it quickly. He knew what he felt for Peigi, but life was complicated for a *dokk alfar* and a clanless Shifter.

"Ah. So that is the way of it."

"Like I said, I don't know what is the way of it." Reid took an irritated sip of whisky. "Can we talk about the problem at hand? Are you sure it's gone?"

"Yes." Cian very carefully didn't name *what* was gone. "I know, the elders of my clan know, and if we don't get it back, everyone else will know. And then we'll die. The situation is simple, and very dire. Will you help us, or not?"

TWELVE

"What do you think I can do?" Reid asked impatiently. "You have warriors, armies, and people who can do *that.*" He jerked his chin at the dancers who spun and kicked in such precise timing that they never touched each other. "I am one person."

"You're an iron master." He used the *dokk alfar* word for it, *syernghan.*

"You're a *ghandeltraum.*" Reid enjoyed Cian's surprise. "Dimitri told me how you dug through rock to get yourselves out of the *hoch alfar* cell."

"I did. The *hoch alfar* do not know, however."

"Well, they're idiots." Reid raised his glass in a toast. "What did you want me to do? Terrify the *hoch alfar* by bending iron while you sneak around them and steal the thing back?"

Cian shrugged. "More or less."

"Ha. Dimitri told me you were crazy."

Cian gave him a tolerant smile. "Determined, rather. The red wolf, on the other hand ... At times, I doubted his sanity."

"He's sharp, is Dimitri. There's a human saying—crazy like a fox."

Cian lost his smile. "He's a being of the Tuil Erdannan?"

Reid blinked. "I didn't mean that literally. Non-Shifter foxes are a common animal in the human world."

His voice was awed. "It must be a strange place, this human world."

"Tell me about it. I've been stuck there fifty years."

"You are here at present, my friend."

Reid studied the room, from the dancers and drummers, the now-shrieking singer and his accompaniment, and the shouting, drinking *dokk alfar* enjoying life.

For a long, long time, Reid had tried anything he could to come back to this, including hunting a Shifter and causing him to be killed. Reid hadn't actually killed that Shifter, but his actions had led to the Shifter's death.

Hence he'd be forever obligated to Cassidy and Diego, not to mention Peigi and the Shifter cubs.

Reid was back home, yes. Maybe not in his own clan's territory, but with his kind, among things he knew.

Instead of relief, though, he felt outside it all, as though he no longer belonged. And maybe he didn't.

"Yes, I'm here." Reid pinned Cian with a stern gaze. "*How* am I? I haven't been able to reach Faerie or go far inside it until today, no matter what I've tried. The spell that exiled me was powerful. How did you manage to bring me back?"

"I?" Cian didn't even try to sound innocent.

"What did you do? Sell yourself to a shaman? How did you negate my exile?"

"I did sell myself," Cian said, his voice low. "My life's blood. For you to come and help save us all."

BEN FOUND IT DIFFICULT TO REMAIN THE NONCHALANT, COOL dude he portrayed himself to be while Angus and Tamsin,

Jaycee and Dimitri, and Reg, the second-in-command of the New Orleans Shiftertown, glared down at him.

"What?" he asked.

Ben stood in a circle of them, red wolf and black, leopard and serval, and most daunting of all, the fox. He never knew what Tamsin would take into her head to do.

Or maybe Jaycee was the most frightening, her golden eyes full of fury. She could strike fast, and it was almost impossible to get out of her way.

"Where are they?" Jaycee demanded. "Eric has already been on the phone to Kendrick, and Kendrick is all over our asses about losing them. Plus … we're just worried." Her voice quavered.

"I don't know what happened." Ben swallowed nervously but spoke the absolute truth. "One second I'm catching up on the basketball game, the next, Reid is teleporting in with Peigi and a Shifter I've never seen before. Then that door opened, and they were gone."

He pointed to the wall in the parlor that was smooth and innocuous. No door in sight.

"So open it again." Jaycee closed in on Ben, her distress sharp. "You can do more magic than you let on."

"Yep," Tamsin said. "Like the glams you throw, and how you once pinned a scummy Feline who was tailing me to the floor." She broke off in admiration. "That was awesome."

"This is different." Ben knew he could disable every single Shifter surrounding him if he wanted to—maybe not all at once, but a couple at a time until they were no longer a threat. Magic to do with Faerie, however, wasn't as simple. "There's ley lines involved, and gates I can't go through, and whatever the house is doing or not doing. I can't just twirl my hand, and *voila*, there's a door." He waved in demonstration.

A fiery tingle shot through his fingers. The wall shimmered, and the outline of a door spread across it.

The six of them turned to stare at it. The door wasn't

substantial—but as though someone had drawn a door frame and door panels on the wall with pencil.

Tamsin went over to study the outline but carefully did not touch it. "Is this what it's supposed to look like?"

"No." Ben, Jaycee, Dimitri, and Angus spoke at the same time.

Ben broke through the circle of angry Shifters and approached the wall. "It should be more like a real door."

The tingle in his fingers increased as he reached for the outline, and he quickly withdrew his hand. He wasn't sure what would happen to him if he crossed through a gate, and wasn't thrilled about finding out.

"If we can't open it, what good will it do us?" Jaycee asked.

"Always so impatient," Dimitri said. "But she has a point."

"I still say we call Lady Aisling," Jaycee said.

"Agreed." Tamsin said eagerly. "I'd love to catch up with her."

Ben knew why. Lady Aisling had revealed that the Tuil Erdannan had created the fox Shifters, and Tamsin must have a lot of questions for her.

Tamsin fixed Ben with her too-knowing gaze. "Remember what Lady Aisling said to the two of us? That you and I had the power to see what was really there, and also to make others *not* see us. The first part might be what we need—you can *see* this door and where it leads. Maybe even find Peigi and Stuart when you do."

"There are too many *maybes* and *mights* in that sentence," Ben said.

"We need to start somewhere," Jaycee said.

"All right, all right, let me think."

Ben reached to the wall again and made himself lightly touch the outlines. He felt power in the insubstantial door, masses of it, but he wasn't certain how to tap it or what to do with it if he did.

The others watched him expectantly, certain old Ben could instantly solve their problems.

True, Lady Aisling, who'd blown him away with her presence, had said that Tamsin could see things for what they were,
and had claimed Ben possessed the same ability.

Ben knew this—he could sense something magical from miles
away. He could also make people not see him. He'd love to do
that now and slip away from the worried Shifters so he could
decide what to do, but they were wise to his tricks and would
find him quickly.

Ben knew he couldn't go back to Faerie, but could he send
others there? Or more importantly, bring Reid and Peigi back?
He liked Peigi and Reid—those two kids needed each other.

If the Fae had murdered them ...

Ben sucked in a breath.

"All right, Jaycee, conjure Lady Aisling. But whether or not
she answers, we're going in. Tamsin, I might need you."

Angus growled, the wolf in him as protective as ever.
"For what?"

"To change this drawn door into a true gate. And then we'll
find Reid and Peigi and bring them home. Agreed?"

Tamsin gave Ben a startled glance that held some fear. Last
fall, she had entered a magical *state*—the only word he could
think of to describe it—and had disintegrated metal. Even iron
masters couldn't do what she'd done. Tamsin had been elated and
terrified at the same time, and she still hadn't processed what had
actually happened.

Behind him, Jaycee took a glittering stone from her pocket.
Dimitri hovered near her as she held it up and said, "Lady
Aisling? Can I bother you?"

Tamsin rested her hand next to Ben's on the wall. "I feel *something*. You?"

"Yep." Ben drew a breath. "But even if it opens, I can't go in,
so it will have to be up to you. And Angus—who is breathing
down my neck, literally. Will you stop that?" He growled over
his shoulder at the scowling black wolf, who didn't move at all.

Only Reg wasn't giving Ben hell, and not because the man

didn't care. Ben sensed him waiting in case Ben eluded the others. Then Reg would be on him.

Ben glanced at the tall black man, and Reg grinned at him. *I'll be watching you …*

Beside him, Tamsin gasped. "I think—"

She broke off as the wall suddenly became a solid door, the door frame full of wild curlicues, carvings of roses in bloom.

She jerked her hand away. "I don't know how I did that."

Ben believed he knew. He'd felt the molecules of the wall change beneath his hand, had seen their structure alter. Tamsin had done this sort of thing before, when she'd changed metal to dust, though that time she'd had Lady Aisling's help. Today, Tamsin had used the ancient power in her blood on her own.

This could prove interesting for the future.

The door banged open, making Tamsin and Ben—and Angus, still at Ben's shoulder—leap back. The door revealed only darkness, but a few seconds later, a tall woman with bright red hair in looped braids appeared on the threshold. She wore gray trousers stuffed into boots, a white shirt, and a hooded cloak. She had a smudge of dirt on her nose—Lady Aisling liked to work in her garden.

"Ah, Tamsin," she said. "And Jaycee. So nice to hear from you. Have you two had your children yet? Oh, yes, you call them cubs."

"Not yet." Jaycee came forward in welcome. "Hasn't been enough time."

"Hasn't it?" Lady Aisling remained in the doorway, the darkness behind her complete. It was eerie, that darkness, and Lady Aisling's brightness cut into it. "Ah well, one loses track of time. Did you need something? Or did you call for a little girl talk? If so, can we go shopping? Perhaps in Milan? I'd love some new shoes."

Ben spoke before the others could answer. "We lost some friends to Faerie. We want to get them back."

"I see." Lady Aisling turned her very dark gaze on Ben. He

found himself out of breath, as though fire had swept through him. "Why don't you go in and get them then?" She stood to one side, gesturing through the open doorway.

"I can't," Ben said, his chest tight. "Exiled. Spelled. No goblin allowed back into Faerie."

"On whose authority?" Lady Aisling's brows climbed. "The *hoch alfar's*? As though I bow to *their* dictates." She again motioned to the darkness behind her. "Come on in, *ghallareknoik-snlealous*."

"Um." Ben studied the blackness, from which an icy breeze began to blow. "Even though I might explode into dust if I cross the threshold?"

Lady Aisling frowned in impatience. "You aren't *trying*. Your friends cannot come with you. They will perish if they enter— there are far too many *hoch alfar* running around trying to kill or enslave Shifters. I had to exert myself for them the last time, remember? Only you can evade the bloody *hoch alfar*. Excuse my language."

Ben swallowed. "Me?"

"Yes, you. Haven't you been listening?"

"Mmm." Ben folded his arms, suddenly far too cold. "I'm not sure about this."

The Shifters had gathered around him again. *"Ben,"* they chorused.

Tamsin patted his shoulder. "If Lady Aisling says it's okay, then it's okay."

"Yes," Jaycee put in. "She'll protect you."

Lady Aisling frowned. "Well, I didn't say *that*."

Ben barely heard her. Her words drifted into the increasingly chilly air, which wrapped itself around Ben and dragged him forward. He held his breath, closed his eyes, muttered inside his head, *What the hell. I can only die once. Right?* and plunged through the door.

———

PEIGI WASN'T QUITE CERTAIN WHAT CIAN HAD BEEN SAYING, but Stuart suddenly went still, any enjoyment he might have gained hanging out in this bar in *dokk alfar* territory sucked out of him.

"What is it?" she whispered to him.

Stuart shook his head. He said something more to Cian, who also shook his head.

"Stuart."

Stuart turned to her. "I agree we need to talk about all this. Somewhere private."

Peigi glanced across the table. "With them?"

Michael focused on her with unnerving suddenness. "What are you whispering about? I know every signal you make, woman."

True, Peigi had lived with the lout for twenty-five years, and he could read the smallest nuance of her body language. It also meant she knew him very well too.

"Trying to decide if you can help or if you're dead weight," Peigi said calmly.

She shook inside to say it, but she met his gaze. Another thing Nell had taught her—be scared, sure, but never admit it to the alpha trying to intimidate you.

Michael immediately grew offended. "Of course I can help. Anything to punch the high Fae bastards in the gut."

"Yeah," Crispin said. "I'll help too." His smirk indicated he'd do anything but.

"And someone needs to keep *him* in line." Michael jerked his thumb at Crispin. "And alive so I can disembowel him when we get home."

Stuart sent Peigi a sidewise glance, but she remained serene. She'd known exactly how to keep Michael from turning on them—appeal to his sense of vanity that he'd be useless in this situation, an appendage. Michael always wanted to be in charge.

"Finish up then." Stuart drained his second glass of *gularain* without blinking. Michael gave him a baleful look, glanced at the drops in his glass, and pretended to ignore them.

Crispin took a final delicate sip, and then Cian rose to lead them out.

Dusk had fallen, but the crowd in the square didn't show any signs of thinning. Lights pricked the darkness, more and more springing up as they walked. Laughter spilled from other taverns, along with more drumming and singing. Stalls with goods were shutting up, but those serving food or drink did brisk business.

Stuart insisted Michael and Crispin follow directly behind Cian, which they did willingly. Michael liked the lead position, which allowed him to keep his eye on Cian and also Crispin. Stuart and Peigi brought up the rear, keeping an eye on the two male Shifters.

Stuart said nothing as they walked, which Peigi understood. Too many ears, and they couldn't be certain that none under-stood human languages. Her heart constricted with worry, wondering what Cian had said to sway Stuart into staying, or at least staying for a while.

They strode from the square through busy streets lined with shops and warehouses, each painted in bright colors, some sporting awnings of broad colored stripes.

Passers-by stared at the Shifters, but like the patrons in the tavern, they didn't faint at the sight of them. Shifters were unusual, Peigi concluded, but not wholly unknown. Meaning the *dokk alfar* had been in contact with Shifters and learned enough about them to know they weren't dangerous unless threatened. Well, except for Michael, who enjoyed being dangerous, and Crispin, who had attacked on command from a high Fae.

The presence of Cian seemed to reassure all, however. The *dokk alfar* watched, but they went about their business.

Stuart, on the other hand, received many blatant stares of curiosity and perplexity. *I was told to find a* dokk alfar *who dressed in the weirdest clothes I could imagine,* Cian's female warrior, who had stayed behind in the tavern, had said. True, Stuart's jeans, sweat-shirt, and short hair stood out among the long-haired, leather-and-fur clad *dokk alfar*.

Cian led them down several streets lined with four- and five-story houses and around corners before he halted in front of a house that didn't appear much different from the others, except its walls were painted blue instead of the bright orange of the next-door neighbor.

Cian opened the front door without unlocking it. Peigi, examining it, saw that there was no lock on the door at all. She glanced around the street, trying to see whether other doors were similar, but she didn't have the chance to decide before Stuart motioned her inside.

Michael wanted to be a traditional male Shifter and not let Peigi enter until he'd checked out the place. Cian only raised his brows as Michael pushed past him.

"Stand down," Stuart said to Michael. "This place is warded out the ass. No one can cross into Cian's territory without him knowing."

Michael halted three feet inside the hall and wrinkled his nose. "Yeah, I smell the stink of Fae magic."

"I'd watch it," Stuart advised. "He'll only put up with your cracks about the Fae for so long."

Michael sent Cian an uneasy glance. "I thought he couldn't understand English."

"He doesn't. But I'll translate for him."

Michael glared. "You're a bastard."

"Yes," Stuart said quietly. "I am."

Crispin entered the house and gave Michael another smirk. Peigi thought Crispin resembled Dylan Morrissey, until he took on a derisive expression, and then Crispin wasn't anything like Dylan at all. Dylan didn't have to sneer and boast. He just stood there, and you knew he could out-fight anyone in the room.

Stuart guided Peigi into the hall, following Cian deeper into his abode. The house had one room fronting the street but ran a long way back into the property, similar to canal houses in Amsterdam Peigi had seen photos of. A staircase bisected the hall, and beyond it opened a courtyard full of plants and a fountain. Behind that, Peigi spied another hall leading to yet more rooms.

"Nice," she said, letting out a breath as they stepped into the courtyard. The trickle of the fountain added a soothing note. "I'd love to remodel our little house like this."

"Good idea," Stuart said. "We'll ask Eric." Peigi caught the teasing glint in his eye and smiled.

Michael watched their exchange, his lip lifting in a snarl.

Crispin, ignoring them, tilted his head to study the walls rising three floors to the roof open to the sky. Balconies ringed the courtyard on the upper floors, decorated with wrought-iron railings. "I thought dark Fae lived in caves."

"Some do," Stuart told him. "Very nice caves, with every luxury. *Dokk alfar* have been around a long time, and our cities are legendary. The *hoch alfar* are uncivilized newcomers."

"Yeah," Crispin said. "That's why they're kicking *dokk alfar* ass."

Stuart was next to him in a heartbeat, crowding Crispin against the fountain. The spray wet Crispin's bare legs, and he flinched. "I warned you," Stuart said. "Keep your mouth shut, or wear a muzzle."

Michael laughed. "I volunteer to put it on him."

Crispin lifted his hands, the folds of the cloak falling from his arms. "Truce." He gave Michael a hostile glance. "But once we're out of here, you're one dead bear."

"Yeah, yeah," Michael said. "Heard it before."

Peigi waited until Stuart backed off Crispin, and Crispin busily adjusted his cloak before she continued her conversation with Stuart.

"You once told me *dokk alfar* didn't have to build glittery castles and hunt unicorns, and all that shit. Your words." She glanced around with admiration. "You never said you had such beautiful houses."

"Functional houses," Stuart said. "The courtyard draws air and cools the house in the heat of summer. The fountain catches rainwater and filters it for drinking. But yes, *dokk alfar* homes can be beautiful. Not glittery."

"Having no glitter is important to you."

Stuart met her gaze, deadpan. "Damned important."

Peigi wanted to kiss him. The need surged to step against him, lift her face to his, lick his lower lip, and then kiss the hell of out him. Never mind Michael and Crispin, or Cian who waited impatiently, wanting to speak to Stuart about dire things.

She touched Stuart's chest, softening her fingers, and saw a flare of need in his dark eyes. Stuart closed his hand on hers, lifted her fingertips to his lips, and nipped one.

Peigi couldn't breathe. She could only see Stuart, the man who'd pulled her back from despair and let her laugh again, felt his hot breath on her skin. The rest of the house and those in it, all of Faerie, in fact, faded to nothing.

Stuart held her gaze for a long time, the frustrated longing in his eyes reflecting hers. He gave her one of his rare smiles and released her.

"Cian," he called. He went on in *dokk alfar*, a phrase Peigi knew. It meant, more or less, *Let's get on with it and back to the gularain.*

THIRTEEN

Cian Tadhg Cailean an Mac Diarmud had to work with what he had: An Iron Master who obviously did not want to be here, his bear Shifter mate, and two disgruntled male Shifters they'd picked up on the way.

The Shifter female called Peigi hovered near Reid, not because she feared Cian or the other Shifters, but to protect Reid from ... everything. Cian recognized the stance. He'd seen it in the leopard Shifter who'd come to rescue his cell mate, Dimitri.

Because of Dimitri and his mate — along with a few other Shifters and a Tuil Erdannan who'd happened along — Cian had lived to see another day. He knew he owed his freedom to Dimitri, who'd been prepared to do battle against a castle full of *hoch alfar* for a *dokk alfar* he'd never met. A man of great courage was Dimitri.

Cian could be kind to Peigi for Dimitri's sake. As for the other two ...

"They need to be isolated," he said to Reid. "You trust your mate, but the others can't know what has happened."

Reid gave him a nod. In spite of the man's odd clothes and shorn hair, he had a weight about him that came not only from the enormous magic Cian sensed in him, but a wisdom that had been gained through suffering. Cian knew all about suffering.

Reid turned to the Shifters and spoke in the strange language of the humans. Cian remembered listening to Dimitri babble and sing all kinds of things in that language, laughing maniacally every once in a while. The kind of man Cian could go drinking with.

The male bear Shifter, Michael, growled in enraged belligerence. They'd have to watch that one, Cian had already concluded. The Feline Shifter with the perpetual sneer, who was weaker than the other, rolled his eyes.

Then they started to argue. Michael snarled, balled up his fist, and went for Reid. Peigi swiftly got in his way, staring down the male bear with anger that went beyond outrage. Those two had a history, Cian surmised.

Reid calmly pressed Peigi aside and scanned the courtyard. Cian winced when Reid's gaze fell on the railing that encircled the second floor balcony. Cian's grandfather had commissioned that from a master blacksmith of his day.

Before Cian could say a word, the railing melted, raining to the first floor in droplets of iron. While the Shifters stared in amazement, the iron reformed into thin bands that flew toward the male Shifters.

They tried to run, but too late. The iron bands whipped around the male Shifters' torsos and lifted them, pinning them together and to the nearest wall. Peigi's eyes widened, but she didn't hide her satisfied expression.

Reid spoke a few more words at the struggling, angry Shifters, then motioned for Cian to lead him and Peigi onward.

Cian took them to his library. Best for discussion, plus he could pull out documents and scrolls with evidence if he needed to convince Reid to help.

Peigi studied the library with appreciation. The room was two floors in height, lined with bookcases filled with scrolls, maps, bound papers, books, loose parchment, and anything else

Cian had filed as interesting to read. Windows overlooked a stretch of garden behind the house, difficult to find in the city, but Cian's family had lived on this land since before the city existed.

"I told them if they were good, I'd let them use the bathroom," Reid said as Cian closed the door. Mirth glinted in his eyes. "Let's be careful, though. Shifter hearing is very, very good."

"Not through these walls." Cian touched the door frame, willing his wards to form. The house was so ancient that the wards came in an instant, infused into the building from generations of Mac Diarmuds. Good house, this. Cian patted the wall in fondness.

Reid spoke to Peigi a moment. She appeared dismayed and darted her gaze to Cian.

"I told her about your blood debt," Reid said. "Now explain it to me."

"It is simple. I need you." Cian turned and unrolled a map on a table, tacking down the corners with round glass weights. "The only iron master I knew about was you, exiled to the world of humans. The spell that kept you out was strong but I heard that you broke it once and fought beside *dokk alfar*. I sought them out. They told me that blood had let you come through, blood sacrificed." He shrugged, trying not to shiver. Cian hadn't been able to get warm since he'd let himself be drained, though his strength had finally returned. "So with the help of my lead spell-caster, I sacrificed mine. The spell was dissolved, and I could pull you in. I apologize for dumping you in front of a *hoch alfar* hunting party. Not my intention, but I could only control so much."

Reid remained fixed in place after Cian finished, his eyes giving away nothing. Peigi, growing impatient with the long speech and the silence afterward, sent a question to him. Reid broke his gaze from Cian and translated.

Cian knew Reid told her exactly what Cian had said, because Peigi bent her dark glare on Cian.

If you're going to piss off a Shifter, one of his friends had warned before Cian had taken this step, *don't choose a bear.*

Cian added to himself, *Especially not a female bear who thinks you're endangering her mate.*

"She admires your courage," Reid told him. "Though not your methods. But we're here." He moved to the table and regarded the map with interest. "Wherever here is."

Cian pointed to a drawn clump of buildings near the northern mountains. Those mountains were remote and wild, reached through territory no *hoch alfar* wanted to traverse, not to mention guarded by the warded barrier. The fact that a hunting party had turned up so close to the barrier warned him that the perimeter was already weakening.

"This city is called Harnsvall. We are closest to where the *karmsyern* resided." He moved his finger to the range of mountains that snaked down about twenty miles from the city walls.

Reid leaned on the table, studying the map. He turned his head and spoke to Peigi, indicating what Cian had showed him. Peigi rested her hands next to his, the two of them at east with each other. They shared the informality of two people so in accord they didn't need to exchange words.

"Any idea how a *hoch alfar* was able to steal it?" Reid asked.

"No." Cian's frustration knotted inside him, but he kept his voice calm. Running around yanking out his hair wouldn't help the situation. "It was guarded by spells, plus the fact that it is pure iron. No *hoch alfar* should have been able to approach within miles of it. That's why I suspect their tame Battle Beasts."

Reid nodded agreement, his lips tightening in anger. His gaze moved from the area in question to a fold of land far to the west, as though drawn there involuntarily. Reid's own territory, Cian realized. The elders had told him Reid came from Berlheim, which was in the west, between the mountains and the sea.

"There are a few problems with the idea that Shifters took it, though," Cian went on. "Shifters don't practice magic—they are magical beings themselves, but don't use magic. They could carry off the *karmsyern* without being poisoned by the iron, but they'd have to negate the spells around it first. Some of those are cloaking spells."

Reid translated for Peigi. Her brows drew together as he explained, then she turned intelligent eyes to Cian and asked a question.

"She wants to know if the *karmsyern* alone keeps out the *hoch alfar*," Reid said. "As in, don't we have guards and other things in place to alert us of their activity? And if not, why not?"

Cian answered Peigi directly. "You hit on a conundrum that has plagued us for centuries. Fought over, in fact. We do have guards, sentries, gates, bridges, warded barriers, and so forth, but the *hoch alfar* have poisoned arrows. If they want in badly enough, they come. Not many can enter at a time or penetrate very far, but they take what they please and disappear. The *karm-syern* at least prevents them from invading in force or staying long."

Peigi's next question was short. "Can't you make another one?"

Cian let out a laugh, feeling marginally better. "I want *you* at the next privy council meeting. Sometimes our leaders have to be hit over the head with the obvious."

"It's a good point," Reid said. "Melt some iron, do some chants, and Peigi and I go home."

By *home*, he meant the world of humans and Shifters, Cian understood. Not Berlheim in Faerie. Interesting.

"Not so simple." Cian tapped his fingers absently on the map. "The original was made not by a *dokk alfar*, but by a Tuil Erdannan, so the legend goes. We don't have records, only oral tales."

Peigi came alert. "Tuil Erdannan?" She turned to Reid and spoke rapidly.

"She wants to know which one," Reid said.

"A dead one." Cian shrugged. "That was centuries ago. Even the Tuil Erdannan have lifespans."

"How about asking another Tuil Erdannan to make one for

you?" Peigi asked through Reid. "Politely," Reid added for himself.

Cian emitted a bitter laugh. "Because a blood sacrifice to retrieve an iron master to help raid the *hoch alfar* and restore the original is easier. Trust me."

"We have a friend who knows a Tuil Erdannan," Reid said. "Peigi is reminding me, as though I could forget. Lady Aisling. She might be able to help."

Cian recalled the mad scramble from the mountain castle of the *hoch alfar* who'd captured him. He was still sore from the injuries he'd obtained during that adventure. A Tuil Erdannan had walked in, set everything on fire, told the *hoch alfar* leader to behave himself, swept up her friends, and departed.

His blood chilled as he thought of it, not that it had warmed much in the last week. "You mean Aisling Mac Aodha, Daughter of Lucas Eoghan Mac Aodha."

"Lady Aisling, yes," Reid said. "Is it worth it to ask her?"

"No." Cian rubbed his arms. "And it's not wise to say her name so casually either. They like respect."

"Even though she's hundreds of miles away?"

Cian checked the corners of the ceiling—watchers and listeners could be anywhere, never mind his wards. The Tuil Erdannan wouldn't even notice the things. "Doesn't matter. They're the most powerful beings in creation. Always show them the utmost courtesy."

Peigi broke in, her voice becoming more insistent.

"She says *she'll* talk to Lady Aisling if we're afraid to." Reid's smile spread. "She's fearless."

Cian wasn't certain if Reid meant Peigi or Lady Aisling, then decided the adjective could apply to both.

"Even if Peigi isn't afraid to talk to Aisling Mac Aodha, that is no guarantee she'll agree. The affairs of *dokk alfar* and *hoch alfar* don't concern them. The only reason she helped us escape Simeon's fortress is because she was doing a personal favor for the red wolf's mate. And then there's the fact that we'd be obligated to a

Tuil Erdannan—a living one—for centuries. Whenever she decides to call in that obligation … it could be bad."

Reid nodded in understanding. "The Tuil Erdannan you were indebted to for the first *karmsyern* is deceased and can't demand any favors."

"Exactly." Cian let out a breath. "I wouldn't ask for your help if things weren't so dire. Retrieving the *karmsyern* will be tricky and dangerous, and I know it. I need an iron master to help me, because you have the best odds of surviving. And *you* are the only one in existence that I know of."

Reid's expression went dark. "That's because the *hoch alfar* killed my entire family, and most of my clan. They wanted to wipe out any chance of another iron master among my people."

"Then let us avenge them." Cian balled his fist on the table. He saw the rage inside Reid, long nursed and frustrated. Cian had researched the man's history, and what he'd found had been horrific. "We will find those who stole the *karmsyern*, take it back, and punish the *hoch alfar*. They won't be able to stop a *syernghan* and a *ghandeltraum* together."

For a moment, Cian thought he'd reached Reid, saw the flame of fury that spelled doom for any *hoch alfar* who got in his way.

Then Reid turned his head and looked at Peigi, who had returned to studying the map, a flush on her face. One lock of dark hair brushed her cheek.

In that instant, Cian saw Reid's need for vengeance, which must have driven his every waking hour since he'd been exiled, evaporate. This Shifter woman had managed to push out the hate, the burning anger Reid had lived with, or at least damp it down a long way.

She'd given him something else to live for.

It was beautiful to see—the two had something with each other that was almost tangible—but it was also frustrating for Cian. He sorely needed an iron master, and Reid was the only one around.

"Let me talk to Peigi," Reid said. He gestured to the window. "All right if we walk in your garden?"

Peigi focused on Cian, her head up, eyes defiant. Again Cian sensed her total protectiveness of Reid, a protectiveness that would knock down buildings for him.

Cian knew she'd try to talk Reid out of it ... Or, maybe she wouldn't. She was no fool and must understand what returning to Faerie meant to Reid. Reid had a chance to help his own people, even if that chance involved a terrible risk.

It had to be Reid's choice. Cian needed him, but he wasn't into forcing people to do what he wanted. Not yet anyway.

"Of course." Cian waved at the garden, lush and green, beyond the windows. "Take all the time you need."

———

STUART LED PEIGI FROM THE LIGHT-FILLED LIBRARY TO THE courtyard, following Cian's directions to the garden. Stuart had his hand on her elbow, the warmth of his fingers comforting.

"Hey," Crispin said as they approached. He scowled, more belligerent even than Michael. Michael seemed resigned, which only meant he was planning something. "If I have to be your prisoner, can I at least not be shackled to a smelly bear? He stinks, and he's a prick."

"Like it's a pleasure being stuck with a traitor," Michael growled. "I'm busy imagining the ways I'm going to take you apart."

"See what I mean?" Crispin asked, petulant. "Aren't there, like, prisoners' rights or something?"

"You're in Faerie," Stuart said to Crispin. "The rules are different. But okay." He brought up his fist and opened it.

The iron band fell away, but just as both Shifter males relaxed, Stuart rotated his hand, and the band split into two. One wrapped itself around Michael like a metal cocoon.

Crispin started to laugh, but then the second band whipped

around him. Crispin's feet left the floor and he sailed upward to be pinned by the band to the railing on the third-floor balcony, the iron around him fusing to the wrought iron there.

He yelled, feet kicking. Michael bellowed with laughter, then cut off the laughter, satisfyingly worried when Stuart turned his gaze at him.

They needed to learn not to mess with him, Peigi thought as she and Stuart continued down the hall to the garden.

"I forgot how much fun that was," Stuart said as he opened the door. "Miss it."

Peigi hid the pang in her heart. "Did you stick people to walls much when you lived here?"

"When I had to. But it's been a long time since I could manipulate iron. It's a feeling that ..." He flexed his fingers, sinews on his arms working. "It's hard to explain."

"Like shifting." Peigi followed him out into a lush and fresh-smelling garden. "It completes something inside me."

"Exactly."

"In the human world you can teleport. Does that feel the same?"

"Sort of, but it's weird. Like I'm being pulled apart and stuck back together. Unnerving. Making iron do what I want ..." Stuart broke off and took a deep breath. "It's powerful."

Peigi didn't answer. Asking him to give up his natural ability would be like someone telling her to cease shifting. She tucked that away in her head for the argument she knew would come.

The garden was small, as it was tucked inside a walled space, hemmed in by other buildings, but beautiful.

The walls were covered in greenery and vines that burst into blue, red, or yellow flowers. Peigi didn't know enough about plants to tell if they were roses or what, but they were big blossoms with a multitude of petals.

Brick walks flowed under trees and around hedges, and flowerbeds filled with blooms provided a carpet of color. While the air was cool, it did not have an icy bite. That plus the abundance of flowers made Peigi speculate it was spring or early summer, at least in this part of the Fae world.

Stuart didn't speak as they wandered the paths. The only sound came from birds enjoying the oasis in the city and the pattering of fountains in corners.

"This isn't the terrifying Fae dominion I was raised to fear," Peigi said after the silence had stretched. "It's kind of nice."

"There are terrifying parts," Reid answered. "Mostly in the lands of the *hoch alfar*. The *dokk alfar* are far more civilized. We lived in happy peace—mostly—until the *hoch alfar* decided our lands would suit them. They'd have killed us off if we hadn't protected ourselves. Not because *dokk alfar* are weaker, but we were taken off guard, not prepared to fight." He sighed. "And we might have to again."

"Unless you can help them find this *karmsyern* thing."

"*If* I can. There's nothing to say the *hoch alfar* haven't already destroyed it. Or if they can't, they might have taken it far, far away. To the human world, maybe. They'd get rid of something iron and spelled as fast as they could."

"It kept them from *dokk alfar* lands, right?" Peigi asked, trying to understand. "I know you and Cian were saying they sent Shifters to steal it, but how are the Fae able to even be around it?"

"Good question. They must have not only sent minions to grab it, but minions to hide it or get rid of it."

Peigi laughed. "Minions."

Stuart shared her amusement. "That's what *hoch alfar* call them—actually, they call anyone who isn't *hoch alfar* that. We call *hoch alfar* dickheads."

"When you're being polite."

"Exactly."

Peigi moved closer to him. "Did you bring me out to explain you're going to stay with Cian?"

"No." He looked at her. "I came to explain that I don't know what to do. Going after the *karmsyern* will be a hopeless quest."

"Cian doesn't seem to think so."

"Because Cian is a powerful man. If Dimitri isn't exaggerating, he's a crazy warrior too. According to Dimitri Cian was imprisoned, beaten, tortured, and ordered to fight Dimitri to the death, and still he got up and kicked ass. Cian must not understand why I haven't grabbed some armor and headed out the door to beat up the *hoch alfar* and bring the *karmsyern* home under my arm."

Peigi let her voice go soft. "So why haven't you?"

"Because."

Stuart faced her and took her hands. His were hard, scarred from his life of fighting, both here and in the human world.

She wanted him to say, *Because I've found you. Because nothing would ever take me away from you.*

And she'd be totally selfish. Stuart had done so much for her, and she could not let him throw away all he believed in, all he loved, to remain in the little house in Shiftertown, working for whatever salary Diego paid him. In the lands of the Fae, he was a leader, a man of strength and honor. The *hoch alfar* had taken that away from him, but maybe Peigi could help give it back.

She'd tried once before, years ago, when he'd wanted to work the spell so he could return to Faerie. Even then he'd done his best to stop her ...

A movement caught her eye, and Peigi stilled, words catching in her throat.

An old tree completed the line that followed this path, a stumpy tree with rough bark and a few shoots of leaves. The movement had been wind in the larger trees that made branches sway, but none of the smaller tree's twigs had so much as budged.

Peigi released Stuart so fast he blinked at her in surprise. Then she was walking away from him, striding faster and faster down the path toward the stumpy tree, which abruptly turned and tried to run.

FOURTEEN

R eid stared in open-mouthed shock at the small, squat tree
scurrying across the lawn with Peigi chasing it.

For something that solid, it could move fast. Peigi tossed
away her shirt and unzipped her jeans, letting clothes and shoes
fall away as she morphed into bear.

It took her a moment to shift, and the tree gained ground, but
then Peigi came down on all fours and took off after it.

The fleeing tree didn't have a chance. Reid jogged down the
path toward them, gathering up her clothes as he went, and
watched her tackle it.

His girlfriend, in bear form, was taking down a running tree.
If anyone from his past had told him this would happen, Reid
would have laughed and said the speaker must be smoking something good.

Reid hit the grass and ran to where Peigi was sinking her
teeth into a branch, just as the tree shrank down and became
Ben, complete with the man's tatts, clothes, and battered
sneakers.

"Shit," Ben yelled. "Peigi, quit! It's me!"

Peigi lifted her mouth away and shifted to her between beast, growing larger, fiercer, angrier. "I know it's you. *Why* is it you? What are you doing here, and why did you run?"

Ben coughed, pushing at Peigi's strong, furry body. "Which question did you want answered first?"

"How did you get here?" Reid put in.

"Another question. Well, let's start with why I'm me. A long time ago—"

"Cut the crap." Peigi took on the tone she used when she had to make Donny admit he'd gone off where he shouldn't—except she never said "crap" or anything stronger to the cubs. "Why did you run?"

Ben sat up, cross-legged, and brushed grass from his shirt. "Because you were having a moment. I didn't want to interrupt. By the way, I've come to rescue you."

"To *what*?" Peigi glared down at him. "It's not that simple."

"You're telling *me* it's not simple? Me, in Faerie after a thousand years isn't simple." Ben surveyed Cian's house visible between the trees, and the buildings beyond the garden wall. "Man, this place has changed."

"Ben!" Peigi growled.

"So many people have been saying my name, lately. At least the short version, which I guess gets the point across. They all come to the house, where I'm trying to eat my lunch, and suddenly there's doors, and Tuil Erdannan, and magic talismans."

"Tuil Erdannan?" Reid asked sharply. "Who? Lady Aisling? Where is she?"

"Not here. She drags me kicking and screaming—I mean, seriously kicking and screaming—through a door, dumps me at the edge of town, shoves a talisman at me, and tells me where Cian lives. I figured I'd park in the garden and blend in, and it would be only a matter of time until you showed up. Which you have."

Reid felt a modicum of relief. "I'm glad. Another powerful being is what we need." With Ben, they might be able to finish the mission faster. Ben was good at moving around without anyone seeing him, he didn't have an aversion to iron, and—

Reid never got to complete the thought. Ben dug into his pocket, and then a deep blue light filled his hand, along with the flash of metal.

"Goddess, I hate this part," Ben groaned, and the garden, houses, trees, and sky ran like watercolors in the rain and were gone.

Gray space filled in where Faerie had been, and then Reid found himself face down on solid, scraping stone. Peigi, still half bear, half human, landed on top him, and Ben's weight completed the pile.

It was dark, stuffy, and cold, and Reid heard thumping, like boots against a door.

————

"I WISH YOU ALL WOULD STAY THE HELL OUT OF MY basement." The Lupine who'd let Peigi and Graham into his cellar when Stuart had first disappeared waited impatiently outside the door he'd wrestled open. "Graham needs to pay me compensation."

"No worries," Ben said. "This should be the last you see of us."

Ben looked awful, his face wan, his dark eyes haunted. Stuart slid out from the bottom of the pile and pulled Ben off Peigi, his movements silent and tense.

Peigi was shaky and sick to her stomach as she dressed in the clothes Stuart had been carrying when Ben transported them. She had to agree with Ben that traveling through the ley line took some getting used to.

Kurt held the door, his planted feet telling her he wanted them out. He slid his gaze to Stuart, probably again thinking of him as *that creepy Fae shit*.

"Thank you for your hospitality," Stuart told Kurt as he exited. "I'm sure Graham will be happy to help you out."

Kurt's eyes flickered. Asking Graham for anything, even the time, was not for the faint of heart. "Just go."

Ben thanked Kurt then ushered Stuart and Peigi out through the basement and up the stairs, bringing up the rear. Covering them, Peigi surmised, in case Kurt decided he'd keep two beings of Faerie and a bear Shifter from his cellar in the most permanent way he could.

Once they were out of the house, striding past Kurt's interested mate and his open-mouthed cubs, Peigi shivered. Her jacket had been good in New Orleans and even Faerie, but the cold of the desert evening was sharp.

"Before anyone yells at anyone else, let's go home and get warm," she said. "We'll have coffee and a meal. I'm starving."

"Yeah, come to think of it, I'm peckish," Ben said. "Dinner would be nice."

"Only if you help," Peigi told him. "I'm not doing all the cooking while you lounge."

"Did I say that?" Ben gave her innocent eyes. "I'd never dream of it, Pegs."

Stuart did not speak at all. Whether he was glad or sorry to be back in the human world or in the Las Vegas Shiftertown, Peigi couldn't tell. He walked beside her, mouth closed, taking in everything, including staring Shifters. They always watched Stuart, and Peigi also. They were oddities together.

Peigi's steps quickened as she approached her house, her joy and eagerness growing with every stride. She wasn't the biological mother of any of the cubs inside the house, but that didn't matter in her heart.

She was running by the time she crossed the yard and darted in through the front door. Plenty of noise led her to the large kitchen and dining room in the back, where four cubs were playing a noisy board game at the table, and the two youngest were engrossed in a separate venture that involved a lot of running and dodging around furniture.

In the middle of the dining room Shane roared, "Will you two stand still? It's almost dinner time, so you four put all that stuff in the living room."

"When's Nell coming?" Donny demanded.

"Yeah," Noelle chimed in. "We want Nell. We want Nell."

The chant was taken up by the other cubs who began pounding on the table. "We want Nell!"

Shane jammed his hands over his ears. Peigi walked in, laughing. "Will I do, instead?"

Shrieks filled the air. There was a blur, and then six cubs were clinging to Peigi, each trying to climb higher up on her than the others.

Shane exhaled in relief and lowered his hands. "Thank the Goddess."

Stuart entered behind her. "I've seen you do battle against hard men, Shane. A few cubs taking you down?"

"Stuart!" More shrieks. Noelle, Donny, and Kevin leapt from Peigi and ran to wrap arms around him. The other three remained with Peigi, kissing and hugging and beaming happy smiles at Stuart.

"About time you got home," Noelle said loudly. "Where have you two been?"

"On an adventure," Peigi answered, ruffling Hannah's hair. "We'll tell you all about it. Shane, you said something about dinner?"

"Mom's bringing it. Or part of it." Shane moved back to the kitchen, visibly relieved. Ben, who'd hung back while all the greeting went on, joined him. "I agree," Shane went on. "About time you got home."

"How long were we gone?" Stuart asked. He sounded curious, not alarmed.

"Five days," Shane said. "Five very long days."

"Five?" Peigi counted two. Three at most. One day to reach

Texas by plane and on to New Orleans that night. They'd spent the next day at the haunted house and then gone out dancing in the evening. This had led them through the gate, where they'd spent half a day at most.

"Time difference," Stuart said. He dislodged Donny but kept hold of the boy's hand as they approached the kitchen. The other cubs let go and actually began to clean up the game at the table.

"Time difference?" Peigi asked.

Ben answered her. "It flows differently in Faerie. Either direction."

"Oh." Something cold formed in the pit of her stomach. They possibly could have been caught there for weeks, or months. She felt dizzy.

Stuart gave her a glance that said he'd explain more later and offered to help Shane prep dinner.

Peigi gave the three cubs she still held a tight hug before setting them down. They wouldn't leave her side, so she joined in helping put away the board game, one that involved many colorful pieces.

"I don't remember this one," she said.

"Nell got it for us," Patrick informed her. "Me and Lucinda are the best at it. We were winning."

Noelle gave him an indulgent nod. "You were. Patrick and Lucinda are very smart."

Noelle was definitely an alpha, praising the strengths of others and not finding them a challenge to herself.

Nell arrived, which entailed more screeching and shouting, including from Nell herself, who reamed out Stuart for keeping Peigi away so long, and Ben for taking his time fetching them back. Jaycee had called and told her all about it.

Shane pretended not to hear as he pan-fried burgers on the stove, or maybe he was so used to his mother yelling that it rolled off him.

In the middle of the chaos, Peigi excused herself to take a shower and returned in fresh clothes to find Stuart had done the same thing in the other bathroom. Peigi satisfied her hunger quickly then lingered at the table to make sure the cubs all had enough, and simply enjoyed being with them.

As the meal wore on, she noticed Ben had slipped away. Of course he had, before she could interrogate him. Or maybe she'd find a small tree had sprouted on the edge of her yard.

Shane and Nell departed after first helping clean up the meal and calm the cubs, never an easy task. But finally, finally, the cubs wound down, tired and unwinding now that Peigi and Stuart were back.

"You won't leave again, will you?" Donny asked as Peigi straightened the covers on his bed and kissed him good night. She sensed the other two boys listening hard. "It's just that the younger cubs were worried."

He spoke with the nonchalance of an eight-year-old who was fine on his own.

Peigi stroked his hair then leaned to Patrick in the next bed, kissing his cheek. "I'm not going anywhere. Not for a long, long time."

She meant it. Peigi had found safety here, and peace. She wouldn't jeopardize that.

"Will Stuart stay too?" Kevin asked from the far bed. "We need him to make pancakes and teach us football."

Peigi couldn't lie to them, but they wanted reassurance. "I'll talk to him. I know he doesn't want to leave either." She was reasonably sure that was the truth.

It was a while before Peigi could turn off the light and leave them, then she repeated the good nights in the girls' room, answering the same questions.

Finally she shut out their light, closed the door, and crept down the hall to the kitchen. She didn't stop walking until she'd grabbed a heavier jacket and was out the back door, off the porch, and into the yard. There she halted, letting out a long breath.

"It's good to be back." Stuart materialized from the shadows of the porch. He stepped down to join Peigi, lacing his arms around her from behind.

Peigi leaned into him, enjoying his strength, his arms encircling her protectively. She rested her head on his shoulder, the wall of his body firm behind her. The night was clear and dry, the stars a wash of light in the darkness.

"I didn't know what to tell them," she said softly. "When they asked whether you would be leaving again, I didn't know what to say."

Stuart was silent a long time, then he released his breath, brushing Peigi's ear. "I don't know what I'm going to do."

Peigi thought that might be his answer. "Cian has you worried."

Stuart unwound himself to turn Peigi to face him. "Cian's not wrong. If the talisman isn't returned, it will lead to a long and bloody war. I liked your idea of making another one, but we can't count on persuading Lady Aisling to do it. The spells might be lost in any case."

"Won't know until we ask."

Stuart gave her a faint smile. "I always like how you think."

"When you have to take care of twenty cubs in a basement, you become resourceful." Peigi studied the half globe of the moon above them. "You know we left Crispin and Miguel bound in iron in Cian's house."

"Yeah." Stuart chuckled. "I feel so bad about that."

"I *suppose* Cian will find some way to cut them free."

"Possibly. He might decide to leave them as decoration."

Peigi's laughter swelled, years of fear and anger flowing out with it. "If I'd known, when Michael kept me prisoner, that he'd end up as an iron-bound ornament in the house of a dark Fae, courtesy of you ..." Peigi's laughter died on a sob. "I wouldn't have been so scared of him. Or angry. Not angry at him—at me. Well, him too. But I loathed myself for deciding to stay with him."

Stuart slid his hands up her arms to her shoulders, his touch both comforting and awakening need too near the surface.

"You never talk about it," he said quietly. "You don't have to."

"Because I was ashamed." Peigi stepped closer to him. "I believed in him. I thought he'd rescue me from my empty life. No one wanted me around, but Michael did. He made me feel good, included."

"It's understandable. Though I'm surprised you say no one wanted you around. What idiots were they?"

"My clan—extended clan, that is. I was orphaned as a cub, and the rest of my clan kind of passed me around—*who gets the cub today?* They made sure I was taken care of, but they weren't interested in me for myself—I wasn't very high in the hierarchy, and I knew that. Plus, Shifters can't mate within their own clans, so I wasn't mate potential. When I ran off with Michael, who at that time was calling himself Michelangelo, they were relieved."

"I'm sorry." Stuart closed his arms around her again, the solidness of him an anchor in the darkness. "Michelangelo?"

"He liked being grandiose. He changed his name to suit the occasion and the locale, which I thought was romantic. See? The idiot is me."

"No." Reid drew her into him, his lips brushing her forehead. "You were young and needed to be needed. Michael is an alpha Shifter. I've seen how Eric and Graham can make anyone think the way they want just by looking at them. You were in a position of vulnerability, and Michael took advantage."

"So were you." Peigi lifted her head, enjoying the darkness of his eyes. "You were alone and vulnerable when you came to Shiftertown. But you don't do what Eric wants just by him looking at you."

He gave a light shrug. "That's because I've kicked around the worlds a bit. I help Eric because I'm grateful to him for giving me a place to stay, and Diego for giving me a second chance."

"I felt the same way about Michael—he gave me a place and

a chance to leave the family who didn't know what to do with me."

Stuart traced her cheek. "But my case is different. Eric respects me and what I can do, lets me be myself. Michael wanted you to be his little groupie."

"He did." Peigi's breath caught. "Even when I realized that, I didn't shun him or try to walk away. He only pushed me aside when I couldn't give him cubs."

That had hurt, kicked her hard, awakened her from her stupor. She'd realized in the space of a heartbeat that Michael had duped her and used her.

"I thought about running," she went on, nestling into him. "But by then, there was nowhere to go. He'd taken me to a place so remote it would have been hard to get away."

"That's not why you stayed with him," Stuart said gently. "You could have found a way to a town if you had to."

"Possibly. By that time, though, Shifters had been rounded up into Shiftertowns. I knew it was useless for me to try to get back to my clan."

"Still not why." Stuart's voice was a point of softness in the crisp night.

Peigi nodded into his chest. "I couldn't leave the other women and the cubs. I could protect them from Michael and his Shifters at least."

"And that is why you are strong," Stuart cupped her face, raising her to him. "The strongest person I know."

Peigi should protest that he was wrong, but she didn't want to talk about it anymore. Not with Stuart holding her, his lips a breath from hers.

She rose to him and kissed him full on the mouth.

FIFTEEN

Peigi's lips were warm in the night, her body soft against his. Stuart pulled her up to him, imbibing her heat, mouths meeting hungrily. He moved his hand down her waist, cupping her hip, his hardness impossible to hide.

Stuart was finished with hiding it. He wanted this beautiful woman. Wanted her next to him, her kisses on his skin, to lie entwined with her in the night.

His wanting had only grown through the days, weeks, months, he'd lived in this house. At first coming over to check on them, which had grown to him spending the night to free up space in Nell's house. And then he'd decided Peigi needed protection from the new Lupines in town, so he might as well stay over most of the time.

Now Stuart couldn't imagine living anywhere but in Peigi's home.

Stuart eased from the kiss, but not because he was finished. Not by a long way.

Peigi gazed up at him, moonlight touching her eyes. She parted her lips as though she'd speak but moved to him for another kiss.

This kiss was stronger, more needy. Stuart responded in kind, their mouths tangling, tasting, wanting.

To have this woman for always, to be with her strength and her caring ... Stuart's heart cried out, urging him to not let go.

His body urged him as well. He wasn't about to admire Peigi from afar. Stuart wanted her *near*, next to him in bed, bodies locked together. He'd do anything to stay with her, to hell with Cian, the *dokk alfar*, and the *hoch alfar* who did nothing but cause Stuart problems ...

"Peigi?" A small voice cut through the night.

It was Donny, his cry tinged with fear and an unspoken wail. *Where are you? Don't leave me.*

Stuart emerged from a place of yearning to find cold air slapping at him. *I'm right there with you, kid.*

Peigi broke the kiss abruptly and swung back to the house. "It's okay, sweetie," she called. "We're here."

"Oh." Donny exuded relief. He cleared his throat and spoke in an offhand tone, though Stuart noted the tremor in his words. "Kevin and Patrick were worried when they didn't hear you and Stuart in the house. I told them I'd check it out."

"We didn't mean to frighten you." Peigi went to him, at her most reassuring. "We were taking a little walk. Not far. Just to get some air."

"No, you weren't. You were kissing." Donny sounded satisfied. "I saw you. Does that mean you're mates?"

Peigi hesitated. Stuart knew she was thinking of a way to tell Donny no, and a reason why she'd been kissing Stuart if not.

Stuart put an end to the question. "Yes," he said. "We are."

Peigi started, rising from comforting Donny. "It doesn't *quite* work that way." Her voice trembled as much as Donny's had, and she too tried to hide it.

"I know. I've been around Shifters long enough, and seen my share of mating ceremonies." Stuart's heart felt light, the rightness of what he was about to do filling him.

"Peigi of the Las Vegas Shiftertown, under the Mother Goddess and in front of a witness, *I claim you as mate.*"

———

HE STILL DIDN'T UNDERSTAND, PEIGI THOUGHT THE NEXT morning as they went to Eric's for what Stuart called a debriefing.

Stuart hadn't taken back the mate claim as they'd walked Donny inside, or discussed it, or even mentioned it. Stuart had put an excited Donny to bed, reassuring him and the other boys that he was there for them, then he'd given Peigi a smile, retreated to his own bedroom, and closed the door.

In the morning, their time had been filled with feeding the cubs and calling Shane again to babysit. Donny had of course told the other cubs about the mate claim, and they were ecstatic, asking questions about when the sun and moon ceremony would be and so forth.

Stuart and Peigi had put them off with evasions. Peigi hadn't accepted yet—how could she, when she hadn't had a chance to get a word in edgewise?

They couldn't discuss it on the walk to Eric's house, because Nell joined them immediately, saying she refused to let Eric interrogate Peigi without her present.

Once they'd settled in Eric's living room, Stuart told the entire story from the time they'd departed on Marlo's plane to Ben's act of dragging them out of Faerie via the ley line in Kurt's basement. Ben still hadn't resurfaced, and Peigi was getting worried about him.

Present for the tale were Eric and Iona, Cassidy, Diego, and Nell, of course. Today Eric directed his questions at Stuart, but Peigi appreciated Nell being there as a buffer for her. Peigi added confirmations and more thorough explanations while the story unfolded, as Stuart's answers could be laconic.

"So what we have," Eric concluded after Stuart and Peigi

had finished, "Is the *dokk alfar* in danger of a *hoch alfar* invasion. The *hoch alfar* have an advantage because they used an agent — you suspect a Shifter, but don't know for certain — to steal the magic talisman. Cian hopes he can locate and return this talisman, but believes he can do it only with your help."

"That's the gist," Stuart said.

Eric, in worn jeans and sweatshirt, lounged back on the sofa, crossing his legs and pulling his bare feet under him. He rarely looked like the leader he was but more like a man ready to nap in front of the television with a beer at his side.

"In other words, the *dokk alfar* want to send one of my best trackers on a seriously dangerous mission inside Faerie," Eric said. "I'll have to think about that."

"And one of my best employees." Diego folded his arms over his black shirt with *DX Security* emblazoned above the pocket.

Stuart nodded silently at them both, as though he agreed with their reasoning.

Peigi grew impatient with the stoic male thing. "It's Stuart's choice. You can't force him to stay and work for you."

Eric gazed at her in mild surprise. "I never said I would. Reid is a free man. I'm just assessing the situation."

His mate, Iona, a beautiful woman with black hair and blue eyes, rested on the arm of the sofa. "Eric likes to assess."

Cassidy laughed her agreement, and Nell rolled her eyes.

"Everyone's a critic." Eric grinned up at Iona, the love on his face evident.

"There's more to consider," Stuart broke in. "I'm of course very worried about what will happen to the *dokk alfar* if the *karm-oyern* is not returned. But things have changed for me. Earlier in my life, I would have rushed at the chance to throw myself in front of a thousand attacking *hoch alfar*, but I have a lot more to lose now. You should all know that I made the mate claim to Peigi."

He tossed out the last words casually, as though his audience would be less than interested in his personal life, but the effect was electric.

Eric came up off the couch, no longer the lazing leopard. Nell whooped, eyes alight, and sprang at Peigi, catching her in an enthusiastic embrace. Cassidy and Iona gathered around her, no less excited.

"It's about time," Cassidy said to Stuart while she waited for her turn to hug.

Eric closed on Stuart, arms open, ready to enfold him in a Shifter hug, but Diego raised his hands. "Wait a sec. Peigi, did you accept?"

The Shifters paused, arrested in mid cheer. Nell released Peigi and studied her. "Well?"

They all watched Peigi, eager—even Diego who'd voiced the question waited in interested anticipation. It was so clear what they wanted her answer to be.

A few years ago, Peigi would have gone into a panic and babbled that of course she'd said yes, whether she had or not, so they'd not be displeased with her. But she'd grown wiser, less afraid of not being accepted. Or so she told herself as she drew a calming breath and prepared to give them the truth, what *she* wanted, not what the group expected her to do.

Stuart stepped next to her before she could speak. "We haven't talked it through yet," he said.

Peigi gave him a grateful look. "It's all right. I haven't answered him," she said to the Shifters and Diego. "Like Stuart says, there's a lot to consider."

Nell watched her a moment, disappointment clear, then she shook her head. "I'm sorry, honey. We were just so excited—we want the best for you."

Iona said, "I know better than most what it's like to be cornered into a sudden mate claim." She shot Eric a glance, and he briefly studied the ceiling. "You can always refuse it—it's your right."

They went quiet, three leopards—one a panther—a bear, and

a human watching her. Stuart was the only one who didn't hang breathlessly on her answer, as though they expected she'd refuse the claim right there and then.

"I know," Peigi said quietly. "As I said, we haven't talked it through. This is between Stuart and me."

Peigi had grown to love these people who'd taken her in and given her such kindness, but at the moment, they all appeared surprised she had the backbone to tell them it was none of their business.

Of course even a year ago, under this much pressure, Peigi would have walked out of Eric's house, striding away rapidly, needing to be alone. She didn't like anything that smacked of confinement or coercion — a bodily reaction set in.

Even now, her feet willed her to run, but Peigi's own convictions plus Stuart solidly at her side let her stand and regard Eric and Nell, both far above her in power, with a measure of calm.

Iona had understanding in her eyes. She'd made the tough choice to leave her sort-of normal life as a half human in human society and live in Shiftertown, but she'd done it to be with Eric. Iona knew what it was to be an outsider, struggling to adjust.

Peigi's situation was a bit different, as Stuart wasn't Shifter, and he too was an outsider wherever he went. Even Cian had regarded him as no longer having a place in the *dokk alfar* realms.

Nell went to Peigi and gave her a light hug — which for Nell meant only slightly bone-crushing. "You take all the time you need, sweetie. I will admit, the fact that you didn't say no outright gives me hope. You need some happiness in your life."

Eric grinned at Nell. "Yeah, because you raced to shack up with Cormac right away. I remember your snarls and growls all the way up until you finally accepted his mate claim. Didn't cause any of us worry or anything."

"I was busy rescuing my son," Nell said, with a trace of the growls Eric mentioned. "I can't do *everything* at once."

Peigi appreciated how Eric had deflected the attention from Peigi and put it on Nell, who could take the teasing.

Peigi couldn't imagine being without Stuart, and the heat that had flared in her heart when he'd made the claim confirmed what she'd already known about her bond to him.

But she was going to have to explain to Stuart what the mate claim, and mating, truly entailed—besides the obvious. Already frenzy stirred within her, which didn't bode well for focusing on a mission.

"If Stuart decides to go back to Faerie and help out," Peigi said, breaking into the banter surrounding Nell, "how will he get there? Ben somehow dragged us out, but he's made himself scarce and he's not answering his phone. The only reason we got through the ley line *to* Faerie is because of the house in New Orleans. It wanted us to go, I think—it was trying to help."

Diego shivered. "I've seen that place, but I still can't get used to it."

"It's powerful." Eric's quiet statement held respect. "A lot of magic on that ley line, I'm thinking."

"I haven't said I was going back," Stuart said, and silence fell. "I came to get your take on it, Eric—actually to hear what all of you thought. I'd like Graham's opinion too. I don't know Cian well. He helped Dimitri, yes, and seems honorable, but do I take his word without doubt? Or does he have his own agenda? Is he sending me into a death trap to spare himself and his own people?"

Eric's brows rose at the mention of Graham's name, but he nodded. "Graham is the most suspicious Shifter on the planet. He'd ask questions I couldn't think of. Makes him a good co-leader."

Peigi felt the ripple of tension despite Eric's easy words. It was not easy for two Shifters to share leadership. They managed it by deliberately leaving each other the hell alone.

"Tell me about Crispin," Eric said abruptly. "Peigi, you said he looked like a Morrissey?"

"Superficially," Peigi answered, relieved at the change of subject. "He resembles Dylan and is a black-maned lion. But he's very unlike the Morrisseys in personality, at least based on the few times I've met any of them."

"He didn't give you his full name?" Eric asked.

"Said very little about himself," Peigi answered. "He wouldn't give us his clan name, wouldn't say why he'd decided to join the *hoch alfar*."

"He also didn't seem very anxious to get away from us and find his Fae prince again," Stuart added. "I couldn't tell if he'd given up or was plotting things in his head."

"He didn't seem very dominant," Peigi said. "Or very submissive either. Like he tries hard to be insignificant."

"Interesting." Eric glanced at Diego, who gave him a nod.

"I'll research him," Diego said. "Reid, can you give me a good description? Crispin might not be his real name." He frowned. "You know, if I needed to take an assumed name, I'd pick something with a little more pizazz."

"Like Michelangelo?" Peigi asked. When blank faces turned to her, she continued, "It's what Miguel used to call himself. Now it's just Michael."

"We've been keeping track of him too," Diego said. "Had a bead on him heading out of Texas, but then he went to ground. My colleagues tracked him to St. Louis and lost him there. I'm sorry, Peigi. I didn't have the intel that he'd gone to New Orleans, or I'd have warned you."

"Not your fault." Peigi shrugged as though it didn't matter. "The New Orleans trip was a last-minute decision. Michael said he was there because he was tracking *me*. He's good at tracking."

"Still, it's my job to keep my eye on assholes and stop them." Diego's scowl showed the determined and resourceful cop he'd been, and the determined and resourceful security expert he was. "My apologies."

"With any luck, he'll be stuck in Faerie for a long time, at the mercy of a *dokk alfar* who doesn't much like him," Stuart said. "Cian doesn't strike me as the type who'll be bamboozled by someone like Michael. Or Crispin. My guess is he'll interrogate the hell out of both of them before deciding what to do with them."

"Which gives a *dokk alfar* access to Shifter secrets," Eric observed, his tone mild. "A *dokk alfar* you don't trust."

"I didn't mean I don't trust him," Stuart said. "I mean I don't know him. And he isn't going to trust *me* implicitly until he knows more about me, and how loyal I am, and to whom."

"All good points," Eric said. "But so is mine."

"About this Crispin guy," Diego broke in. "I know how we can find out if he's one of the Morrissey clan."

"Yes?" Eric lifted his brows.

"Ask a Morrissey."

Eric flashed a grin. "I love you like a brother, Diego. Since you bring it up ... Dylan called this morning. He's on his way, and he wants to talk to you two." He pointed at Peigi and Stuart. "All right with you?"

SIXTEEN

R eid didn't share the group's trepidation at the mention of Dylan's name. He'd been working with Dylan for a while, off the books, and had learned how to deal with him. Dylan had a lot of power, true, but plenty of wisdom and deep-rooted kindness to go with it.

"Let me know when he shows up," Reid said to Peigi. "Mind if I go have a talk with Graham? I told him I would."

Eric nodded. "If you don't, Graham'll be in my face telling me to send you over. I asked him to this meeting, but he couldn't make it. Cubs."

Everyone assumed expressions of amusement. Graham wasn't happy unless he dominated everyone … except the cubs in his life. They pretty much led him around by the tail.

Reid knew the feeling. Donny's fear last night that he and Peigi would leave him had hit Reid hard. Soldiers, cops, fire-fighters—anyone who worked for the good of others went through that, he knew. The choice between helping the world and making sure your own child was safe, protected, and happy was the toughest one there was.

Eric gently pulled Peigi into an embrace. It was the hug of a

Shifter leader passing reassurance to one of his own, letting her know he was there for her, whatever choices she made.

Reid watched Peigi loosen under Eric's touch. She'd badly needed someone like Eric when she'd first been rescued, with his true promise that he would protect her, unconditionally. Michael, who'd been her leader, should have done that for her, but hadn't.

Eric led unselfishly while Michael had only wanted to dominate. Eric had sacrificed himself for others—Michael sacrificed others for himself. This was the difference between a good and bad leader, Stuart had learned, and why he trusted Eric with his life.

Nell and the ladies insisted on hugging Peigi after Eric moved off. Diego bent an eye on Reid.

"Not gonna hug you," he said. "But don't worry about coming in to work until you get this sorted out. Your desk will still be there."

"Xavier that happy working my case load, is he?" Reid asked.

"Xavier needs more to do." Diego spoke with the sternness of an older brother for a younger. "It's good for him."

"I'm sure he's thinking that," Reid said without cracking a smile. "Tell him I'll be back as soon as I can. I like my job."

This had surprised him at first, but Reid had discovered he was a good police officer and enjoyed detective work. Finding a bad guy and stopping him had been satisfying, making his lonely exile more bearable.

Diego, who had started the DX Security firm when he'd quit the police force to mate with Cassidy, had given Reid a way to continue stopping bad guys, for which Reid would be ever grateful. The bad guys had learned to fear Reid, Xav, and Diego, and the words *DX Security* could send a tremble to the most hardened drug dealer's heart.

Reid and Peigi finally left the house—with all the Shifters still hopeful Peigi would accept the mate claim. They'd ceased saying so, but Reid knew it, their excitement barely dampened as they said their good-byes.

"Ready to face Graham?" Reid asked Peigi as they walked down the long street in the direction of the Lupine section of town.

"Sure. I'm interested in his opinion too." Peigi's hand hung stiffly at her side, near but not touching Reid's. "Will you tell me something honestly?" she asked. "If it weren't for me and the cubs, would you be running through a gate to find Cian and take on the *hoch alfar*?"

Reid swallowed, knowing the answer. "Yes."

"Thought so."

Stuart took her rigid hand and pulled her to a halt. Peigi turned reluctantly, but she faced him.

They'd stopped at the edge of another Shifter's yard. Reid knew the Shifters inside the house would be watching out the window—no one minded their own business in Shiftertown—but this was too important.

"Let me tell you why." Reid stood close to her, toe to toe, sneaker to sneaker, and let his voice go quiet. "Because if you and the cubs weren't here, or didn't like me around, I'd have nothing to lose."

Peigi's dark blue eyes flickered with competing emotions. "I never want to stop you."

"You don't." Reid lifted their twined hands to his lips and kissed her fingers. "You've given me something to live for—*you*. I don't want to lose what I've found. I know you believe I stay in Shiftertown and help you and the cubs because I have nothing better to do, but that's not why."

Peigi flushed. "I did think that," she said softly. "That you'd leap at the chance to go back home."

"No leaping." Stuart kissed her fingers again, then leaned to her and pressed a swift kiss to her lips. He imagined the Shifters—a family of Felines—in their living room, watching avidly, maybe passing around popcorn. "It's killing me that everyone expected I'd want to go, to leave you like it was nothing to me."

"Is that why you made the mate claim?" Peigi's question held trepidation.

Stuart felt his smile come. "No. I made it because you're seriously hot."

Peigi didn't laugh as he intended, remaining worried. "You shouldn't joke about that. Do you know what a mate claim does to a Shifter?"

"Makes their friends want to throw a party? With hugging. Lots and lots of hugging."

"It triggers the mate frenzy." Peigi's breath touched his lips. "You've never experienced Shifter mating frenzy."

"I've seen Shifter mates barely able to keep their hands off each other. Is that what you mean?"

"Do *ðokk alfar* have mating frenzy?"

Stuart drew closer. "If you mean deep, all-consuming need, then yes. I'm kind of feeling that right now."

Peigi's eyes darkened. "Trust me, it's nothing like mating frenzy." She rose on tiptoe and licked his ear. "I'm very strong."

Heat shot through Reid's body, and his heart banged. "So am I."

"Uh-oh."

Reid jerked his head up and glanced around, thinking someone was coming upon them, but Peigi had her gaze fixed on him.

"Uh-oh what?" he asked nervously.

"We'll have to have Shane or Nell stay over again. Because once the frenzy takes hold, we won't be doing anything else for a while."

Reid growled in his throat, a very Shifter sound. "I am so looking forward to that." He was tempted to start immediately, but he knew that if Graham expected them, he'd storm around and pull Reid out of the house, even if Reid was deep in bed with a mate-frenzied Peigi.

"I'm looking forward to it too."

Peigi's whisper chased the fires already burning inside him.

Reid kissed her, harder this time, fingers threading her hair, but instead of relieving tension, the kiss only ramped it up.

When he eased from the kiss, Peigi gazed up at him, a half-smile on her lips. Reid knew that if Peigi refused him it would be the hardest thing he faced in his life. Even the *hoch alfar* dumping him in the human world and sealing him from his home would be nothing in comparison.

Peigi unwound their fingers and walked on, her back view enticing. Reid waved at the Shifters he knew lingered behind the window, and quickly followed her.

———

GRAHAM WAS AT HOME, AS ERIC HAD SAID, DEALING WITH A cub thing. That turned out to be Kyle and Matt on the roof attempting to set up a skateboard run. They'd already constructed a few ramps, Misty told Peigi and Stuart when they arrived, which Dougal, Graham's nephew and second, quickly dismantled, but Kyle and Matt rebuilt as fast as Dougal tore down.

Graham stood on the roof yelling at everyone, but Misty was in the kitchen, calmly making tea. Her cub, a boy called Hamish, sat in a high chair, slamming his fists against the tray, threatening to topple the baby bottle on it and making almost as much noise as Graham on the roof. Hamish had a thick quantity of black hair on his head and penetrating wolf-gray eyes.

"Want some tea?" Misty asked cheerfully after she invited Peigi and Stuart inside. "I heard Stuart made the mate claim."

Peigi halted, eyes widening. "How did you know that?"

"Nell called me, right after you left Eric's." Misty's smile widened. "She also told me to keep it quiet, as you hadn't given your answer yet, but I thought I should warn you. All Shifter-town will know within the hour, I'd bet."

Stuart showed no alarm at the prospect. "I don't mind." He

brushed the back of Peigi's arm, sending pleasant tingles through her. "Think Graham's in the mood to chat?"

"I think he's in the mood to chain the cubs in the basement. Not that chains would keep them in." A huge *bang* on the high chair caught her attention. Misty rescued the bottle that six-month-old Hamish had smashed to the tray, and set it upright. Both tray and bottle were made of sturdy material, built to withstand the strength of a baby Shifter. "You can always try. You'll have to go up on the roof, though. Graham won't come down until the cubs do."

"I can deal with that." Stuart kissed Peigi's cheek. "Be right back."

He vanished with a pop. Peigi, used to it, didn't even blink in the rush of air he left behind. Hamish stared, wide-eyed, then he squealed with laughter and banged the tray with gleeful enthusiasm.

"He wants an encore." Misty went to Hamish and brushed a tender, motherly kiss to his head. "So, the mate claim," she said to Peigi. "Are you ready for that? Everyone at Eric's was trying to push you into it, right?"

"They were." Peigi sighed, the weight of their expectations pressing at her.

"That's because they want you to be happy." Misty moved to the counter, poured a cup of steaming tea, and brought it to Peigi. "If you're happy, they can stop worrying about you. Problem solved—for them."

Peigi took the warm cup, inhaling the tea's rose-scented fragrance. "Cassidy and Diego rescued me. Eric mate-claimed me temporarily so the male Shifters wouldn't pounce on me as fair game. Nell has made me an honorary member of her clan so she can protect me further. I owe them everything."

"Do *not* accept a mate claim because you feel obligated to Eric and his family," Misty said sternly. "Or Nell and hers. It's not fair to you, and it's not fair to Stuart."

"Stuart." Peigi repeated his name with longing. "Is it fair to him for me to *accept*?"

Misty gave her a sage look. "You mean keeping him with you when he's being asked to help his people, don't you?"

"Yes." Peigi sipped the tea but decided she was too restless to handle dainty bits of porcelain and set the cup on the counter. "How can I keep him with me when *ðokk alfar* might die by the hundreds if he doesn't go? At the same time, I know if Stuart fights, there's a good chance he'll be killed himself. I mean, high Fae with poisoned arrows? Against Stuart and a few people Cian puts together?" Peigi realized Misty might not know the whole story and what she was talking about, but her fears poured out of her. "It will be slaughter. Stuart can do tricks with iron, but even with that, he can't take on the entire Fae army by himself. And there are Shifters working for the Fae, who aren't bothered by iron touching them, or bothered by killing *ðokk alfar*."

Peigi ended up in the middle of the room, arms jammed over her chest, tears on her cheeks.

Misty went to her. The smaller woman reached up and wrapped her arms around Peigi, pulling her close. Misty smelled a bit like rose petals herself, and her softness was comforting.

"I know," she said. "Trust me, Graham gets himself into horrible situations, and I can only wait and worry. You, on the other hand, are a kick-ass bear. You can make sure Stuart survives."

"And if we're both killed?" Peigi asked. "What happens to the cubs?"

Misty pulled away but rested comforting hands on Peigi's arms. "In this Shiftertown? If Nell and Cormac, or Iona and Eric, or Cassidy and Diego don't take them in, I know Graham would. He's all growly, but he adores cubs. The more the better."

At that moment, Graham's voice rattled the windows. "Matt! I said *no*! Put that down!"

The two women looked at each other and burst out laughing. Hamish banged the tray, gurgling baby squeals, happy in his

mother's presence, with his father's voice ringing down from
on high.

————

THE ROOF OF GRAHAM'S TWO-STORY HOUSE WAS MOSTLY FLAT,
as was typical in this older desert neighborhood. A large AC unit
and various exhaust fans and pipes poked out of the roof at inter-
vals like stunted metal trees.

The two wolf cubs had built a series of ramps out of plywood
and crates, plus a wide plastic board that had once been a slide
on a play set, and PVC pipe of various lengths. Dougal, the wiry
young wolf who was Graham's second, and Graham himself, had
given up trying to dismantle the obstacle course and settled for
making certain it was sound. Matt pounding at anything and
everything with a hammer wasn't helping with the noise.

"Uncle Stuart!" The little boys shouted in unison when Reid
abruptly teleported onto the roof.

"Hi, Uncle Stuart!" Kyle ran at him while Matt continued to
smash his hammer against PVC pipe until the pipe broke. "We
didn't rescue you this time," Kyle yelled. "Uncle Ben did."

"He did indeed," Reid said. The view from the roof was good,
the house taller than those around them. From this vantage
point, Graham could observe all Shiftertown. "By the way, have
you seen Ben?" Reid asked Graham.

"No," Graham growled.

Matt raised his head. "I have. He was just here."

"What?" Graham demanded. "When was this?"

"You were busy arguing with Dougal. He explained how to
make that." Matt pointed with his hammer to a complicated
setup of four low ramps bolted to a wide crate.

"Yeah?" Graham asked. "How did he get up and down
without me seeing?"

Matt and Kyle glanced around, brows furrowing in perplexity. They went to the lip of the roof and glanced over at the long

ladder against the side of the house as though expecting Ben to
be clinging to it. "Maybe he can fly," Matt suggested. "Or teleport, like Uncle Stuart."

Graham turned his scowl on Stuart. "Perfectly good ladder
right there. Why didn't you use it instead of scaring the shit out
of us?"

"I wasn't scared," Kyle said confidently.

The ladder was spindly, resting on two narrow feet far, far
below. A Shifter wouldn't think anything of climbing it, but Reid
shuddered.

"No thanks," Reid said with feeling. "I wanted to make it
without broken bones."

Graham continued to scowl. He always had to growl to Reid
about his teleporting—it was like a greeting ritual.

"Eric called me and told me some of the shit you went
through," Graham said. "So how did it feel to go home?"

"Weird. I haven't had time to think about it." Emotions clam-
ored for Reid's attention, but he pushed them aside. "I came to
ask what you would do." He filled in details of his discussion
with Cian. "I'm interested in your opinion," he said when he
finished.

"Huh. I guess I'm flattered." Graham paused to hammer
a stout nail next to a bent one Matt had pounded into a
piece of wood. "You want the truth? I'd bounce this Cian
guy on his head until he told me everything he wasn't
telling me. Then I'd find whoever stole this whatsit, rip his
limbs from his body, take the thing, and go home." Amusement glinted his eyes. "Not what you wanted to
hear, right?"

"Actually, it's helpful. Refreshingly direct."

"Yeah, well, that's me. Direct. Eric can think a thing to death.
Or have endless meetings about it."

"Sometimes the problem has solved itself by the time all his
meetings are finished," Reid pointed out.

"True enough. Eric's a crafty bastard. Anyway, want me to go with you and kick some Fae ass? Some Shifter ass too if necessary?"

"I'll hold you in reserve," Reid said. "Haven't decided to go back, if I even can."

Graham nodded, with a glance at Kyle and Matt. Dougal was desperately trying to explain that a piece of string wasn't strong enough to hold heavy pieces of wood together.

"I get that," Graham said. "Mate and cubs changes everything." He pinned his gaze on Reid, the softness leaving it. "If Peigi hasn't accepted the mate claim, it's because she's afraid you'll vanish and leave her hurting and alone. Not because you're a weird, fucked-up dark Fae shit."

"Thanks," Reid said. "That's almost a compliment, coming from you."

Graham huffed a laugh. "You're not so bad."

"Stop it," Reid said, deadpan. "You're starting to embarrass me."

"All right, all right, I'll shut the fuck up. Eric said Dylan's coming to give you the third degree. Want backup?"

Reid shook his head. "It's all right. I'm not afraid of Dylan."

Graham's eyes widened. "Just when I think I've figured you out, you say stupid shit like that. We're all afraid of Dylan. Like and respect the guy, but damn, he scares even me."

Stuart shrugged. "Maybe he doesn't intimidate me because I'm not Shifter."

"No, it's because you're ignorant and lack common sense. I'll come anyway, because if he dicks with you, Peigi and Misty will be all over my ass for not protecting you."

"I'm touched," Reid said dryly.

"Touched in the head." Graham tapped the side of his. "Do me a favor, climb down the ladder."

Reid glanced at it and shuddered again. "*That* terrifies me. See ya, Graham."

He picturing the ground in front of Graham's back porch, and willed himself there. Reid broke into a grin at Graham's frantic *Son of a bitch*, as he popped out of existence and reappeared on the back doorstep.

————

STUART TRIED TO TALK PEIGI OUT OF ACCOMPANYING HIM TO see Dylan. Peigi and he had a loud argument about it, which Peigi decided to win.

"I'm not your mate yet," she growled, halting on the road that led from Graham's to their house. "I don't have to obey you." The day had clouded, and cold rain began to fall, dripping into Peigi's eyes. "And anyway, I won't have to obey as mate if I think you're wrong. Mates don't give orders. They give *suggestions*."

"Not what I've heard," Stuart said, folding his arms.

"Only because you talk to male Shifters. You think Nell does whatever Cormac tells her?"

She had him there. Stuart glared back at her, but she knew his irritation came from worry. He stood close to her, as he had when he'd kissed her—in front of this same house, Peigi noted. The Shifters inside were getting an eyeful today.

"If I am your mate," Peigi went on. "That means I protect *you*. It goes both ways. And like hell I'm okay with you meeting Dylan alone."

"I won't be alone. Dylan will bring trackers, and Graham volunteered to back me up. Eric will either be there or send Brody or Shane."

"All the more reason," Peigi said. "They're all Shifters, and you are not. I know Eric and Graham go on and on about how much you've done for them, but in the end, you're still a being of Faerie. When the shit goes down, Shifters will save Shifters. I will save *you*."

"And what about you?" Stuart demanded. "They still see you as the victim they rescued from that warehouse. Proud of you for coming this far, but you're still not one of them. If Dylan had decided you should live in *his* Shiftertown, you'd be there, no matter what Eric said. Dylan could demand you be moved any day, and Eric and even Graham would send their seconds over to help you pack."

Peigi had drawn a breath to yell more arguments, but she knew Stuart spoke the truth. The Shifters had been very kind, but they did scramble to obey Dylan.

"Is *that* why you made the mate claim?" she asked, voice shaking.

Stuart looked at her with his midnight eyes that held so many secrets. "I think I told you why. This is another reason."

"To protect me from Dylan." Peigi's heart thumped.

"To protect you from all Shifters." Stuart's hands warmed her arms, his body shielding her from the falling rain. "From the whole fucking world."

SEVENTEEN

Peigi stared up at Stuart, her heart thumping. His eyes blazed with anger, but also determination and behind that, desire. Stark, mirroring her own. That desire had been in him a long time, and so had Peigi's, hidden until all the barriers were down.

"Because I'm fair game." Her voice barely worked.

"Not anymore you're not," Stuart said fiercely. "By Shifter rules, any Shifter who wants anything from you, even to borrow a cup of sugar, has to come through me. Including Eric. Including Nell. Including Dylan."

Peigi swallowed, then nodded. She was shaking, from cold and from his declarations. She also tasted triumph as she saw a chink in his reasoning.

"By Shifter rules, we protect *each other*," Peigi said. "So I'll be going with you to see Dylan."

Stuart started, as though he'd been certain he'd won the day. He blinked a few times, his scowl remaining in place.

"You're devious," he said.

Peigi slanted him a smile. "I don't know why that's so surprising."

"And it's sexy how you turn my arguments around on me."

"Is it?" Peigi brushed her lips across his. "That's what I was going for."

Mating frenzy rose in her, hotter than before. She didn't know if she'd be able to contain it much longer. She slid her arms around Reid, flowed into his body, and deepened the kiss, deciding to give the Shifters watching from their window a show worth seeing.

———

DYLAN MET THEM LATER THAT EVENING IN THE MOST NEUTRAL space in the Las Vegas Shiftertown—a level cement platform in the middle of the back yards between Eric's house and Graham's street.

Visitors to Shiftertown sometimes asked if the cement slab was a sacred place, perhaps dedicated to rituals to the Goddess, but this was not the case. It was where Shifters set up their barbecues and makeshift bars for community celebrations.

Reid saluted Dylan's wisdom for meeting there—if Dylan had gone to Eric's house, Graham and his Lupines would have been furious. If he'd gone to Graham's, Eric's Shifters would have feared that Graham was about to turn on Eric.

The barbecue slab was a stroke of diplomacy, even if the rain kept coming, and Shifters stood around getting wet. None of them, including Reid, owned an umbrella.

Dylan arrived, flanked by two men, one bulking tall with orange and black striped hair, the other black-haired and blue-eyed, like Dylan, the hilt of a Sword of the Guardian rising above his left shoulder.

Reid easily recognized Tiger. The Guardian was Sean, Dylan's son.

Dylan nodded a greeting to Stuart, and Peigi behind him. Peigi had won the argument about coming along.

Dylan's dark hair was touched with gray at the temples, his

eyes a deep blue. Sean looked much like him, not only in hair and eye color but in the shape of his face, his easy stance.

Graham headed over with Dougal, approaching from a different angle than Eric and Diego. Reid usually enjoyed watching Graham and Eric dance around each other, but today he was impatient to get on with things.

Stuart didn't bother to greet Dylan or wait for the others to be in place. He knew from experience the Shifters could stand around a long time talking about nothing before getting to the point.

"What are you here to tell me to do?" Stuart asked Dylan abruptly.

Dylan was a difficult man to startle. He didn't change expression as Reid's words echoed in the wet air.

Sean let out a laugh, his breath steaming. "He's taken your measure, Dad. You wouldn't have run down Marlo and hopped on his plane if you didn't have an agenda."

"Thank you, Sean." Dylan kept his gaze on Reid. "I think everyone knows why I'm here." He flicked his focus to Peigi and gave her a grave nod. "How are you, Peigi?"

The question was genuine, not mere politeness. Dylan always asked after Peigi and the cubs, his concern true. Dylan was a hard-ass and a control freak, but he also took care of Shifters, even when they might be unaware of it.

"I'm fine," Peigi said. "Really."

"You don't have to accept his mate claim, you know. It is your choice."

"That news has gone around the world, hasn't it?" Peigi stood next to Reid, her arm touching his, refusing to shy from Dylan's gaze.

Dylan shrugged. "We're Shifters. We like a good mate claim, hope a sun and moon ceremony is around the corner. Eric was on the phone immediately to my son Liam, who called *me* ..."

"And Liam's talking to Shifters all over," Sean put in. "Bowman in North Carolina, Eoin in Montana, Zander ..."

"Zander?" Graham growled as he approached. "That walking furball? No secret is safe with him." He gazed up at Tiger, who had remained in the background in silence. "How's it going, crazy?"

Tiger took a moment to consider the question. "It is going well. A mate claim is not a secret. That is the point of one."

"Fair dues." Graham nodded at Dylan and Sean, then stepped back as Eric and Diego arrived.

This meeting was technically between Reid and Dylan, but the others had insisted on standing by as referees. Reid wondered whether they feared what Dylan might do to Reid, or what Reid might do to Dylan.

Tiger held Peigi with his golden gaze. "Congratulations. My mate told me to tell you, 'It's about time.'"

"I haven't accepted yet," Peigi said quickly.

Tiger looked Peigi up and down in silence. As Dylan began to speak, Tiger mouthed to Peigi, *Yes, you have.*

Peigi flushed, but Reid had to switch his focus to Dylan before he could think about what Tiger implied.

"I'd like you to go back to Faerie," Dylan said. "As you probably guessed I would ask you to. It's important."

Reid frowned. "Why? To help Cian and the *dokk alfar*? Or to scout for you and your upcoming war?"

"Both," Dylan answered without missing a beat. "You can find out more easily than most which *hoch alfar* are gearing up, where, and with what. If the *dokk alfar* have a spelled iron talisman that can stop them, so much the better."

Reid didn't move. "If you mean, when I find the *karmsyern* I should deliver it to you instead of Cian, you are talking to the wrong man."

"I mean no such thing. The *karmsyern* ought to be returned to Cian and protect the *dokk alfar* people. I'd never steal something so important." Dylan stuffed his hands into his jacket pockets. "But I might ask to borrow it a while."

"I can suggest it to Cian," Reid said. "He might be amenable. Then again, he might not."

"Huh," Graham broke in. "I bet he tells you to take a flying leap. Why would this dark Fae care about protecting a bunch of Shifters, especially if it means his own people might be mowed down in the meantime?"

"That's why I'll *ask*," Reid said. "Not simply take it."

Was Dylan disappointed? Hard to tell under his poker face. Dylan liked to get his way. That way usually did a lot of good, but at the same time, he could bulldoze over people to make things go as he planned. Dylan was reasonable enough to know he had to compromise, but at times he'd throw compromise to the wind and be utterly ruthless.

"What I'm proposing is an alliance with the *dokk alfar*," Dylan said, an edge to his voice.

"I know." Reid refused to back down. "And I'll *ask*. That's the best I can do."

They went silent, matching stare for stare. Dylan was used to Shifters dropping their gazes before him, but Reid wasn't Shifter. In terms of Reid's clan, he was no submissive either. He'd not been at the absolute top of his clan, but pretty near. He'd learned never to give in to a leader without long thought about what that leader really wanted.

Dylan moved his gaze to Peigi. If he expected *her* to knuckle under, he didn't know her. This woman could convince Donny and Noelle to clean their rooms and do the dishes, and that took some serious maneuvering.

"I don't want to see the *hoch alfar* come in and overrun us," Peigi said to Dylan. "But I won't risk the safety of the *dokk alfar* either. If the *karmsyern* can be borrowed—if it can even be found and rescued—then it has to be up to them."

"I agree," Dylan began, but Peigi wasn't finished.

"And it isn't fair to expect Stuart to go in and browbeat them. Stuart is loyal to you, but by his choice, because he likes you and is grateful to you, and Eric and all. But that doesn't mean he'll throw the *dokk alfar* under a bus so Shifters might have an edge in a fight."

"The *dokk alfar* don't have busses," Stuart murmured out of the corner of his mouth.

"Whenever they invent busses," Peigi said heatedly. "You won't throw them under."

"No." Stuart's answer was firm. "I won't."

Dylan regarded them in silence. Rain spattered down, thoroughly wetting Stuart's hair and dripping into his eyes. The Shifters didn't seem to notice, but they'd just shake it off. Bears and wolves—and tigers—liked the rain.

"As I started to tell you," Dylan said, "*Yes, I agree.* I'd like it if Cian gave us the damned thing without hesitation, but no, I'm not asking you to submit your own people to slaughter. If I can't use it, I can't." He let out a breath. "But I have to try."

"It won't be enough."

Tiger's voice cut in from behind Dylan. Stuart jumped a little and was satisfied that Dylan jumped too.

"What did you say, Tiger?" Peigi asked.

"The *karmsyern* won't be enough to stop the *hoch alfar*." Tiger spoke steadily, without anger. "They might have discovered its secret, or learned how to withstand it. The *hoch alfar* want to beat Shifters at all costs. The *dokk alfar* are a barrier to their power, so they want to destroy them too."

Tiger snapped his mouth shut, as though a recording had been clicked off. He resumed his stance of mild impatience, waiting for the meeting to be done so he could go back to his mate and cubs.

Graham raked a hand through his short, rain-soaked hair. "Whenever the big guy speaks, he's usually right."

"And I listen," Dylan said. "Even so, the *karmsyern* could give us an edge. Find it, and talk to Cian about borrowing it. That's all I'm asking."

"Which could get Stuart killed," Peigi protested.

Dylan's look to Peigi was surprisingly gentle. "That's why I'm *asking*, Pegs. It's his choice."

Stuart had the feeling that if he, Stuart, refused the task, Dylan would set about finding someone else to recover the *karm-syern*. A Shifter, maybe, who wouldn't be as conscientious about talking to Cian before taking it.

"I'll think about it," Stuart said. He already knew he'd go, because he couldn't risk Dylan doing exactly what Stuart envisioned. His hesitation was only so he could talk to Peigi first.

"A question for you, Dylan," Peigi said. She'd stood in close contact with Reid for the entire meeting, her warmth the only thing keeping him from shivering. "Do you have a Shifter in your clan called Crispin?"

Dylan blinked and then he appeared, if anything, embarrassed. "Crispin," he said in resignation. "What's he done this time?"

"Joined the *hoch alfar*," Stuart said. "He was working for a Fae prince."

Sean glanced heavenward. "The Goddess go with him. I mean that for when Dad gets his paws on him."

"I knew he had run off to Faerie to be a Battle Beast," Dylan said. "Crispin is a distant cousin, and was always full of stupid ideas. I'd given him up as dead. But I had no idea he'd gone so far as to throw in his lot with a Fae prince." His lip curled.

"Right now, he's Cian's prisoner," Peigi said. "Stuart wrapped an iron bar around him." She smiled rapturously. "It was awesome."

Sean laughed. "Ah, Peigi, you're as bloodthirsty as any of us."

"Only for asshats," Peigi said.

Eric chuckled. "I'll remember that."

"*If* you decide to return to Faerie," Dylan broke into the mirth. "Will you bring Crispin back for me? I'd leave him to be offed by *dokk alfar* or the *hoch alfar* when he finally pisses them off, but I'd rather take care of him myself. He's family."

"You want a Guardian to send him to dust, you mean," Sean said, his laughter fading. The Sword glinted, even in the rain. "Leaving his soul to be stolen would be cruel, even if he is an asshat."

Dylan shoved his hands deeper into his pockets and didn't answer Sean. "I'll wait for your answer, Reid. Meanwhile, it's bloody cold. Will I be breaking all kinds of protocol if I ask one of you to take me inside for a beer?"

―――――

PEIGI STRODE BESIDE A SILENT STUART AS THEY HURRIED through the rain, heading home. She seethed about Dylan's demands, plus his assumption that Stuart would be going back to Faerie, but Stuart remained stoic, no emotion on his face.

They opened the front door, stepping out of the wet, to find all six cubs in the living room with Nell and Shane, the cubs lined up by age. The line was uneven by height because the bear cubs were already taller and bulkier than the wolves, but they presented a united front.

"The kids have something to say to you," Nell said, her eyes a mystery. "Got to go. Bye."

Shane was nearly bursting with laughter as he gave them two thumbs-up and followed Nell out the door Peigi and Stuart had left open.

The cubs chorused, "Bye, Aunt Nell! Bye, Uncle Shane!" Shane slammed the door and was gone. Peigi heard Nell's and Shane's laughter drifting to them as the two passed the front window.

Instead of brushing past the cubs to continue wrestling with his own problems, Stuart slid off his jacket and hung it on the coat rack, brushed the rain from his hair, and faced the cubs.

"What's up, guys?"

Peigi hung her jacket next to Stuart's. She'd been less both-ered by the rain but it felt good to be in the warm, dry house.

"We have something to discuss," Donny said, his face serious. He nudged Noelle. "You tell them."

Noelle stepped forward, a piece of notebook paper in her hands. Donny retreated, as though relieved to leave the confrontation to her.

"We had a meeting," Noelle said. "We've drawn up a list of reasons why Peigi needs to accept Stuart's mate claim. Also, we've set out a schedule that lets us each have time with you, and you with your cubs when they come, and gives you two alone time so you can form the mate bond."

EIGHTEEN

Peigi's love for her cubs surged. Noelle, with the brown and blond hair of her grizzly, regarded her so gravely with deep brown eyes, the line of cubs slowly sidling behind her as their point of contact.

"This is very thoughtful of you. Did Nell help you at all?" Peigi imagined Nell gleefully suggesting adding the part about the mate bond.

"She helped us with the words when I wrote it down," Noelle said primly. "But what came out of the meeting was our idea."

The other cubs nodded solemnly. Kevin, now behind all the others, said, "We want you to have cubs but not forget about us when you do."

"Sweetie." Peigi knelt on the carpet in front of them, putting herself at their height. "I'd never, ever forget about you. You're *my* cubs."

Noelle held her paper in front of her as though it were a shield as she addressed Peigi. "Aunt Nell says we can't expect you to accept the mate claim. But we have places for you to sign for what happens if you *do* accept the claim, and what happens if you don't."

Stuart remained standing, but his voice was gentle. "May I see? I'm curious as to what happens if we don't have the mating ceremony."

Noelle handed the paper up to him. "Basically everything remains the same, but I think the schedule for spending time with each cub should be imple— implem—" She gave up trying to twist her mouth around the word. "We should do it. There are six of us, so that's one for each day of the week, plus a day for you and Peigi alone."

Stuart folded himself up on the floor next to Peigi, his long leg touching her knee. "You put a lot of consideration into this. I commend you."

"We want what's best for all of us," Noelle said. She stepped next to Donny, hands behind her back.

Stuart read through the paper, written in Noelle's careful hand, turning it over to study the other side before he passed it to Peigi. "Well, I will have no trouble signing this document. Pegs?"

Peigi's fingers trembled as she read. *While Peigi and Stuart have alone time to form the mate bond, the six current cubs, and any subsequent cubs, will be taken out for pizza and ice cream by Aunt Nell or Uncle Shane.*

"It seems fair to me," she managed to say.

Donny and Noelle high-fived each other, and the four littler ones exchanged hugs. They'd been worried, Peigi realized, that she and Stuart would be angry with them. Noelle must have had to talk long and hard to get them to go along with the plan.

"I used to be in a family," Stuart said.

The cubs ceased celebrating and blinked at him. Peigi was surprised as well—Stuart rarely spoke of the family he'd lost, only saying that they'd been killed, nearly every member of them, before he'd been ejected into this world.

"We didn't always get along. We fought about a lot of things, and not only in words. My brothers and I ... we could fight harder than anyone I knew. With swords and all. But in the end

—we were family. We knew that when all was said and done, we
had each other's backs. And we did, right up until the end."
Stuart's voice caught, and he cleared his throat. "What I'm trying
to say is, *you* are my family. You six, and Peigi, whether she
accepts the mate claim or not. I couldn't ask for a better one. I
know you're worried that without something like this ..." he
touched the paper Peigi held ... "we'll fall apart, but we won't.
We're in it for the duration. Together."

Peigi's heart squeezed to a point of pain. "We are," she
agreed. "All of us."

Living in this Shiftertown, protecting these cubs from the
world, with Stuart at her side, had given Peigi a reason to get up
in the morning. She could have easily succumbed to despair
when she'd first moved here, knowing herself safe but forgetting
how to live.

The fact that none of the rescuers had truly known what to
do with the motherless cubs had made her angry, and from that
anger had sprung her compassion, and then love.

They'd saved her life, they and this man sitting beside her.

Peigi drew a breath, laid down the paper, and reached for
Stuart's hand, clasping it between hers.

"Stuart Reid, under the light of moon—wherever it is behind
all the rainclouds—and in front of witnesses, *I accept your
mate claim.*"

For a moment all was silence. The cubs stared, open-
mouthed. Stuart looked at her, stunned, his dark eyes at last
letting her see into them.

She read shock in him, fear, hurt so profound she couldn't
understand it—far beyond anything she'd expected. A longing
for happiness, coupled with Stuart's realization he might have
found it, and great fear he'd have it taken away.

Then the room erupted in noise. Six cubs vaulted at Peigi,
knocking her to the floor. Hugs and kisses followed, love pouring
over her in waves. The cubs hurtled from her to a laughing

Stuart—he went down like a father lion with cubs crawling all over him.

They bounced up, Patrick and Hannah doing a jerking dance that involved fingers pointing at the sky. Noelle whooped, arms in the air, Donny gyrated in place, Kevin imitating him, and quiet Lucinda twirled and twirled, her ponytail in a graceful arc.

Stuart leapt to Peigi and sent her to the carpet with him on top of her, his mouth seeking hers in a long, hot, and frenzied kiss.

———

PEIGI WOKE IN THE MORNING, HER BODY LIGHT, THE URGE TO sing at the top of her voice strong. She didn't know any current songs, so she sang ones from her childhood. That should have the cubs curious.

She was alone in her room, had gone to bed alone. She and Stuart had shared the passionate kiss on the floor and then had realized they needed to make dinner for the cubs. Six little ones in the house was a good damper for mating frenzy.

Peigi showered, dressed, and combed her hair, singing all the way.

The happiness pouring over her startled her, the back of her mind wondering what was wrong, when the other shoe would drop.

But she realized as she charged out her bedroom, on the way to the kitchen to start another meal, that she was no longer afraid.

Peigi halted in the middle of the hall, dazed. She felt about in her mind for the sensations she'd been living with for years. The daily fears—would Miguel find her again? Would she be strong enough to protect the cubs from him, or any other Shifter? Or Shifter Bureau? Would Stuart run away screaming if the cubs asked him one more time to teleport?

She'd feared Stuart didn't care for her the way she'd started to care for him. That he stayed with her only to make sure the cubs were okay, the natural concern of the rescuer for the rescued. Or because he didn't have anywhere else to go.

Last night when she'd made the leap of accepting the mate claim, throwing off the ropes of uncertainty and diving into the unknown, she'd cut the last knot that tied her to fear.

She loved Stuart Reid, and she wasn't afraid to let the world know.

Peigi resumed her light-footed dance to the end of the hall. Before she could emerge to the kitchen, Stuart came out of it to meet her at the end.

"Morning," she said, smiling.

He slid arms around her, and she him, gathering him in for a long, tangling kiss.

Peigi tasted a bite of coffee and his spice, the goodness that was him. Stuart's strong arms cradled her, protecting her from the world. But not binding her. That was the difference.

Heat ran in a fiery tingle from Peigi's heart to pour through her body. One day soon, she'd let her full mating frenzy come out to play, and satisfy every craving she'd buried for too long. Maybe then Stuart really would run away screaming.

She pictured it, and laughed.

"Good morning to you too," Stuart said, his hands on her back.

Peigi rose to him for another kiss. It was so much fun to be in love.

"They're kissing again!" Donny shouted from two feet away.

Peigi jumped, but Stuart finished the kiss and smiled. "You'll be seeing us do that a lot, lad," Stuart told him. "We're mates."

"Woo hoo!" Noelle said. "Breakfast's almost done, Peigi. Stuart cooked it already. And Ben's in the kitchen."

Now Stuart started. He and Peigi unwound themselves from each other and ran for the next room.

Ben sat at the table, about to attack a steaming pile of pancakes. "You were busy, so I thought I'd help myself."

In spite of his glib words, he did not appear to be well. The hand that held his fork trembled.

Peigi grabbed a cup from the cupboard and poured dark coffee Stuart had brewed into it. She set the cup at Ben's elbow and took a seat next to him. "Where've you been? You left without a word."

Ben shuddered. "Don't ask."

"You don't have to talk about it if you don't want to," Peigi said. "I'm just checking that you're all right."

Behind her, Stuart herded the cubs to the counter to start carrying the food to the table. He waited until the cubs were settled before he sat down to his pancakes.

"Dylan get to you?" Stuart asked.

"I haven't seen Dylan, lately." Ben gave another shudder. "Thank the Goddess. No, I've been exploring ley lines since Lady Aisling lifted my curse. Or *possibly* lifted my curse. Be careful what you wish for. I've been searching for any other goblins, anywhere, but haven't found them. Going back and forth is playing hell with my metabolism." He shoveled in several mouthfuls of pancakes and washed them down with coffee. "One thing Faerie hasn't figured out is good coffee. Thanks, Peigi."

"Stuart made it. I just poured." Peigi cut into her own pancakes, letting syrup and butter ooze onto the plate, and lifted her fork. "If using the ley lines exhausts you, maybe you should stop doing it for a while."

"Great advice." Ben ate a few more mouthfuls. "But while the Fae threaten Shifters, I'll be using them. Keep an eye on the bas —" He caught six cubs watching him and coughed. "Keep an eye on the bad men. They'll never come through on my watch, don't worry."

"Peigi and Reid will kick their asses," Noelle said with confidence. "So will Nell and Cormac, and Eric, and Graham, and everybody."

"That we will." Stuart stated this with quiet belief.

Ben continued to eat—a lot. He hadn't lied when he said he'd run down his metabolism, but Peigi realized some of his peaked-ness came from sorrow. He must've hoped that a few of his people might have survived the long-ago devastation by the *hoch alfar*, and he'd found no evidence of it.

Impulsively, Peigi patted the tattooed hand that rested on the table. Ben gave her a weak smile, one that said, *I'll be all right*. His resignation broke her heart.

He drew a breath, some of his robustness returning. "So, mate claim, eh?"

"She accepted," Noelle said with satisfaction. "We just have to plan the sun and moon ceremony. Full moon is in two weeks. I looked it up."

"Can we stay up all night for the moon ceremony?" Donny asked immediately. "It will be a special occasion, right?"

"We'll talk about it," Peigi said.

Donny decided to take that as an affirmative. She saw him putting arguments in line if she took a stand against his night-long party.

Breakfast ended in a jubilant mood. Peigi knew she shouldn't be so happy, as they had much to worry about, but she couldn't help herself. She'd accepted mate claims in the past—Michael's and then Eric's nominal one—but those were for expediency. This time her whole body danced, and joy flooded her heart.

This was *right*.

Peigi assumed Stuart would want to talk with Ben about Dylan and his requests—rather, his thinly veiled demands—but Stuart said nothing at all. He helped clean up after breakfast, asking Ben what he thought about the Tuil Erdannan, and somehow the discussion ended up being about soccer—or footy as Ben and Stuart called it.

Peigi left them to it.

She did ordinary things, such as make certain the cubs were bathed and dressed, their dirty clothes from yesterday in the laundry—activities that today were easy. She found herself humming again as she worked, which infected the cubs, who started singing or bellowing tunes along with her.

"How many cubs will you and Stuart have?" Noelle asked her after lunch. She held a steno pad and pen and appeared to be taking notes. A young human girl would have been tapping on a tablet, but Shifters were still restricted from certain technologies.

"We haven't got that far yet," Peigi said, flushing. "Haven't even started on the first one."

Noelle regarded her without embarrassment. Shifter cubs knew all about sex and what it was for, though they had only a cursory interest in it until their Transitions when they were in their mid-twenties. *Then* they would pursue sex with mindless adrenaline.

"Once the cubs start coming, we'll need a bigger house," Noelle said. "We'll have to tell Eric. We might be able to stay in this one but build on." She assessed the end wall of the living room.

"Early days, my girl," Peigi said breathlessly. She'd thought the same at Cian's house—maybe Eric would okay a courtyard and another floor, she thought with nervous hilarity.

"In any case, Stuart should move into your room right away, and we can start turning *his* room into a nursery."

Ben leaned on the open doorway to the kitchen, coffee mug in hand. "You mean he's still sleeping in the guest room? Seriously?"

As Peigi's face grew hotter, Noelle nodded. "They haven't spent the night together *at all.*" She shook her head, disappointed in them. "Cubs will take forever if they don't change that."

Ben took in Peigi quivering with embarrassment, the other cubs listening in avid interest, and Stuart pretending not to hear as he banged dishes in the kitchen, then reached behind him and set the coffee mug on the kitchen table. "Tell you what, kids. How about I take you out for sundaes?"

Instantly the cubs forgot about Peigi and Stuart's personal
life and shouted their pleas.

"Can we, Peigi? Please, can we?"

"I suppose it will be all right. But take your coats—" Peigi's
admonition was drowned out by a chorus of delight.

Noelle abandoned her position of family organizer, flung
down her steno pad, and dashed for her coat. Ben herded them
toward the foyer as Stuart emerged from the kitchen to help
bundle them up.

Ben bumped fists with Peigi. "You two have some things to
work out," he said. He grabbed his leather jacket from the coat
rack and followed the cubs out the front door, hollering at them
to wait for him.

The door slammed shut, and the cubs' voices receded and
faded as Ben loaded them into the SUV Eric had given Peigi.
The engine turned over, and the SUV pulled away.

"I never gave Ben the keys," Stuart mused. He leaned on the
doorframe where Ben had.

"Neither did I."

"Good to know he'd make an excellent car thief."

"Maybe he is one." Peigi tried to smile, and the corners of
Stuart's eyes crinkled.

They studied each other, the silence like a barrier rising
between them.

Peigi swallowed. "They expect us to ..."

She trailed off, unable to voice it. She hoped, she wanted,
and yet was uncertain. Shifter frenzy was strong, but Stuart
wasn't—

Stuart pushed himself from the door frame before she could
finish the thought. "And why not?"

His dark eyes fixed on her as he came to her, purpose in
every step. Before Stuart reached her, he pulled off his sweatshirt and tossed it to the sofa, his bronze-colored skin molded to
hard muscle beneath it.

Peigi made a strangled noise in her throat. She grabbed her own shirt and jerked it off over her head. Her bra followed a moment later, right before Stuart drew Peigi into his arms and kissed her with a fierceness that took her breath away.

NINETEEN

To touch this woman, to taste her … Stuart had waited so long—too long.

He skimmed his hands down her arms, absorbing her heat, her softness. Peigi was strong, her body firm, and at the same time smooth and curved.

Reid pulled her against him, taking her with a kiss that contained all his need. She met his kiss with her own, seeking, their mouths coming together in desperation.

The hall was short, the rooms along it small. Peigi's was at the end, the tiniest in the house, which she'd taken, claiming she didn't need much room. Stuart backed her toward it, unable to cease kissing her. She'd mentioned mating frenzy, as though Stuart wouldn't be able to understand it, but he understood plenty. *Dokk alfar* could out-frenzy Shifters any day.

Peigi laughed as Stuart spun her in the hall so he could open her door. He danced her inside, holding her tight, until they bumped against the bed.

He kicked the door shut. Though the house was empty, he wanted privacy for Peigi in case the ice cream party came home early.

They paused, breathing hard, studying each other in the gray light. The open blind showed rain streaking the window, mist beyond it like a curtain shrouding the world.

"Stuart," Peigi whispered.

Not a protest or a hesitation. She said his name as though she liked saying it, pronouncing each syllable with enjoyment.

Stuart couldn't answer, finding no words. He kissed her again, tasting the salt-sweet of her lips as his arms stayed around her, her breasts against his bare skin.

He wanted to take her down to the bed, but they were still wearing too many clothes. Stuart released Peigi long enough to unbuckle his belt. He unbuttoned and unzipped in record time, letting his jeans fall around his legs, underwear after it. He kicked out of the fabric to see Peigi watching him, a smile on her lips, a gleam in her eyes.

Goddess, she was beautiful.

She studied him without shame—she'd never been shy about staring at his body. Stuart went incandescent as her gaze dropped to his full erection. He couldn't help it sticking straight out in her direction, his wanting for her obvious.

He ceased breathing altogether when Peigi undid her jeans and let them drop. Her hips were a sweet curve cupped by underwear that was at once practical and feminine.

She slid her fingers under the waistband, and without hesitation, slid the panties down her legs.

Stuart wanted to die. He'd seen Peigi nude before, when she shifted, but she'd been bear very quickly after her clothes were off.

Now she stood in her bedroom, her body bare for him, and welcomed his gaze. Her breasts were round and full, nipples dark. Her waist nipped in slightly before her hips curved out, a dark twist of hair between her legs.

Stuart found his voice, though it came out whispery and wrong. "I see the Goddess's touch on you. She made you beautiful."

A flush spread across Peigi's face. "You aren't so bad yourself."

"For a weird dark Fae shit?"

"*I've* never called you that. You are the most gorgeous male I've ever seen. Of any kind." Peigi smiled at him, her eyes shining, and suddenly Stuart felt like the strongest man alive.

He forgot anything he planned to say to her, any declarations he could have made or sonnets he wanted to recite. None of that mattered. Stuart went to her, hands on her waist.

He kissed her, wanting that intimacy, words superfluous. She met his kiss with a powerful one of her own, her yearning matching his.

Stuart couldn't wait any longer. He wanted to touch her all over, explore her, taste her.

He eased them down to the bed, the small mattress sagging under their weight. Peigi held Stuart with her gaze as he came over her. He read the urgency in her eyes as she parted her lips, lifting herself to him at the same time she wrapped her arms around him. Her body fitted against his, welcoming, her faint sound of need undoing him.

Stuart touched her thighs, which readily opened for him, and groaned as he slid home inside her.

———

PEIGI HAD ALWAYS BELIEVED THAT SURRENDER MEANT LOSS OF freedom, confinement, and fear. Today, she discovered that surrendering could be a different thing.

She didn't expect Stuart to catch her, comfort her, or wrap her in a blanket. Surrender today didn't mean submitting to one stronger than herself and hoping he'd be kind—it meant surrendering to *love*. To the need to make the world better for that person, to make certain he had everything, even if she didn't.

Stuart kissed her throat, her breasts, his breath hot on her

skin. Having him inside her made her complete, her last uncertainty gone in a puff of wind.

It also made her cry out in ecstasy—why not? Stuart opened
her and touched her deepest places and it felt astonishing. No,
astonishing wasn't a strong enough word. It was wonderful, tight,
glorious, and plain fucking fantastic.

Stuart's midnight eyes held the gleam of magic he constantly
tried to hide. It flared, and she saw *him*, the powerful being who
kept himself contained so he wouldn't destroy others.

The Shifters didn't understand what they'd taken in, with
Stuart. But Peigi did. She always had.

Stuart's power surrounded her, tingled through her, touched
the latent magic within all Shifters. A surge of wildness hit her,
blotting out the rain, the gray mist, the cold of the winter day.
She and Stuart were solid, hot, together, and she wished this
would never end …

But then the heat where they joined expanded to drown her,
and she spiraled toward a screaming peak. Peigi came and came,
and Stuart, holding her, let out a shout that rang through
the room.

Mine, mine, love, mate. The words tumbled through Peigi's
mind and might have come out of her mouth.

Stuart pounded the mattress with his fist. He moved inside
her, the friction hot and driving, as though he'd lived his entire
life for this moment, this loving.

His cries joined hers, as they came together, finally, finally
finding a haven from their long and weary existence. Wrapped in
each other, they fell together, panting, laughing, tears wetting
Peigi's cheeks and falling from Stuart's beautiful eyes.

———

"Ben's keeping them out a long time," Peigi murmured
much later.

It was mid-afternoon. Whatever daylight had formed was gone, and mist pressed the window in swirling white-gray.

Reid, his whole body rested and satisfied, traced a pattern on Peigi's bare arm. Satisfied, yes, but he knew he could do more, and more. They were only stopping to rest.

"We'll have to find a place to be alone as our family grows," he said. His voice was scratchy. "Noelle is right—it's a small house."

Stuart hadn't been able to speak at all as he loved Peigi, until passion had taken him, and he'd yelled his release in the cozy room. He'd gone on and on until he could only rasp.

"If the family does grow," Peigi said.

She sounded so wistful that Stuart lifted on one elbow to look down at her. His arm was sore—they'd made love a long time.

"You're afraid you can't have cubs?" he asked gently.

A swallow moved Peigi's throat. "I was twenty-five years with Michael and never ..."

Reid touched her face. "You were also stressed, on the run, confined, afraid ..."

"So were the other women. They conceived and bore cubs just fine. That's why we have our six."

Reid liked that she spoke of them as "ours." "Can I ask a very personal question?" he ventured. "Did you have mating frenzy with Michael?"

Peigi's cheeks went pink. "I thought I did, at first. I was young, not long past my Transition. I knew Michael wasn't the ideal Shifter, but I thought the alternative to staying with him would be worse. I'd be stuck in a Shiftertown, probably with members of my clan who didn't want me. Shiftertowns are decent places now, but back then, they weren't at all."

"I know." Stuart hadn't been assigned to the newly formed department that handled Shifters when Shiftertowns first opened, but he'd seen the crowding and misery whenever he'd had to handle complaints from humans who lived nearby. "You were right to try to avoid it."

"I convinced myself I should be with this strong Shifter who took care of me. But when I didn't have cubs, he easily turned to other women. I had enough dominance that he couldn't put them above me, but he let me know I'd disappointed him. I was still head mate, but it became pretty awful."

Reid kissed a tear from her hot face. "I wasn't trying to make you remember bad things. I'm sorry."

"No, I need to remember. I need to immerse myself in how much better my life is, living in this house, in the middle of a Shiftertown, with six cubs and a *ðokk alfar* lover."

Stuart gave her a mock glare. "Wait, you have a *ðokk alfar* lover? Who is he? I'll kill him."

Peigi laughed shakily. "He's a shit. I don't know if you'd like him."

"Probably not." Stuart slanted her a smile. "One more question. Did any of Michael's other women have cubs? None of ours are his—I've always known that." Their cubs' fathers were Michael's trackers and seconds, some of them dead. None of the ones alive had bothered to find out what had become of their cubs.

"The women there took several mates each," Peigi said. "Michael's idea, as there are always more Shifter males than females. A more diverse gene pool, he said. But thinking it through, I'm not sure any of the women had cubs by Michael."

"Did *you* ... um ... take another mate?"

"No." Peigi shook her head adamantly. "I didn't want to, and Michael figured I was infertile, so he didn't insist. I also think he didn't want to share the alpha female."

Reid brushed her lower lip with his thumb. "I'm thinking Michael is the one who wasn't fertile. Probably had his trackers take the same mates he did to cover up the fact he couldn't make little Shifters."

Peigi didn't gasp or clap her hand to her head in shock. She nodded slowly. "I've thought about that. He was very careful not to show any weakness. He made sure he was in charge at all times."

"Conclusion—you might be able to have cubs after all."

Peigi's eyes clouded with tears. "I want to have hope. I'm afraid of hope, though."

"I understand that, believe me." Stuart brushed back a lock of her hair. "All the years I tried to get home, when hope after hope was dashed … Hope can be a cruel thing."

"I don't want to hope then." Peigi let out a breath. "All right?"

"Fine by me." Reid propped himself on his elbow again, the better to see Peigi's beautiful face and her plump breast exposed by the sheet. "We have six wonderful cubs to take care of already. If more cubs come along, that's fine too. And you know, we can keep trying. Day and night, indoors, outdoors, wherever, whenever. Keep doing what it takes. Forget about hope—let's just put in the effort."

Peigi was laughing by the end of the speech. "I think I can agree."

"Good. How about we start now?"

More laughter. Peigi drew him down to her, the longing in her eyes flaring. Stuart pushed aside worries and his renewed rage at Michael and lost himself in Peigi's warmth once more.

————

PEIGI WOKE WITH A START. THE ROOM WAS PITCH DARK, and cold.

Stuart slept next to her, curled in a nest they'd made in the small bed, one leg snaking out from under the blanket.

As awareness returned, Peigi started to sit up, panicked. Where were the cubs?

She heard them, six voices raised in happy contentment with their outing. Ben's gravelly voice answered, and Peigi relaxed in relief.

She should get up, dress, go out and be with them, thank Ben, and send him home. Let Stuart sleep while Peigi prepared the cubs for bed. She'd tuck them in, kiss them good night, and thank the Goddess she could be with them.

Wind blew past the window, swirling the mist. A branch of a nearby tree tapped on the pane, its scratching bringing her even more fully awake.

The mist swirled again, precise patches drawing away until it resembled a face peering in through the window—two voids of eyes and a gaping mouth.

Peigi sat up, the bear in her snarling. She leapt from the bed, shifting to her between beast as she went. The face drew back, then stretched into a hideous form, the maw of mouth widening.

Sucking her in. She must be dreaming—the face was a trick of wind, light, her half-sleeping state, nothing more.

But she felt the cold, barely warmed by fur that sprouted on her body. Ben's voice faded, and then the cubs' did too, as though a muffling curtain had been lowered between the bedroom and the rest of the house.

Behind her, Stuart jumped awake. He stared at the widening blackness at the window before he rose, backwards, off the bed. As though someone had plucked him up, he was lifted into the air and flew toward the window, which started to dissolve into thicker mist.

At the last minute, Stuart reached to the foot of the bed and grabbed his jeans. Then Peigi was jerked off her feet and slammed sideways into the thick fog where the window had been. She grabbed Stuart's hand as he passed her, and hung on.

Cold clamped her, and then blackness. Peigi felt only Stuart's grip, a lifeline in the freezing darkness, and then nothing.

TWENTY

Peigi landed on prickly ground, in the darkness, her eyes stinging. This was no dream. Icy chill swirled around her, far colder than a Las Vegas January night.

Where the hell was she? She inhaled, but there were too many confusing scents. Wood smoke, animals, snow, the acrid smell of burning debris, and … Shifters.

Before she could register what Shifters and where, Stuart, whose hand she'd lost hold of, slammed into her. His presence sent relief through her, though she remained alert, wary.

"What the fuck?" he asked in a quiet voice.

"Where are we?"

"Faerie, I'm guessing." Stuart climbed laboriously to his feet. He pulled on the jeans he'd been able to grab and hastily buckled them. He was barefoot and bare-chested, the cold prickling his flesh. "Where, I have no clue."

The scent of Shifter increased, and then Peigi heard them, growls and roars that grew louder until they melded into a single din. Shifters attacking. Peigi instinctively put Stuart behind her as she crouched in a defensive stance.

They poured from the mists that rolled back to reveal the black trunks of trees, like dark cutouts in the white.

Lupines, bears, Felines, not attacking at random but in coordinated columns, divided into where each Shifter could give others the most cover. They ran with determination and with enough wildness to strike fear into their enemies.

All this for her and Stuart?

The moment the thought formed, Stuart grabbed her and forced her down. Over their heads flew bolts, fired from crossbows by a line of warriors in leather and metal.

Iron and steel, not silver, Peigi realized immediately. They were *dokk alfar*.

One of the *dokk alfar* shouted and a second line of crossbows fired. Shifters went down, screaming. Others raced aside, sprinting to flank the crossbowmen and get behind them.

Peigi roared and dropped to all fours as bear. Shifters attacking *dokk alfar*? For the Fae, or on their own—and why?

Stuart's voice sounded in her ear, "We need to get out of here."

No kidding. Peigi slammed her shoulder into Stuart, who caught on quickly and climbed onto her back.

She ran. Choosing a path perpendicular to the action, Peigi charged away, Stuart clinging to her back, head down. He hung on with ease, as though riding a fleeing bear was no big deal to him.

Peigi ran until the sound of battle receded, then she slowed her steps. As Stuart slid off to his feet, she morphed into her half-beast, her heart pounding, breath coming hard.

"What the hell is going on?" she gasped.

"A very good question. We need to find Cian."

Peigi glanced around wildly. "How did we even get here? A gate came to find *us*?"

Stuart rubbed his short hair, flinging droplets of mist from it. "Again, I'm thinking Cian. He half-pulled me into Faerie once before. Maybe he figured out how to do it all the way."

"I hope not. For his sake." Peigi snarled, her blood pumping high. Screw hiding in the shadows waiting to feel better—she wanted to thump heads, lots of them. "How do we find him? Every direction looks the same to me."

As when they'd first entered Faerie, the trees that surrounded them, marching into mists, appeared identical—each view mirrored the other.

"We retreat to the *dokk alfar* side," Stuart said. "Even if these aren't Cian's men, *dokk alfar* lands will be in that direction."

"What if those Shifters are ours?" she asked. "I mean, sent by Dylan. And the *dokk alfar* want them dead for some reason?"

"Accidentally being shot with a crossbow bolt won't answer that."

He had a point. "All right," Peigi said. "We find Cian and slam him against a wall until he explains everything."

Stuart laughed, a startling sound in the dank air. "My mate is kick-ass. Don't mess with her."

"Damn straight." Peigi sent Stuart a smile, probably alarming in her half-bear, half-human face. "Want to ride again?"

"It would be faster." Stuart bumped himself into her. "Besides, your fur is soft."

"Sweet talker." Peigi dropped down to become full bear. Stuart climbed aboard, and they were off.

Behind them, the battle raged on. Shifters shrieked, dying, and *dokk alfar* screamed as they went down under the Shifters who'd broken through their lines.

Peigi tried not to listen, tried not to let her heart break. Shifters had fought so long and hard to free themselves from the Fae, and they were throwing it away rushing against *dokk alfar* in the world they'd wrested themselves from long ago. The cry in her mind was *why?*

She knew how to move unseen—she'd learned that while in Michael's thrall. Peigi skirted through trees, using sound and scent to guide her. The misty woods made her a bit claustrophobic—she'd grown used to the vast Nevada desert where she could see fifty miles by standing on a slight rise of ground.

The tumult of what must be a camp ahead came to her—the odors of horses, cooking fires, roasting meat, and the sounds of people moving about, shouting to each other, men running in from the line of battle to babble news, others running out again.

Peigi stopped and rose, Stuart sliding from her as she shifted to human.

"If I go any closer as bear or my between-beast, someone might shoot me," she said, out of breath.

Once her bear receded, the cold hit her with a slap, and Peigi shivered. She hadn't had time to grab her clothes, and she'd been shifting once the gate had taken them.

"Stay put." Stuart put his hands on her shoulders, gave her a quick kiss on the lips, and disappeared into the trees.

Peigi morphed to her half beast simply to stay warm, but Stuart was back quickly, tossing a bundle at her.

She reverted to human again as she shook out clothing— leggings and a long leather shirt. Stuart had taken a tunic for himself and boots for both of them. The boots didn't fit Peigi well but at least kept her feet from the wet ground.

"Who's going to yell at us for stealing their clothes?"

"Probably no one," Stuart said as he settled his tunic. "These clothes are as generic for *dokk alfar* as jeans and T-shirts are for us, so maybe no one will miss them. I stole them from the laundry tent."

Peigi tied the shirt's drawstrings with chilled fingers, the leather feeling odd against her bare skin. "Is Cian there?"

"Didn't see him, but I plan to ask."

He held out his hand. Peigi took it, and they walked together toward the camp, like a *dokk alfar* and his lady out for a stroll … In deep woods near a battle scene. Sure.

The *dokk alfar* moving hurriedly about the camp didn't notice two more people, dressed similarly to them, entering. They glanced at Stuart and then in puzzlement at the tall woman next to him, then went back to what they were doing.

"Great security," Peigi murmured.

"Mm," Stuart said in agreement. "That's how I could steal the clothes. Let's find someone in charge."

Not all sentries were lackadaisical. One man with a sword on his belt snapped around, saw them, and was in front of them faster than fast. He snarled something at Stuart, and Stuart answered. Stuart made his voice hard, refusing to wilt under the guard's stare.

The guard eyed them in suspicion, but gave Stuart a nod. He motioned for them to follow and started toward the tents, calling another guard to bring up the rear.

The tent the first guard took them to was no larger than the others, and no fancier. Peigi wondered if it was a brig until she saw Cian standing outside it, listening hard to a *dokk alfar* with a bruised and cut face. Cian waited until the man finished speaking and then barked a few orders. The *dokk alfar* saluted and melted back under the trees, already running.

Cian turned to Stuart and Peigi, unsurprised, as though expecting them at his party. The tent flaps parted, and out walked Michael, who took up a stance behind Cian.

"Who let you off your leash?" Stuart demanded.

"He did." Michael, smug, jerked his thumb at Cian. "He wanted my help fighting Shifters. I know how to do it."

"You speak *dokk alfar*? That's interesting."

"Don't have to. Interpreter."

Another jerk of the thumb showed them a Shifter sitting inside the tent, this one bound to a chair. Crispin. He'd acquired clothes, the same *dokk alfar* leggings and tunic Stuart said were common.

"I need him when you're done," Peigi said. She wasn't certain Dylan would let Crispin live for betraying Shifters, but what Crispin knew about the high Fae could be invaluable to Dylan.

She understood that perfectly—and Dylan didn't want a member of his clan dying alone in Faerie.

Michael gave her a puzzled look. "Whatever."

Cian cut him off and started talking to Stuart. He spoke with authority, no apology. For whatever reason he'd come out to attack Shifters, he'd made the decision and was sticking with it.

Stuart scowled as he listened then turned to Peigi. "The *hoch alfar* were building up on his territory's borders. They have a small Shifter army backed by *hoch alfar* archers. The leader is our Fae prince who was hunting in the woods. At least, he's their leader nominally. Cian believes a general is using the prince's money and influence to let the attack go through."

Peigi watched a *dokk alfar* set down a wooden crate, wrench off its lid, and start handing iron-tipped crossbow bolts to men who lined up to receive them. "Why are they attacking Cian?"

Stuart shrugged. "*Hoch alfar* and *dokk alfar* have never needed an excuse to fight. Each of us existing is the excuse. Now that the *karmsyern* is gone, the warded borders are weak—still patrolled and guarded, but weak. This attack took out border guards along the river, which is that way." Stuart gestured in an indeterminate direction toward the trees. "That's why there's so much mist. Slight warming trend near the river, and we're stuck in a cloud. Cian responded with a thrown-together army. For him, it's been about a week since we left."

Peigi digested the information. "Is he hopeful he'll turn them back?" She hugged her arms to her chest, unable to get warm. "Those are *Shifters* dying out there. Even if they made the choice to join the *hoch alfar,* they're still Shifters."

Michael growled. "You mean traitors. What kind of fucked-up Shifter joins the Fae?"

"You've joined the *dokk alfar,*" Stuart pointed out.

"Under coercion. But yeah, I'm happy to help this Cian guy take out the Shifter shits. If they get their asses kicked and turned into fur rugs, it's their own fault."

Many Shifters would think so, Peigi knew. She thought of

Graham, who never hid his opinion that Shifters who were betraying them were total bastards who deserved no mercy. On the other hand, Graham would work to save them, take them back to the human world so he could personally thump them on their heads. Michael was ready to let them be slaughtered.

Stuart said something to Cian. Cian glanced at Peigi and let out his gravelly laugh.

"What?" Peigi demanded.

"I told him you were ready to slam whoever led this show up against the wall. He said he didn't blame you."

"Good." Peigi glared at Cian. "What do we do? Why are we here, anyway?"

Stuart scanned the camp, the crossbowmen hurrying out to reinforce the line. As before when they'd entered Faerie, Stuart became stronger, steelier, reaching out to embrace the magic of this world. "An iron master can turn the tide, he says."

"In other words, he wants you to save his butt?" Peigi continued to glower at Cian, who looked amused in his hard-ass way.

"He's resourceful," Stuart said. "Cian claims he didn't bring us through personally. He knows there's a ley line nearby and was trying to line up his spell-caster to summon me, but the *hoch alfar* attacked sooner than expected. He figures one of his under-lings must have heard him and the spell-caster brought us across. How the ley line was moved to your house, he doesn't know. He only knows what happens on this side."

"I see." Many things to ponder. Cian had recruited Michael with a promise of—what? Cian had obviously decided Crispin would be useful, and now he had Peigi, another Shifter on his side. Resourceful indeed.

Peigi wouldn't kill other Shifters. She had to draw that line ... Well, unless they were trying to kill her, or Stuart, and there was no other way to get away from them.

But she also wouldn't sacrifice herself to save Shifters who'd willingly put themselves under Fae power, becoming Battle

Beasts in truth. She was done with sacrifice to Shifters who did nothing but abuse those who wanted to help them.

The thought made her switch her gaze to Michael. What was he up to?

Michael met her stare, as he'd used to when he was in charge of his fawning feral Shifters.

Then his expression changed from self-satisfied to surprise, then shock, then outrage. He swung on Stuart. "You *mate claimed* her." His snarl rang into the mists.

Stuart gazed back at him calmly. "I did."

"I accepted," Peigi said before Michael could start blustering. "I told you, I considered us broken up. That's good enough under Shifter law, especially when we had no sun and moon ceremony, to accept another mate claim. So suck on it."

"You were always a feisty bitch," Michael growled.

Peigi lifted her chin. "You say that like it's a bad thing."

Michael continued to growl, then his smile abruptly returned, in a way Peigi didn't like.

"Yeah, I know Shifter law too." He pinned Stuart with his gaze. "You mate claimed her, *dokk alfar*. Okay then ... *I Challenge.*"

TWENTY-ONE

S tuart saw Crispin inside the tent jerk upright. Even Cian, who hadn't understood the English words, stiffened.

Stuart was familiar with a Challenge, with a capital *C*. When a Shifter mate claimed a female, another male could Challenge the first to a fight. Prize, the female, although only if she accepted the winner.

Archaic, deadly, and perfectly reasonable according to Shifters. In the bad old days, the strongest males mated with the strongest females so that cubs had a better chance of surviving. These were far from the bad old days—more or less—but the tradition survived.

"No," Peigi said swiftly.

"Not up to you," Michael said. "Even if you're a feisty bitch."

"Up to me if I cut your balls off." Peigi lunged for him, claws sprouting, but Stuart locked his hands around her arms and held her back. It satisfied him, though, that Michael took a worried step away from her.

"It's all right," Stuart said to her. "I accept the Challenge."

Peigi faced him, eyes wide. He saw that she thought he'd lost

his mind, feared that Michael would crush him into a stack of
dokk alfar bones.

Crispin rapidly translated for Cian, and Cian took on a frown
of disapproval. "There's no time for this shit."

Stuart didn't answer. He knew he had to deal with Michael
or the man would never leave Peigi alone. Killing him would
solve a lot of problems, but Cian was right—having Michael's
information on Shifters and what rebel ones might do was
valuable.

"Good." Michael's nod to Stuart held a modicum of respect.
"Since we're obeying Shifter rules, the Challenged gets to choose
the time and place."

"I know." Stuart took a step away from Peigi. "I
choose … *Now.*"

He spun and grabbed the iron crowbar the *dokk alfar* had
used to pry open the crate of bolts. He was back before the
breeze of his passing had died, the crowbar already twisting in
his hands.

Michael shifted to grizzly, but as Michael's bear formed,
Stuart flung the iron at him.

The iron bar wrapped itself around Michael and lifted him
into the air, flinging him backward about fifty feet. He flew past
the tents and slammed hard into a tree, halfway up its tall trunk.
Immediately the iron slid away and sailed back to Stuart's
open hand.

Michael hung suspended for a moment, his roars panicked,
and then he fell down, down, down, bear limbs flailing all the
way. He crashed into the ground, a bellow of pain exploding
from him. He lay for a time as a groaning pile of fur, before he
climbed resolutely to his feet and limped back toward Stuart.

Stuart met him halfway, the iron bar in his hands forming
into a sharp-pointed rapier. Stuart marched to Michael and
thrust the rapier against Michael's bear neck, letting the tip
draw blood.

With a crackle of bone, Michael became his between-beast.

He bulked above Stuart—a huge grizzly-man, but Stuart kept the tip of the sword on Michael's throat.

"Not a fair fight," Michael croaked.

"You fight your way, I fight mine. Yield?"

Michael growled at him. "No."

"I was hoping you'd say that."

Michael went for him, claws, teeth, and roars. Stuart side-stepped his striking paw and whirled his iron sword in a competent slice. Michael barely missed having his stomach cut open, and only because Stuart pulled back at the last moment.

Michael reared up, drawing on his strength. Stuart swung the sword again, the blade whistling in the air. Michael took another hit, but he raised his bear paws high, ready to crush Stuart.

Peigi charged. Her clothes fell away as she shifted, then she slammed into Michael and tumbled over with him in a cloud of dust.

———

BEFORE MICHAEL COULD RIGHT HIMSELF, PEIGI WAS ON HIM, roaring her rage, her paws smacking his face, his gut, his stupid face again.

Every fear and hurt he'd ever caused her, every hurt and terror of the cubs and the women under her watch, welled up inside her. That anguish changed to pure rage and poured out through her giant paws. She smacked him and clawed him, over and over, bashing at his hated face.

She felt hands on her fur, trying to pull her back. She recognized Stuart's touch and then the wiry hands of Cian.

They didn't want her to kill Michael. They needed him. Peigi didn't give a shit.

Michael began to whimper. Blood gushed from his wounds, flowed from his mouth and nose. His belly was a mess of matted fur stained with red. He opened his mouth and let out a pathetic roar.

Peigi blinked down at him, her bear realizing what had just happened. She'd defeated him, out-dominated him. In the Shifter world, this meant a change in the hierarchy, and now Peigi outranked him, Michael sliding further down in the order.

Crispin, who'd watched avidly from inside the tent, and probably heard everything too, realized it. "He's down," he called out, voice filled with new respect, almost fear.

Peigi rose on her back legs, roaring her triumph. Her voice stirred the mists, a Shifter defeating her enemy. Didn't matter that the enemy was male and her former mate. Shifter instinct took over and rearranged things to where they should be.

Peigi came down, sniffed at Michael with a derisive huff, then turned her back on him and walked away.

Stuart started for her, but Peigi kept walking. If she didn't keep up her dignified pace, she'd halt, shift, and do cartwheels around the camp.

For you Donny, Noelle, Hannah, Lucinda, Patrick, Kevin. For you ladies and cubs who endured with me. For all of you.

Peigi allowed herself a little sideways hop as she strolled back to her clothes. Michael was no longer a creature of terror, of control, of cruelty.

He was a pile of limp bear fur, and would be forever after. Better than killing him, Peigi thought, tasting triumph. Far, far better.

———

STUART WATCHED PEIGI, KNOWING WITH HIS WHOLE BODY that something had changed in her. He knew, because he felt a change within himself.

Michael remained on the ground, breathing hard. Alive but winded, wounded, and defeated.

Hey, don't mess with my lady.

Stuart would have to explore the ramifications of Peigi besting Michael at length, but at the moment they were in the middle of an army camp, and Shifters and *hoch alfar* were battling Cian's men not a mile away.

Stuart wiped the iron bar clean of Michael's blood and returned to a bemused Cian. "What's your plan?"

Cian raised his brows. "You two done teaching him a lesson?"

"It needed to be taught," Stuart answered calmly. He gave Cian a shrug worthy of Eric. "It's a Shifter thing."

"He did need an ass-kicking. I just thought you'd do it later."

"He'll be easier to control this way. Your plans?"

Cian shook his head and returned to the matter at hand. "Already in place. My men are leading the *hoch alfar* and their Battle Beasts into a warded pocket near the river where they will be defeated. But a temporary defeat, unfortunately. My scouts tell me more *hoch alfar* are amassing."

Stuart flipped the sword in his hand. "We'll just have to get that damned hunk of iron back."

"That would be ideal," Cian said dryly. "Any thoughts on how?"

"I have one or two, in fact."

Stuart turned from him and went to Michael. He prodded his groaning form. "Get up. She didn't hurt you that much. Neither did I. Shifters heal quickly, and we didn't damage you permanently."

"You don't understand." Michael shifted back to human, his body covered in scrapes and bruises. "You can't. You're not Shifter."

"I understand she kicked your ass. You deserved it." Stuart gave him a steely look. "But we can't afford to have you moping around. Shifters with the *hoch alfar* will die if they lose this battle, and I don't want that. Dylan won't want that—a lot of them have families in Shiftertowns. So I need you to keep them alive."

Michael jerked his head up, brown eyes narrowing. "You

want me to help a bunch of traitor Shifters who went over to the *hoch alfar*? They want to be Battle Beasts so bad, they can die as Battle Beasts."

Stuart flipped his sword again, end over end. Iron didn't frighten Shifters, but the sword was sharp, and Michael winced.

"Not what I said. I need you to take those Shifters prisoner and keep the *hoch alfar* from killing them and cutting their losses. We'll get the Shifters home and let Dylan deal with them."

Michael perked up. "*That* I can get my head around." He got to his feet, something like his old arrogance entering his eyes. "Yeah, I'll take those bastards prisoner. Won't Cian and the *dokk alfar* just kill them, though?"

"No, because they're not complete dickheads. But I need you to keep the Shifters intact. They'll have intel we need."

"True." Michael rolled his shoulders as though trying to shake off his defeat. "Please say I get to do some interrogating. I'm good at interrogating."

He meant he was good at beating on people until they coughed up what he wanted to hear. Stuart had worked with cops like that.

"Just keep them alive." Stuart turned his back on him, both to show he was finished with the conversation and also that he was not afraid of having Michael behind him. Shifters could strike fast, but Stuart was faster than Shifters and always had been.

He strode to the tent where Crispin waited and went inside.

Crispin, with the benefit of Shifter hearing, had followed the events outside. His face had a greenish tinge, no evidence of the ferocious black-maned lion about him anymore. He must be from a lesser branch of the Morrissey clan, low in the hierarchy. Dylan hadn't said so outright, but he'd implied it. Crispin had probably decided to join the *hoch alfar* because he knew he wouldn't gain power any other way.

"I heard you talking about Dylan," Crispin said before Stuart could speak. "That you'll give the Shifters to him." He shuddered. "You don't know how cruel that is."

"I have a good idea," Stuart said. "I've worked with Dylan a while. Let me guess, you want me to spare you that."

"You don't understand." Crispin swallowed. "He's my clan leader. I won't be just another rebel Shifter to him. It will be personal."

"No kidding. How about we cross that bridge later? Right now, I want you to tell me where the *karmjyern* is."

Crispin started. "The what?"

Stuart leaned closer, but not close enough to get bitten or slashed if Crispin suddenly decided to shift and attack. Crispin was bound thoroughly with chains, but even fettered Shifters could be deadly.

"You know. The funny iron talisman that keeps *hoch alfar* from overrunning the world. You know exactly where it is, don't you?"

TWENTY-TWO

C rispin went ashen, his eyes widening in fear. "How do you figure that?"

Stuart tested the weight of the sword he'd created. It wasn't quite right—he'd been in a hurry. He willed the iron to rearrange itself slightly to make it perfect. Crispin watched the iron undulate, and swallowed.

"You allied yourself with a Fae prince," Stuart said. "Related to Walther le Madhug, who has his eye on becoming emperor. Interesting choice—one that would bring you a lot of power if you played it right. Did you steal the *karmayern* for them?"

"No!" The fast and adamant answer held a ring of truth. "All right, all right—the prince did take it for him. Wants to be Walther's favorite toady. But I had nothing to do with it. He sent in Shifters I didn't know, and they stole it. I guess he didn't trust me." Crispin sounded hurt.

"Sucks, when the master you betrayed your own people for betrays you." Stuart folded his arms, the sword pointing downward. "Where did he put it?"

Crispin drew a breath. Stuart watched him calculate what to tell him—the man was cunning. "I can show you."

Stuart heard Peigi come in behind him, sensed her presence. She moved to stand next to him, dressed again in the form-fitting leggings and tunic that suited her tall body.

"He'll tell you anything to get out of his chains," Peigi said to Stuart.

"I caught that." Stuart edged closer to her, absorbing her warmth. "But be doesn't have to be loose to help."

Crispin looked disappointed. "You want your iron thingy back, right?"

He was up to something—the signs were obvious. Stuart had been a soldier, a cop, and a security expert long enough to know when someone else's ulterior motives smacked him in the face.

Crispin played his own game, and working for the Fae prince had only been part of it. He must figure that aligning himself with Stuart and betraying the Fae was in his best interest. And he was probably right.

"You're going to take me to it—" Stuart began.

"And lead you into a trap?" Peigi glared at him. "No way am I letting that happen."

"I won't let it happen either." Stuart turned back to Crispin. "You've seen what I can do. One wrong step, and those chains kill you."

Crispin gulped. "I know."

Peigi scowled. "If he lets a Fae kill you first, it won't matter."

"I have the feeling Crispin won't be the favorite of his Fae prince anymore, even if he brought me to him trussed up and gutted. Fae princes don't tolerate failure. He'll have installed another Battle Beast in his place by this time."

"I knew what I was getting into with him," Crispin admitted. "It was nice to be top Shifter for a while." He sighed, crestfallen. "I'm going with you, because I know it's my best choice. And when we get out of Faerie, you'll tell Dylan I assisted you."

"He'll be briefed," Stuart said. As this point, Crispin would promise anything to save his own ass.

"One problem." Crispin moved his bound arms so the chains

rattled. "It will be hard to get into a Fae castle in these. The Fae can smell iron."

Stuart gazed down at him expressionlessly. "We'll find a way. Not letting you out of those, or you out of my sight. Got it?"

"Yeah." Crispin glanced away. "You just signed my death warrant, but okay."

"We should be able to get in and out with no one the wiser," Stuart said. "Even if you clink and stink."

Crispin shrugged. "We'll have to be stealthy, but maybe if it's just the two of us ..."

"The three of us." Peigi gave them a level stare from her gorgeous eyes. "I'm not letting my mate run off alone to a Fae castle with a Shifter turncoat for company. Someone has to keep an eye out while you find the *karmsyern*."

Her defiance was beautiful. She expected Stuart to argue, to tell her to stay behind where she'd be safe-ish, to wait for him to return.

Screw that. Peigi was resourceful, strong, and more powerful than she knew. Stuart would be a complete idiot to not want her fighting at his side.

"No way am I doing this without you," Stuart said. "When the danger is greatest, it's best we *split up*? Don't think so. We make a hell of a team."

He wanted Peigi safe from harm, yes, but she'd been born to be a fighter. Stuart recognized that in her. Keeping her enclosed, forbidden to do what she did best, would kill her. She'd been slowly dying under Michael's rule, and the asshole hadn't realized that.

Stuart would do anything to let this woman be who she needed to be.

"Awesome." Peigi beamed a smile at him as big as Donny ever gave. "Let's go rescue a hunk of iron."

———

CIAN'S BATTLE RAGED ON AS PEIGI, STUART, AND CRISPIN slipped away through the woods, carrying the bare necessities of supplies. Peigi's scent sense told her they moved away from the river as they skirted the area of the skirmish, the woods becoming dryer and less dank.

Stuart led the way, holding Crispin by a chain, with Peigi bringing up the rear. The mist began to clear as they went, and she felt the path gain elevation, if ever so slightly.

They were making for a ridge, Crispin explained. Presently the climbing became more obvious, tree roots forming stair steps in the earth as the hill grew steeper.

The air dried as they climbed, though Peigi couldn't see much better through the thickness of the trees and underbrush than she had in the mists. The cold also increased, the garments she wore barely staving off the chill.

After a time, Stuart announced softly that they'd left *dokk alfar* territory, though how he knew, Peigi couldn't say. The landscape didn't change much, and the visibility was nil.

"These are the borderlands," Stuart said. "Disputed territory for centuries. A dangerous place to linger."

"How does the *karmsyern* keep the *hoch alfar* out?" Peigi asked, more to make conversation than anything. "Does it have a range?"

"It's made of spelled iron that strengthens the warded barriers—sort of spreads the effect of iron through the bones of the earth and the air itself. *Hoch alfar* can have only so much contact with iron before they're weak and sick, or dead. It works on their metabolisms like heavy metal poisoning, but faster."

"A magical iron barrier sounds like a good idea then," Peigi said, her breath heavy from the climb.

"The *karmsyern* was forged a thousand or so years ago," Stuart said. "A long time after Shifters left Faerie forever. Funny how it was stolen just after Shifters started voluntarily coming back." He gave Crispin a pointed glance.

"Don't look at me," Crispin said quickly. "I didn't touch the thing."

"It makes me wonder if the Fae plans to enslave Shifters again were part of this—to help them get rid of the *karmɔyern*. To overrun the *ðokk alfar* and kill them off, taking over all Faerie."

"I thought Dylan said it was to take over the human world," Peigi said. "Using Shifters to fight humans and then get rid of the iron."

"Which would be one hell of a job. I don't think the Fae understand how large the human population is and how much iron has taken over that world." Stuart halted, hands on hips as he caught his breath. "The question is, was stealing the *karmɔyern* part of the overall plan to dominate Faerie, or did a few *hoch alfar* simply seize the opportunity? Or is this Walther's bid to rise in power?"

"Again, don't look at me." Crispin took a rest by sitting down abruptly. "The Fae prince gave me a cushy suite and whatever I wanted, but he didn't let me in on his secret plans, if he had any. Enthusiastic guy, but not gifted with brains."

"Then why did you want to work for him?" Peigi asked.

"Didn't you hear me? Cushy suite, anything I wanted, people to wait on me. Better than being treated like bottom-of-the-clan crap back home."

"I've been treated as bottom of the pile most of my life," Peigi said serenely. "Never occurred to me to jump to the Fae side. I'd have missed out on a lot if I had." She sent Stuart a warming glance.

Crispin stood up again, brushing off his leggings. "Yeah, well, we all make our choices."

He didn't sound regretful, or self-flagellating, or even self-pitying. He stated the fact and continued up the hill.

The fortress was some distance from the battlefield—about thirty miles, Crispin said, if he figured correctly. They walked all the rest of the day, slept in shifts watching over Crispin that night, and continued early the next morning.

Stuart missed teleporting. When he'd discovered his ability once he'd been exiled to the human world—and once he'd finished freaking out about it—he'd mourned that he'd had to lose his iron master powers for it.

Now he'd happily trade. Teleportation left his feet a lot less sore, for one thing. Plus, it made it so much easier to catch cubs darting across Shiftertown before they accidentally violated a crabby Feline's or tetchy Lupine's territory.

Being an iron master never had given him the joy he felt standing in the kitchen, slinging hash, watching Peigi surrounded by cubs, laughing with them, the house full of happy sounds.

Didn't even compare.

He needed to find the *karmsyern* and shove it at Cian, then figure out how to get himself and Peigi the hell home. Stuart had been ripped out of sated slumber, Peigi's body warm next to his, and he longed to go back to that place with everything he had.

The activities he'd have to do to reach the sated state wouldn't be bad either. He remembered being inside Peigi, gazing down at her beautiful face as she rose to him. The sensation of her surrounding him, holding him, hadn't left him, no matter that he was back in a cold world, hiking up a mountain.

She completed him, wove warmth through his heart, and excited him like no one ever had in his life. Stuart was in love with Peigi, for always, and he had no intention of denying it.

———

THE CASTLE THEY HEADED TOWARD PERCHED ON A CRAG THAT overlooked the river. They'd hiked around a big loop of that river, which then bent out of sight to flow eventually to the battlefield where Cian had parked himself.

As with most fortifications on the borderlands, there were no doors that Stuart could see, and only tiny windows toward the top of the walls for ventilation. Crenellations lined the roof, where *hoch alfar* archers could hide to shoot their famous poisoned arrows down on approaching enemies.

"How do we get in?" Peigi gazed up at the keep, wind stirring her dark hair. "Secret stairs? Long exhausting tunnels?"

"I was thinking I'd just walk in," Crispin answered. He rubbed his face, which was stubbled with beard, his blue eyes bloodshot with exhaustion. "The *hoch alfar* can believe I escaped your attack and finally made my way back. 'Course, it would be easier to do without these." He shook the chain around his middle.

"We've discussed this," Stuart said. "No."

"See, this is why people are fighting you," Crispin said sullenly. "*Dokk alfar* are mean. You know how hard it is to take a leak while you're in chains?"

"You're managing." Stuart squinted at the keep. "I agree that walking in would be easier than trying to find passages and fighting guards. But we do it my way."

Stuart handed his sword to Peigi and turned to Crispin, who took an uncertain step back.

Stuart never needed to make sharp gestures or shout words when he worked iron. It was fun and scared the shit out of his enemies, but not necessary.

He brought his fingers together and willed the iron in the chains to stretch. The links melded into each other and thinned at his command, becoming cords instead of thick chains.

At first Crispin grinned, as though readying himself to shift and slip out of his shrinking bonds. Then the grin died, and his expression turned to near panic as the chain thinned to become almost invisible cords that burrowed through his clothes and clung tightly. The cords appeared delicate, but they retained the strength of the chains, holding Crispin fast.

"Holy shit," he whispered.

"One step out of line," Stuart said. "Like I said, I can squeeze you in half. Understand?"

"Yes," Crispin said, the word hoarse.

"What do you want me to do?" Peigi had watched the process in fascination, showing no fear. She'd never have anything to fear from Stuart.

"Do you mind going the last part in your bear form?" Stuart asked. "Crispin can pretend you're a new recruit, and I want you able to fight if we have to."

Peigi nodded, already unlacing her tunic. "And you?"

Stuart grinned. He hadn't had so much fun in a long time. "I'll be your prisoner. A pathetic *dokk alfar* you captured for Crispin's master."

Peigi eyed him doubtfully. "Okay, if you think you can pull that off. But I'll need some rope."

Wordlessly, Stuart pulled it out of his pack. The smile Peigi flashed him made the entire trek worth it.

———

TWENTY MINUTES LATER, PEIGI, AS HER BROWN BEAR, followed Crispin, who hid his nervousness surprisingly well. Stuart lay trussed up on her back.

The bonds were loose — Peigi had snarled warnings at Crispin, who'd tied the rope. Stuart had his sword beneath him, out of sight, and Peigi felt it hard against her back. Reassuring, though. If they had to defend themselves, Stuart could easily break free and come out swinging.

A road led up to the keep, not as harrowing and steep as Peigi had feared. Crispin explained it was the route for farmers and suppliers who hauled in necessities. The road crossed a wooden bridge over a chasm — the bridge could be easily dismantled and thrown into the abyss, thus cutting off the castle from attackers.

Peigi peered over the edge of the bridge as she crossed. Mist rose from where the river crashed below, the updraft cold. She shivered and quickly returned her gaze to the solid rock at the end of the bridge.

Crispin had been correct about simply walking into the castle. The guards at the back door recognized him, eyes going wide at Peigi with Stuart on her back. They cringed from them, their trepidation toward Peigi apparent. Hopefully they'd move far enough aside that they wouldn't sense Crispin's iron bonds or Stuart's sword.

They did stare hard at the *dokk alfar*, seemingly unconscious, on Peigi's back. One guard growled something and another laughed.

Crispin joined the laughter, gesturing at Peigi. The guards stepped back even more and Crispin walked inside. No respect showed in the guards' eyes as they let Crispin pass, but at least they didn't stop him, or Peigi either.

"If I had time, I'd gut them," Stuart whispered in her ear.

He didn't enlighten her as to what the guards had joked, by which Peigi concluded it was something extremely derogatory about a female Shifter carrying a *dokk alfar*.

Crispin had chosen the entrance well. Few were using these passages, though Peigi heard voices and banging in the distance that suggested a kitchen. Pounding down another corridor and a whiff of smoke indicated a smithy. The *hoch alfar* worked in silver and bronze, and were experts at it, so she'd heard.

She followed Crispin up, and up and up, a narrow staircase, her bear almost too bulky to fit within its tight, curving walls. But she'd learned how to squeeze into small spaces when she'd been confined with Michael, and also days when she'd had to search for tiny Kevin, who'd decided hiding would be the most entertaining thing he could do.

"Why aren't there more guards?" Stuart whispered to Crispin. "They have to know someone will try to steal it back."

"Don't know," Crispin said. "There were more before I left."

Worrying. Could be the *hoch alfar* had already gotten rid of the *karmsyern* —dropped it in the chasm maybe, or sent it far, far away. If the talisman was as strong as Stuart had told her, it should have made every *hoch alfar* in this castle sick, but the guards had seemed perfectly healthy.

Something wasn't right, and her bear knew it.

They'd climbed a hundred and twenty steps by Peigi's counting, before they emerged without challenge to the topmost part of the keep. Cracks in the ceiling above them showed the gray afternoon sky. It was colder up here, the draft icy.

Crispin led them down a short, dark corridor and paused before a door made of plain slabs of wood held together with bronze bolts. The door handle and lock were also bronze. Crispin tried the latch, but not surprisingly, the door didn't budge.

"Can you open that?" Crispin asked Stuart. "You know, with …" He wriggled his fingers.

Stuart moved the ropes and slid from Peigi's back, taking the hard sword with him. "Iron master, not bronze master."

Peigi shifted to her between beast. "I can break it open," she offered.

Crispin looked pained. "I hoped we'd get in and out without making noise and drawing attention. You know we're in a castle full of *hoch alfar* with sharp weapons, right?"

"I do." Peigi leaned to study the lock, letting her bear claws recede. The bronze was cool beneath her human fingers, but the lock mechanism was simple. "All right then, I'll pick it."

"You can pick locks?" Crispin asked in surprise.

"Sure. Nell taught me. I just need some lock picks."

Stuart handed her two. Peigi threw him a startled glance and realized he'd fashioned them from a piece of his iron sword.

"No wonder the *hoch alfar* are afraid of you." Peigi smiled and took the picks, wanting to kiss him, but she'd save that for later.

The lock was new and clean, which meant someone wanted whatever was inside protected. A clean lock was also much easier to pick. Peigi inserted the metal wires into the hole and played around with the mechanism, as Nell had showed her. Nell had learned lock picking when she'd had to retrieve her sons from wherever they'd gotten themselves stuck as cubs. Shane and Brody had been holy terrors, according to Nell.

Not long later, the lock made a satisfying click, and the door creaked open.

Neither Stuart nor Crispin charged inside, instead hanging back and studying the opening with care. They expected traps—poisoned darts or a dying guard with a sword—like in every good treasure-hunting movie Peigi had watched with the cubs.

Nothing happened. Stuart peeked around the door, then blew out his breath. "Come on."

Peigi motioned Crispin to follow Stuart in while she brought up the rear. The room they entered was dark, the only light coming through cracks around a worn shutter opposite the door. Peigi carefully skirted the room and pulled open the shutter to reveal a small square window, about eighteen inches on a side.

"Fuck," Stuart said behind her.

Peigi jerked around, terrified Crispin had found some way to attack, but Crispin stood next to Stuart, gazing at what he did in almost as much dismay.

A much-carved, thick-legged wooden table held court in the center of the room. On its broad top lay a pool of metal, edges cracked, most of it a collection of gray ash and red rust.

Stuart reached out a finger to it, and the metal where he touched it crumbled to powder.

"The *karmʌyern*," Stuart said in a hushed voice. "Or its remains. They've destroyed it."

TWENTY-THREE

"How?" Peigi, still in her half-beast form, demanded. Stuart's heart pounded in rage. If Crispin had known this, if he'd brought them here to trap them ...

He swung around, and Crispin flung up his hands in alarm. "I didn't know. I swear, I didn't know. It was fine when I left."

The *karmsyern*, the sacred talisman of the *dokk alfar*, the one thing that had kept the *hoch alfar* from being more of a collective pain in the ass than they already were, was a wreck. A heap of rust and slag on a table.

"How?" Peigi repeated. "*Hoch alfar* can't work iron, right? This looks like it was left out in the rain for a couple hundred years."

"A very, very good question."

Stuart understood why the *hoch alfar* weren't guarding it closely, and why no one in this castle was sick and dying from it. They still wouldn't come too close, hence the thing was alone in a locked room high in the keep, but at the same time, there was nothing more to fear from it.

"*Shit.*" Stuart flung his sword to the floor. It rang as it skittered across the stone.

"Remember when I said you should make another one?" Peigi asked. "I think you're going to have to."

Stuart retrieved the sword before Crispin could snatch it up. "The technique was lost, the spells too. *Damn* it, this is so not good."

Peigi came to stand next to him. "Not necessarily. We know Ben and Jaycee, who know a Tuil Erdannan. Ben said she broke the spell that kept him out of Faerie, which means she probably likes him. We can ask Ben to find her and ask. Jaycee too if we need her. Lady Aisling might know how to create another one, or point us to someone who can."

"A huge risk." Stuart let out a breath, but took comfort in Peigi's nearness. "Lady Aisling might not have any interest, or if she asks another Tuil Erdannan to help, they might decide that destroying the *dokk alfar* is more fun."

"Listen to the iron master," a new voice rumbled from the shadows. "Best not to involve the Tuil Erdannan. We are growing bored with your little games."

Crispin gasped in stark terror. "Oh, son of a *bitch*."

Peigi growled, her bear-beast exuding fury. A chill gripped Stuart as he turned, sword ready, to confront a person who was Tuil Erdannan but definitely not Lady Aisling.

The man, tall and disdainful, had the flame-red hair of most Tuil Erdannan and dark eyes that could suck out souls. Stuart felt the press of his magic, an all-encompassing power that would crush them out of existence with the flick of his finger.

Peigi came right up against Stuart, a bulk of strength. "Did you do this?" She pointed at the ruined *karmsyern*. When the man gave her a grave nod, she demanded, "Why would you help the *hoch alfar*? I thought Tuil Erdannan didn't like them."

"*Like* has nothing to do with it." He stepped out of the shadows, his dark gray cloak the same color as the stones. "Nor does hate. In your language, Shifter-bear, I do not give a shit."

Stuart realized the man was speaking English—either he'd

learned it somewhere or magic was translating the words for Peigi's benefit.

"Then why?" Peigi insisted.

The Tuil Erdannan shrugged. "Amusement. Perhaps. Or to throw off the balance, or possibly restore it—who knows? Or to make Aisling Mac Aodha understand she can't have everything her way."

The room took on an icy sharpness. "You are an enemy of Lady Aisling?" Stuart asked.

"You could say that." The man didn't move, but Stuart felt the power humming inside him increasing, like a rumbling beneath the earth before a volcano spilled forth. "I am her husband."

He lifted his hand, and a blasting wave of magic sent Stuart, Peigi, and Crispin straight toward the open window.

The wall blew outward, bricks exploding to widen the passage that the three flew through. There was nothing outside the window but a vertical drop, and they plunged together down into the misty abyss.

———

PEIGI LATCHED ON TO STUART—AS THOUGH SHE COULD STOP his fall, she thought hysterically. Or maybe she just wanted to die with him. Crispin flailed and cursed, his big cat snarls cutting the air. Stuart said nothing at all, only assumed an expression of grim determination.

He flung something from his hand, and the two of them jerked to an abrupt halt. Stuart's sword had become an iron grappling hook that found purchase in a beam jutting from the castle, the ropes they'd used to bind him to Peigi their lifeline. He'd grabbed the ropes, with great presence of mind, on their way out the window.

Stuart brought up his hand, and the iron cords around

Crispin drew outward and likewise latched themselves to the rope.

Crispin shouted as he was brought up short, swinging on the rope's end. After a moment of swearing, he grabbed on to the line, using his Shifter strength to hang on and find footholds on the wall.

"Great." Peigi gazed the long way down, water churning at the bottom of the drop. "What now?"

Stuart grunted with effort as he held them all steady. "Now, we climb."

In the next hour, Peigi learned the absolute power of an iron master. Stuart not only changed the iron in his sword and Crispin's chains to climbing spikes but made the iron flow between minute cracks in the wall and affix themselves harder than any pounded wedge. Every few yards downward, he'd summon out the spikes and reaffix them for the next haul.

Stuart's physical strength was incredible. Peigi realized how much he'd been holding back as he lived among humans and Shifters, letting them believe he was no stronger, and in some cases weaker, than they were. He climbed effortlessly, steadying the ropes for Peigi and Crispin, muscles working as he clung to the spikes and willed the iron to do as he wished.

There was no wonder the *hoch alfar* had feared him.

If the three of them had been human, they would have died in that passage downward. But Shifters had strength and agility, which was matched and surpassed by Stuart. Peigi's greatest fear was that the Tuil Erdannan would throw his terrible power down on them again, disintegrating metal and ropes to send them plummeting into the gorge.

She peered upward from time to time in worry, but the hole in the wall the Tuil Erdannan had created remained empty. Perhaps he didn't believe they'd survive, or he simply didn't care.

Lady Aisling's husband. *Hmm.* Jaycee hadn't mentioned him, nor had Dimitri or Ben. Peigi reasoned they hadn't known about him—she didn't imagine any of those three would have kept quiet about Lady Aisling's dangerous spouse.

They weren't home free when they reached the bottom of the castle wall, because the keep had been built on the edge of the precipice. The road they'd ascended was around the other side— this side was right over the gorge. The going was slightly easier once they started descending into the canyon, as the rock walls offered more footholds, if precarious ones, but it was still tough.

At long last, Crispin released his hold of the rope and landed on his feet in the shallows of the river. Stuart dropped after him, and Peigi shifted to bear as she let go. She splashed into the water and shook herself, very, very happy to have all four feet on the ground.

She didn't often find a good stream in Las Vegas, so she didn't fight the urge to romp, kicking up water with her huge paws. Bears liked water, and she was no exception. The cubs would love a river like this.

Peigi especially enjoyed batting water at Crispin, who hissed and snarled at her. *Cats.*

Stuart had gathered all the iron to him in one lump. The moment Crispin brushed water off himself and caught his breath, Stuart reformed the chains and made them wrap themselves around the Feline again.

"Aw, come on." Crispin grabbed a chain and held it up in disgust. "What do I have to do?"

"Can't risk you running back to the keep and unleashing a dozen *hoch alfar* guards on our asses." Stuart coiled the ropes and hoisted them over his arm. "I'll let you out when we're home."

"Great."

"I say we make ourselves scarce." Stuart eyed the castle, half-hidden by trees growing out from the gorge's walls. "Before our new Tuil Erdannan friend decides to come after us, or send out the *hoch alfar.*"

"Surprised he hasn't already," Peigi said as she rose out of her bear form into her between-beast.

Stuart motioned them toward the bank, and they all splashed toward it. "Tuil Erdannan sort of live outside the rest of us, as though what happens to us isn't any more important to them than what bugs are doing under the ground is to us."

"Sure," Crispin said in disgust. "The bugs aren't important, until you're infested with termites."

"Exactly my point. The Tuil Erdannan only crush things when they're annoyed. I'd bet the guy up there has already forgotten about us."

"We can hope." Peigi shuddered. "Do you believe him when he says he's Lady Aisling's husband?"

"Who knows? If we ever see her again, we can ask."

Peigi wondered why the two were estranged, and whether the man had left Lady Aisling or she'd kicked him out. She decided she wouldn't want to be between them when they fought.

They made their long way back to Cian's camp, no one speaking much. The *karmsyern* was gone, and the Tuil Erdannan were more involved than any of them had thought. Unsettling; the outlook bleak.

Peigi traveled as her bear, keeping an eye on Crispin, who walked ahead of her, disconsolate. He'd gambled everything when he'd defected to the *hoch alfar*, and he'd lost.

They spent another night in the damp forest. Peigi was hungry, but Shifters could stave off hunger and thirst for a time, drawing on energy reserves until their next feast. Bears were particularly good at this, which was why they could nap for a month and wake up none the worse for wear.

Stuart also remained stoic, as though hiking through woods without food or water was a stroll in the park to him. Crispin didn't complain, but he clamped his lips together sullenly, making sure they knew he suffered in silence.

Stuart and Peigi cuddled together at night. She wondered what Stuart would do now that the *karmsyern* was no more — Cian would need the iron master more than ever.

This was Stuart's home, his true home. Peigi loved him, and she believed he loved her, if what she'd seen in his eyes was true. But the choice had to be his.

Peigi pulled him close, warming him as he kept watch, pain in her heart.

They reached Cian's camp the next afternoon, and found it in chaos.

The battle had resumed, Cian told Stuart as he and Peigi hastened to where Cian stood over his map in the middle of the site. Tents fluttered as they were dismantled, *dokk alfar* hastily piled carts and wagons with supplies, and wounded soldiers lay everywhere.

Stuart translated for Peigi. Things were going poorly, Cian said. He'd have to retreat or be killed to the last man.

Stuart should have been exhausted from their three-day trek with nothing to show for it, but he straightened his shoulders and took on an expression of hard determination. He asked Cian a question, and Cian motioned him to his map spread out over flat boulders.

The map was beautiful, exquisitely drawn to the last detail, very different from a relief map or a hastily scribbled plan of battle. Peigi saw a flicker of movement on it and leaned closer.

She sucked in a surprised breath. This was a real-time depiction of the battle, with tiny figures moving around trees and rocks, as though a GPS satellite beamed images down to the sheet of paper.

Stuart rested his hands on his thighs as he scrutinized the battlefield, he and Cian speaking together in the *dokk alfar* language. Finally Stuart straightened up, gave Cian a nod, lifted the iron sword he'd reformed, and strode off under the misty trees.

Peigi, as bear, ran after him. Stuart turned to her as she crashed through the brush, but he didn't admonish her or tell her to go back and wait for him. He rested his hand on her shoulder, and together they walked toward the battle.

The armies were fighting hand to hand by the time Peigi and Stuart reached them, bloodily hacking and cutting each other. Men shouted, screamed, died. Shifter bodies lay everywhere, motionless, while the Shifters still alive fought in tight groups, harrying *dokk alfar* who had to divert from fighting *hoch alfar* or be torn apart by Shifters.

So much for rounding up the Shifters and keeping an eye on them. Peigi saw Michael, roaring as his grizzly bear, his scarred face fearsome. He shifted to his between-beast as he fought a leopard who was lithe and fast.

"Stay down, you fuckers!" he yelled. "Stupid bastards. No Guardians, you assholes."

The slain Shifters would simply be dead, no Guardian to release their souls to the Summerland and render their bodies dust. Shifter souls floating free could be enslaved, with no hope of reprisal. It was the worst fear of a Shifter, and Peigi shared it, to die out of reach of a Guardian.

No one was winning this battle—they were simply killing each other. The *hoch alfar* fought with mad hatred, as did the *dokk alfar*. The Shifters only added to the madness.

"Screw this," Stuart snarled.

He strode forward. The mists silhouetted him as he lifted his arm and spun his sword like a quarterstaff.

Mist swirled from the sword and gathered around him like a cloak. Peigi hung back, not wanting to hamper him, poised to rush to his aid.

Stuart flung the sword high. It flipped end over end in perfect arcs, rising higher, higher. When the sword reached its apex, Stuart bellowed a single word.

That sound reverberated from the trees, amplifying itself above the noise of battle, above cries of man and beast. The vibrations of power that touched Peigi were no less formidable than what had come from the Tuil Erdannan in the castle.

Fae soldiers halted in sudden worry. Shifters were slower to respond—when Shifters hit killing frenzy, they were difficult to stop—but at last they ceased, breathless and wondering.

The iron sword splintered. It became thousands of shards, dull black against the mist, thicker than a swarm of locusts. A darkness formed around it like black fog.

Peigi had seen this before, when they'd fought the *hoch alfar* just inside a gate in the ley line outside Las Vegas. As they had then, the *hoch alfar* looked skyward in collective terror, and then they ran.

The *hoch alfar* soldiers fled through woods and underbrush, scrambling and slamming into each other, anything to escape the deadly bolts falling from the sky.

The Shifters stared in bafflement as the *hoch alfar* changed from attacking fury to screaming masses of terror. The shards began to rain down on the Shifters as well—they weren't affected by iron, but a thousand bullets falling on them was going to hurt.

The Shifters roared and yelled, and tried to run. Michael had retreated under the trees when the shards began to fall, but he reemerged, realizing they weren't falling on *him*.

He started driving the Shifters toward the river as Cian had directed him, using plenty of foul words as well as fists and roars. Peigi joined him, charging at the confused Shifters until they ran, snarling and yowling into the river. There they cowered, beating off the shards that stung them.

"Nice." Michael's voice held admiration. He held up his hand-paw for a high five as Peigi flowed from bear into her half-Shifter state.

Peigi studied the hand a moment, which hovered, waiting for a sign of comradeship.

She could give Michael a withering glance and turn her back. She'd won their dominance fight, and he couldn't do anything about that.

Or she could acknowledge him, start healing herself by letting the anger out of her heart.

She slapped his palm with hers. Michael started, then grinned crookedly.

Someone should have slammed him in a dominance battle a long time ago, she decided. Might have made him turn out better.

The *dokk alfar* recovered from their dazed surprise at the iron master's magic and chased the fleeing *hoch alfar*, their cries of triumph receding into the distance. Stuart lowered his hands and strolled toward Peigi, none the worse for wear. He wasn't even breathing hard.

"So that's done," he said.

Peigi morphed into her human form, wrapped her arms around him, and kissed him.

TWENTY-FOUR

Peigi kept shooting Stuart smiles full of hot promise as they returned to camp, Peigi dressed again, and Stuart's blood burned. The kiss they'd shared on the riverbank had been sizzling, making Stuart want to carry her away and make love to her, screw the battle, screw ruined iron talismans.

Only the cold, damp ground, the snarling Shifters, and the wild screams of celebrating *dokk alfar* had stopped him. He wanted Peigi somewhere warm, soft, and private.

Cian's expression was bleak as Stuart told him in more detail about the destruction of the *karmsyern* and the appearance of the Tuil Erdannan. Cian let out a few colorful words Stuart hadn't heard since he'd been much younger.

"We're fucked," Cian concluded.

"Maybe," Stuart said. "What we're hoping is that Lady Aisling will be amenable to making another one for the *dokk alfar*. If she hears her husband is involved, that might motivate her on your side. I got the feeling the two aren't exactly on the best terms."

Cian remained cynical. "The Tuil Erdannan do what they

damn well please. As we discussed before, we can't count on her."

"I know," Stuart answered. "But we have friends she likes. I'm going to gamble on that friendship." He let out a breath. "Face it—it's all we've got."

Cian growled. "I suppose we don't have a choice." He trailed off into phrases that would make a human howl and flee if they knew what they meant. Human swear words were sparkles and glitter compared to the ones in *ðokk alfar*.

"We'll need to go back through the ley line, or bring our friends to us," Stuart said, and waited.

Cian frowned. "I told you, I didn't bring you through this ley line. I have no idea how to send you back."

Stuart didn't like the qualm his words gave him. "It doesn't matter—if we find the ley line and have a spell or a talisman that can get us through, good enough."

Cian shook his head. "My spell-caster was wounded and hasn't regained consciousness. He's hurt too badly to do any chanting any time soon. And I'm fresh out of talismans."

"Um ..." Crispin, who'd been helping bandage wounds of the captive Shifters, rose from kneeling beside a hurt Lupine and came to them. He spoke *ðokk alfar* and would have understood the entire conversation. "I have a talisman you can use. It's how I crossed over in the first place."

He reached into his tunic. Stuart grabbed his hand, not trusting he wasn't going for a weapon, and searched Crispin's pocket himself. He closed his fingers around something warm and metal, and brought out a small silver medallion fashioned into a Celtic knot.

Stuart studied the medallion in his palm, feeling its tingle of magic. "Why are you volunteering this? I can't believe you're suddenly excited to help the *ðokk alfar*."

Crispin shrugged. "The Tuil Erdannan dude will tell the *hoch alfar* I sneaked you into the keep, so I won't be good for anything but a lion skin if I go back to the Fae prince. Besides." He deflated. "I should go home anyway. Throw myself on Dylan's mercy."

Stuart closed his hand around the medallion. "Good choice."

He didn't trust Crispin entirely—any Shifter who had chosen to go over to the *hoch alfar* couldn't have his priorities straight. But it was worth a try. He would have Cian keep an eye on Crispin while Stuart checked out whether the medallion worked. If the medallion did anything it wasn't supposed to, Stuart would ... Well, he'd think of something.

Cian showed him on the map approximately where Stuart and Peigi had been when they arrived, and where the ley line ran.

The closest point was about a mile from camp. Stuart explained the situation to Peigi, and together they walked out of the teeming camp, making for the ley line.

"That was hot," Peigi said.

He started. "What was? Asking how to get to the ley line?"

Peigi walked closer to him. "You alone facing the *hoch alfar*. Whirling your sword like a bad-ass."

Stuart grinned at her, then he sobered. "Cian was right that he needed an iron master. I didn't realize what he was up against. And I never guessed the *hoch alfar* would be able to destroy the *karmsyern*."

He didn't like the tension his words put into Peigi's eyes. "What will you do?" she asked, voice calm.

"I don't know yet."

She meant would Stuart remain in Faerie, lending his magic to Cian? Stuart had learned on his brief journey here years ago to save Cassidy and Diego that his family and all close to him were dead. He'd decided there was nothing left for him. He'd gladly gone back to Shiftertown to be with Peigi and take care of the orphaned cubs.

Now Peigi was his mate. But *dokk alfar* could die by the thousands if he did nothing. They were strong fighters, but without the *karmsyern,* and with Shifters turning on them, Stuart's people needed all the help they could get.

Peigi pulled him to a halt before Stuart could continue. Mist surrounded them, and against it, Peigi's eyes held warm comfort.

"I know you have to make a choice," she said. "I've struggled with this decision, because I know this is your life, your people, your home."

Stuart's body went cold, his heart like lead in his chest. She was going to tell him to leave her, to stay in Faerie with Cian, to save the lives he could. To say good-bye to her, to the cubs, to all he'd come to love. Because it was the right thing to do.

Stuart drew a breath to speak, but Peigi put her fingers to his lips.

"Let me finish. I've decided that, whether we're stuck here, or we go back, or you decide to stay, I stick with you. Doesn't matter what."

His throat went dry. "Peigi ..."

"*Doesn't matter what.* We're mates. Mates protect each other. Remember what you said to me? That it was stupid that when things were the most dire we split up? Well, I agree." Peigi slid closer to him, moving her fingers so her breath could touch his mouth. "We stay together. Until this is done."

The knot in Stuart's heart dissolved, until he felt light, floating, as free as the mist. "Yeah?" He swallowed. "You're not just saying that?"

"Nope." Peigi smiled, which was like sunshine bursting through the worst rainy day ever. "You're stuck with me. But once we finish what you need to do, we'll have to go back to Shiftertown, because we promised the cubs. Remember?"

"I remember," Stuart said, voice gentle. "When I said I didn't know yet what I'd do, I meant whether or not to come back and help Cian from time to time. I'm definitely going home with you right now. So help me, Goddess."

Peigi's smile widened, and she kissed him, quietly and with

tenderness. Stuart kissed her back, getting lost in the sweetness of her.

She eased from him after a long, satisfying interval. "I'm glad that's settled, and without hours and days of drama." Peigi straightened. "Let's go find this gate."

"If Crispin isn't shitting us about this medallion."

"Ben was in the house when we were sucked across," she reminded him. "If anyone can find the residual magic of that and act on it, it's Ben."

"Here's hoping."

Peigi leaned to him and kissed him once more. "Let's go find out."

———

PEIGI SENSED EXACTLY WHEN THEY REACHED THE LEY LINE and the thin veil that separated this world from the other. The air vibrated, as though an electric power plant hummed nearby.

Except for that, this part of the woods looked no different from any other—she'd have never found the place without Cian's directions.

"So how does this work?" she asked, trying not to shiver.

Stuart slid the medallion Crispin had given him from his pocket and dangled it from its chain. "Hey," he addressed the air. "Open up."

Peigi stifled a laugh. "Very mystical."

Stuart flicked a gaze to her, every line of him taut. "I'm a fighter, not a magic user."

"And this isn't an RPG."

"I wish it were," Stuart said. "Then I'd just roll dice or click on something."

Peigi cupped her hands around her mouth. "*Ben!* Are you there? We need you."

They waited. The woods remained quiet, the only sound moisture dripping from trees to the damp forest floor.

"The gate won't necessarily come out in our bedroom," Stuart said. "Or Kurt's basement. Or anywhere near our Shiftertown, for that matter. The pockets in between space and time move around. Trust me, I did plenty of research on this, for years."

Peigi didn't like the sound of that. What if they emerged in the middle of Antarctica? How did they get home then, if they didn't simply freeze to death?

"So do we charge around waving the medallion and see what happens?" she asked.

Stuart handed it to her. "You try. I'm realizing that whenever I've come through, you've been with me. When we went after Diego, there you were—and I hadn't been able to open a gate before that, no matter how much I tried. The first time Cian summoned me, I got stuck. Maybe the gates still don't work well for me, but they do for you."

Peigi wasn't certain about this theory, but she had nothing to lose by trying. The silver knot was warm from Stuart's hand and quivered faintly with magic, mirroring the hum she perceived from the gate.

Maybe frequency was the key. Perhaps when the sound waves from the gate and the medallion either melded or canceled each other out, the gate opened.

Peigi held the medallion high, closing her eyes. She could hear better this way, letting the Shifter in her listen.

Earlier this year, Donny had become obsessed with learning how to play guitar. Cormac had brought him one and taught Donny to tune it.

When Cormac plucked two strings—one fretted, one open—to produce the same note on each string, the vibrations between the two produced a faint *wah wah wah* sound. That discordance was more pronounced the more out of tune the strings were to each other, and disappeared when the two were perfectly tuned.

Peigi heard a similar sound between the gate and medallion. Now to figure out how to tune it. Peigi couldn't simply turn a nut to loosen or tighten a string—she had to loosen or tighten a *gate*.

"Ben?" Peigi called. "Seriously, we need your help." She thought about how they'd unstuck Stuart from the gate in the basement. "Maybe Matt and Kyle too, if Misty will let them go. They seem to navigate gates without any problem. Also, we're going to need a Guardian. Unfortunately." Her words fell away, flat against the damp. "Tell the cubs I love them. If you can hear me, wee ones … *I love you.*"

Her words caught on a sob. Stuart put his arm around her and drew her close.

The dissonance surged, pushing on Peigi's eardrums, and then abruptly the two notes merged into one clear, sweet tone.

On top of that came noise, voices talking over each other, each one rising higher to be heard. Over *that* sounded a stronger, more gravelly voice, far more frustrated.

"If you will all let me hear myself think …" Graham bellowed. "Matt, Kyle, come back here. The rest of you *sit down.*"

"Oh." The voice was Ben's. "I think it's too late."

Three cubs charged out of the mist, two wolves and a small grizzly bear. They slammed into Stuart and Peigi, and all five went over in a tangled heap of fur, excitement, and fervent face licking.

TWENTY-FIVE

"Settle down!" Graham roared. "Aw, damn it, I never wanted to see *this* place again."

Peigi pulled herself up, the grizzly cub firmly in her arms. "Noelle, what are you doing here?"

The two wolf cubs rolled from Stuart and shifted as they gained their feet. "She said we had to rescue you, *rescue you*," Matt and Kyle babbled, one overlapping the other. "Do you need us to rescue you, Uncle Stuart?"

"I do now." Stuart sat up, brushing wet leaves from his tunic. "Two wolves just knocked me down."

Matt looked pleased with himself. "We like to knock people down," Kyle said.

Peigi hugged Noelle, who was nuzzling a cold wet nose into Peigi's neck. "What happened?" Peigi asked Graham. "Why are you here?"

Graham stared at her in disbelief. "What do you mean, why? You were shouting down your hall to Ben, that's why. Telling him to bring Matt and Kyle. He came barging into my house saying he needed them, but like hell I was letting them go without me."

"Which he explained loudly." Ben emerged from the mists carrying a duffel bag. "You said you needed a Guardian, so I called Neal. You guys okay?"

Peigi blinked. "It was like fifteen seconds after I said that when you crashed in. Oh, wait, must be the time difference."

"Yeah, jet lag has nothing on ley-line lag," Ben said. "Why do you need a Guardian? What happened?"

"Tough battle," Stuart said. "Dead Shifters. Can't leave them."

Graham scowled but Peigi saw the flare of grief in his eyes. "Stupid …" He cleared his throat. "Well, come on. We're rescuing you. Let's go." He swung back to the empty mist he'd entered through, finding nothing. "Shit."

"Ben, we need you to talk to Cian before we go." Stuart sounded unworried that the gate seemed to be closed again. "He needs a huge favor."

Ben went wary. "I can't donate any body parts. Physiology not compatible."

"No body parts," Peigi promised. "The favor is, can you ask Lady Aisling to talk to Cian? Or have Jaycee ask her?"

Ben grew still more wary. "Why?"

"The *karmsyern* has been destroyed," Stuart said flatly. "I'm going to ask her to make another one."

"The fuck." Ben's mouth dropped open. "*Destroyed?* Are you sure?"

"Saw it ourselves," Peigi told him unhappily.

"How can it be destroyed?" Ben's disbelief hurtled itself at them. "Who the hell could do that?"

"Lady Aisling's husband," Peigi said. "At least, he claimed to be her husband."

Ben's outraged perplexity died in shock. "Lady Aisling is *married?*"

"Apparently."

"Shit." Ben thumped his palm to his head. "I gotta process this."

"Can you talk to Cian while you process?" Stuart asked. "The *karmɷyern* …"

"Yeah, I know what the *karmɷyern* is." Ben ran his fingers through his damp hair. "But you don't need Lady Aisling for that. No Tuil Erdannan made the *karmɷyern*."

"How do you know?" Peigi demanded. "Who did?"

Ben assumed an expression that held embarrassment, sorrow, and a tiny bit of pride. "That would be me."

Stuart wasn't often shocked, but he stilled, his eyes becoming very focused. "*You* did?"

Ben nodded. "It's one of the reasons the *hoch alfar* wanted to be rid of me. I got in the way of their world domination plans." He stared off into the mists, his outrage returning. "All that work, all that magic, all those *liveɷ*, and a Tuil Erdannan just flicks his fingers …"

"The *karmɷyern* was made a thousand or so years ago," Stuart said, dumbfounded.

"I was young." Ben opened his hand. "Full of myself. I never thought the *hoch alfar* would wipe out all goblins everywhere for it." He shook his head. "When I catch up with that Tuil Erdannan … Lady Aisling's husband, you say?"

His awe and fear of the Tuil Erdannan was departing in the face of his anger. Peigi had the feeling that if he *∂i∂* find the man who'd destroyed the *karmɷyern*, that Tuil Erdannan would be in for a rude awakening.

Ben had power, which he kept buried most of the time, like Stuart. But when Ben ever let it out … Peigi wasn't certain whether she was eager to see that or not.

Graham stared at Ben. "Just when I think I've figured you out …"

"I have a lot of history," Ben said. "You know, hidden depths."

Peigi, her arms full of bear cub, reached to Ben and touched his broad shoulder. "You risked everything to help others. That was wonderful."

"Yeah well." Ben cleared his throat. "It wasn't the only reason the *hoch alfar* came after us, but one reason. It showed them how powerful we were."

Stuart had recovered himself enough to give Ben a glance of compassion. "I hate to ask you to do it again, but the *hoch alfar* will wipe out *my* people if you don't. They've already started."

Ben growled under his breath in a language Peigi had never heard, ending in a snarled *hoch alfar*. Then he heaved a resigned sigh.

"I'm going to need iron that's as pure as can be found. Some Fae gold, if any is lying around, some silver, dried sage, and a forge to work on. Oh, and beer. Lots and lots of beer."

———

BEN HAD BROUGHT CLOTHES FOR THE CUBS IN THE DUFFEL bag. Noelle went with Peigi behind a tree to slide into sweat pants and shirt, but Kyle and Matt argued.

"We don't mind running around Faerie like this," Matt declared in his ear-shattering voice. "We've done it before."

"No!" Graham bellowed.

"Please?" Peigi asked them.

Matt and Kyle ceased chasing each other in circles as Peigi spoke, grabbed clothes from the duffel, and pulled them on.

"I don't know how you do that," Graham growled.

"It's a magic she has." Stuart sent Peigi a glance that had her wanting to say to hell with the *hoch alfar* and rush him home.

When they reached the camp, Stuart took Ben to Cian, and the three began speaking together in *ðokk alfar*.

Peigi did *not* want Noelle to see Michael and wished Ben and Graham had left her at home, but she likely had rushed after Matt and Kyle before anyone could stop her. Peigi didn't know how much Noelle remembered of Michael, and how much trauma encountering him again would cause.

Before she could decide what to do, Michael came out of the

tent where he was tending to, and reaming out, the wounded Shifters. He halted when he saw Peigi with cubs, puzzled, no recognition in his eyes.

Peigi's anger at him wound up all over again. He didn't know Noelle, one of his tracker's cubs, probably hadn't ever noticed her when she'd lived in his compound.

Noelle, on the other hand, studied him a moment and nodded gravely. "I remember you. Looks like someone kicked your ass."

"That was Peigi," Stuart, who'd turned around to watch the encounter, said.

"Yeah?" Noelle gazed at Peigi in profound respect and swung her fist through the air. "'Cause she's *awesome*."

Peigi relaxed. Noelle would stare trauma in the face, and spit on it.

Michael, still not understanding what had just happened, returned to the Shifters.

Peigi moved to help him and Crispin, Noelle at her side. Graham joined them, his belligerence mitigated by compassion when he took in the injured Shifters.

The most wounded were inside the tent, groaning softly in pain or simply staring. Some were contrite, realizing they'd thrown away their lives joining the *hoch alfar*, but others were defiant. Shiftertowns sucked, they said, and Shifter leaders were selling them all straight to hell. Graham had a few loud words to say about that.

Peigi bandaged wounds and cleaned up blood and bile, comforting where she could. Noelle helped without a qualm. She tended wounds in all seriousness, having had plenty of experience ministering to her brothers and sisters when they got themselves hurt—Shifter cubs inevitably did. She knew how to clean cuts and wrap limbs and lend reassurance, telling her patients that all would be well and not to worry too much. Even the most recalcitrant Shifters were charmed by her.

Neal Ingram, the Guardian of the Las Vegas Shiftertown,

arrived not long later. Peigi went to meet him as he walked into the camp.

"How did you find your way through?" she asked him curiously.

Neal, a tall Lupine with gray eyes, was habitually a quiet man. Most Guardians kept to themselves, but Neal had made an art of it.

Neal touched the hilt of his sword resting above his shoulder. "This lets me pass through the gates. The Shifter souls crying out were a clue where they were too. I'll go help them."

He strode unerringly toward the end of the clearing where the dead Shifters had been laid out. Neal drew the Sword as he walked, and Peigi heard him begin a low chant to the Goddess.

"Goddess go with them," she whispered, and then returned to the Shifters who were alive and needed her.

———

BEN DECIDED TO REMAIN IN FAERIE, AT LEAST FOR A TIME, TO attempt to forge a new *karmsyern* for the *dokk alfar*. Cian would take him home, he told Stuart, and Ben could work on a forge Cian planned to have built for him.

Stuart was not surprised Ben decided to stay, and was grateful. "Take care of yourself," Stuart told him.

Ben held up his hands for a fist bump. "You mean don't let a *hoch alfar* catch me and spear me. I'll keep that in mind. Tell Jasmine I'll be back to look after her house as soon as I can." He hesitated. "Tell her to tell the house too. I wouldn't want it getting upset at me."

Stuart agreed. An angry sentient house was a thing he did not want to experience. He completed the fist bump, advised Ben to send for him whenever he needed help, and left him to it.

What did surprise Stuart was that Michael wanted to stay.

"I'm a Collarless Shifter," Michael explained when Stuart asked. "And I hurt and pissed off a lot of your friends. If you

take me back, Dylan will get his hands on me, and either kill me
or shove a Collar on me. Screw that. If I stay here, I can keep my
eye on the Shifters who have joined the other side. Maybe catch
some, beat sense into them. Who knows?"

He shrugged and turned to another hurt Shifter. Michael was
good at field doctoring, Stuart had already seen. He'd probably
had to learn it while leading feral Shifters.

Stuart would never forgive the ass for what he'd done to
Peigi, the women he'd sequestered, and their cubs. But at least
Michael might do some good, if Cian kept an eye on him, to
make up for part of it. Peigi winning their domination fight had
also subdued him a bit, Stuart could already tell. Noelle was
right — Peigi was awesome.

Matt and Kyle also wanted to stay in Faerie, to both see what
it was like and attack a few *hoch alfar* for the fun of it, they said.
Graham told them a firm no.

This time, he used a tone that Matt and Kyle obeyed. They
slunk next to him, dejected, but perked up again as soon as they
marched with Graham toward the ley line gate. They were
going home.

Stuart and Peigi walked behind them, the two of them
holding Noelle's hands between them. Neal, downcast from
dispatching so many Shifters today, followed with a bound and
shivering Crispin.

Peigi had kept Crispin's silver medallion. She'd tried to relin-
quish it to Ben, so he could return to the human world when he
wished, but he'd waved it off, saying he had his own talisman.
She remembered the light in his hands when he'd dragged them
home from Cian's garden, and wondered if it had been he who'd
opened the gate outside their bedroom window. She'd started to
ask, but Ben had gazed at her as though he had no idea what she
was talking about.

Sure, he didn't. The gleeful expression on his face when he'd
turned away had confirmed her suspicions. He'd known they
were needed and somehow sent them back.

Neal opened the gate this time, the Sword of the Guardian leading the way. The mists parted and Peigi walked into her own kitchen, which was full of Shifters. Not only her cubs, but Nell, Cormac, Shane, Eric, and with him, Dylan Morrissey. The cubs' yelps of gladness drowned out any questions or hope of conversation.

Crispin waded through the throng and stood in front of Dylan, the chains around him clinking. They'd have to be cut off, as Stuart was no longer an iron master on this side of the gate.

Dylan studied Crispin for a time, his blue eyes dark. Crispin returned the gaze, head up, though he trembled.

Then Dylan abruptly reached for Crispin and dragged him into a tight, heartfelt, Shifter embrace.

"Thank you," Dylan whispered, his eyes misting. "It's a brave, brave thing you did, lad."

Crispin returned the hug the best he could, and when Dylan released him, he was smiling, his eyes also full. "No problem, cuz. Give me a harder assignment next time, will you?"

TWENTY-SIX

"So he was Dylan's plant?" Peigi asked. She and Stuart lounged on the back porch in the moonlight much later. It was still cold, but Peigi wanted the night and its silence—as silent as it ever got in Shiftertown. "Damn, he had me fooled."

Stuart, in the porch chair drawn next to hers, sipped the coffee he'd brewed after they'd fed the cubs' dinner and at long last convinced them to go to bed. It had been a task getting them to settle down, but finally, they'd ceased listening to Noelle's tales of her brief adventure and dropped off in exhaustion.

"Dylan told me before he left tonight that he sent in Crispin to give him the rundown on the Shifters who'd defected," Stuart said. "How many, who they were working for, what they were expected to do—basically any intel he could gather."

Peigi pulled the afghan Misty had given her closer around her. "Crispin was good at making us believe him a disgruntled Shifter at the bottom of his clan."

"He *is* at the bottom of the Morrissey clan. Dylan decided he'd be perfect for the job, because no one would question a Shifter low in the hierarchy running off to find a place of his own. People ignored him, or despised him, or felt sorry for him."

"*I* felt sorry for him," Peigi said with wry humor. "He was probably laughing his ass off at me the whole time."

"No, he was grateful." Stuart slid his hand under the crocheted afghan and touched hers. "Deep cover is tough, believe me."

He took on a haunted expression, leftover from his years of moving from one identity to the next while he tried to find a way back to Faerie and home. The expression changed, however, as he met Peigi's gaze, pain and distress leaving him. Now when he said *home*, he meant this house, Peigi, and the cubs.

"So that's why he stuck with us instead of trying to escape and return to the *hoch alfar*." Peigi ran her thumb across the back of Stuart's hand. "I wish Dylan had told us. I wouldn't feel like such a fool."

"The fewer people who know about a cover, the less easy it is to have it blown. I know that from experience too. Dylan holds his cards very close to his chest. Not many people are on his need-to-know list. Apparently not me either, in this case."

"I understand, I think," Peigi said. "But why didn't Crispin try to get home to Dylan once he was away from the Fae prince?"

"To gather as much intel on the situation as he could. Plus, I didn't give him a lot of choice, did I?"

Peigi laughed softly. "We played right into his hands."

"He told me today he was grateful to us. Hanging out with the *hoch alfar* could make anyone lonely."

Peigi let out a breath and rested her head on the back of the chair. "I hope Ben doesn't feel the same way about *ðokk alfar*."

"I think they'll get along fine. Ben and Cian are a lot alike, doing anything to stop the hated *hoch alfar*. Cian will go far, I'm sure."

"I'll feel better when Ben is back, anyway." Peigi turned to look fully at Stuart. "Thank you for coming home with me."

"I had to," Stuart said in a light tone. "I signed Noelle's agreement, remember?"

"No, you didn't have to." Peigi folded her fingers around his. "You can return to Faerie, be the iron master, save the world. They need you."

Stuart bowed his head for a time, moonlight touching his black hair. When he straightened up again, his eyes were quiet, no more indecision. "Maybe Cian and Ben will find another iron master—I can't be the only one in existence. We're rare but not unique." He untangled their hands from the afghan, raised her fingers to his lips, and kissed them gently. "I made my choice, Pegs. I made it a long time ago, when I saw you walk away from Eric after he brought you here, ready to face whatever life threw at you. I fell in love with you that day, and that love has never wavered. I love you still." He kissed her fingers once more. "And I know I'm going to love you always."

Peigi's heart burned with her connection to him, the mate bond, the tether that would never loosen.

"I fell in love with *you*," she said, "when you were ready to give up your chances of going back to Faerie so you wouldn't hurt Cassidy or any other Shifter. You wanted to go home so much—it was killing you—and you let it go, so others could live and be happy."

"Yeah." Stuart's voice was quiet. "I'm awesome."

"You are."

"What is grabbing me and throwing me over the moon in that speech is *I fell in love with you.*"

"Well, I did," Peigi said. "And I love you now."

Stuart leaned closer. "Time moved while we were in Faerie. The full moon is in a couple of days, so Eric will do the sun and moon ceremonies."

"Yep." Peigi rested her hand on his firm shoulder. "What's your point?"

"My point is, I don't want to wait."

Peigi's mating frenzy, which she'd tamped down during their adventure and soothing the cubs afterward, roared high. She was off the chair and onto his, her legs around him before he finished the sentence.

"Me neither," she said breathlessly, and kissed his mouth.

Stuart smiled into the kiss, which turned deep, longing, needy. He slid his hands under her shirt and up her back, dragging her against him. His hard cock fit right between her legs, rigid through the layers of fabric between them.

The kiss was a point of heat, his hands pouring fires through her. Peigi eased back but remained a breath away while she rubbed against the delightful hardness of him.

"It's warmer inside," she whispered.

"More cubs in there," Stuart pointed out.

A cold wind poured down the porch, making wind chimes sing. Peigi shivered. "I think we should risk it."

"Nuff said." Stuart rose, lifting Peigi so he cradled her in his strong arms.

They laughed when he navigated the doorknob with his arms full of Peigi, then he set her on her feet in the kitchen. Another kiss there, this one body to body, the two tightly against each other. Then they moved as silently as they could down the hall and into the dark bedroom.

Stuart firmly shut the blinds. "No dragging us back to Faerie tonight."

"No." Peigi cupped Stuart's face when he came to her again. "Someday, though. They'll need you."

"Crispin promised to keep open communication with Ben and Cian. But right now …"

"Right now …"

Right now, she was with Stuart, the man who'd woken her from the stupor in which she'd existed for years, who'd taught her how to live again. The cubs snored down the hall, and bright moonlight leaked around the blinds, the Goddess bathing Peigi in cool radiance.

They undressed each other in the silence, hands and mouths seeking, bodies entwining as they fell to the bed. The mate bond

snaked around Peigi's heart as Stuart began to love her, a bond
she gathered to her with gladness.

The last of the chains of fear and loneliness fell away, and
Peigi welcomed Stuart with love, wrapping herself in the mate of
her heart.

EPILOGUE

How all the Shifters from the far ends of the country managed to arrive in time for the full-moon ceremony, Stuart didn't know, but come they did.

Bowman and Kenzie from North Carolina with Kenzie's formidable uncle, plus a Fae woman who stayed near him. The entire Morrissey clan from Austin, along with Liam's trackers: Spike, Ellison, and Ronan and his mate and extended family. Tiger came with his mate, Carly, their baby son, Seth, and the wild young tiger woman he'd rescued. Mason McNaughton and his brothers brought their mates, including Jasmine, the woman who owned the haunted house.

Jaycee and Dimitri traveled with Kendrick's family, and Angus and Tamsin had hitched a ride with them. From Montana came Zander, the giant polar bear who was a healer, with his mate Rae, her Guardian's Sword glinting on her back.

Of course, the entire population of the Las Vegas Shiftertown showed up to make sure Peigi and Reid got themselves mated. The members of Eric's household, Graham's, and Nell's mingled, with Diego's brother Xavier pairing up once more with Lindsey, a lynx Feline.

Ben had stepped through the ley line earlier that day, emerging in Kurt's basement, to that Lupine's supreme annoyance. Ben had softened the blow by bringing Kurt a keg of *dokk alfar* ale.

The *karmsyern* was coming along, Ben assured Stuart. Tricky, but doable. Cian was proving a good host, and Ben, to his surprise, found he was enjoying the visit.

"Not forever, though," he said, fondly taking in the vast dry desert running northward out of Shiftertown, the bright sky, the Shifters already partying hard. "I like this crazy, fucked-up human world."

Stuart had to agree.

Cubs ran everywhere, with Peigi's and Stuart's bunch pleased to act as hosts. Noelle told the story again and again of how Peigi and Stuart fought valiantly inside Faerie and how she and Matt and Kyle had helped rescue them.

Stuart barely saw Peigi all day, as she was pulled from one family to the other, congratulated, hugged, kissed. She laughed, and wept too, discovering how many Shifters from multiple Shiftertowns had her in their thoughts.

Eric had performed the sun ceremony earlier that day, completing the first half of the mating ritual. Peigi had been whisked away immediately afterward by Nell, Cassidy, Iona, and Misty for whatever female bonding they did for the rest of the afternoon.

As much as Stuart longed to be with Peigi—in private, celebrating their own way—he didn't see her again until the full moon was well up, and the Shifters gathered in their circles for the second part of the ceremony, the most important one.

Dylan had taken the opportunity during the down time, of course, to ask Stuart all about what had gone on in Faerie and about Ben and the *karmsyern*. Plus whether Cian would be amenable to form an alliance with him. The *hoch alfar* would move on Shifters sooner or later, and if the *hoch alfar* had a Tuil Erdannan on their side ... Things could be bad indeed.

Stuart was all for strategizing, but today, Peigi took precedence. Dylan's mate, Glory, came for him while he and Stuart were talking on Peigi's back porch, and to Stuart's surprise, Dylan left with her abruptly, saying they'd have plenty of time to discuss things later.

As the night began to cool, the moon became bright enough to cast sharp shadows. The sky was cloudless, stars pricking out in thick clusters. Venus, brightest planet in the darkness, glowed like a white candle near the horizon.

Peigi emerged from the house in a white dress that hugged her beautiful curves and showed off her legs. A multicolored jacket kept her from the cold, and her dark hair held a circlet of hothouse roses, courtesy of Misty's flower shop.

Stuart didn't know if the ladies had spent all afternoon and evening dressing Peigi, but the result was worth it. Peigi was beautiful in sloppy T-shirts and jeans, and she was stunning in the form-fitting dress that revealed the complete beauty of her.

He couldn't say a word as she joined him in front of Eric, his mouth dry.

Fortunately, only Eric had to speak. Shifters didn't make vows or promises—all that would be done once they were mated and could remember how to talk after the ensuing mating frenzy.

The Shifters formed circles around them, the general population of Shiftertown and visitors in the outer one, the inner filled with their closest friends—Diego and Cassidy, Eric and Iona, Graham and Misty, Nell and her family, and of course, the cubs.

Noelle kept throwing up her hands and dancing. Donny tried to calm her, which would last about thirty seconds, before she started again. The younger cubs, loving to see Noelle cut loose, imitated her. So did Matt and Kyle, those two yelling at the tops of their voices.

Finally Graham bellowed, "Let him get on with it!" and the cubs at long last quieted enough for Eric to step forward and raise his hands.

"Let me join in the voices I've heard all day," Eric

announced, "and proclaim to Peigi and Stuart Reid—*It's about time!*"

Laughter roared across the circles of Shifters. Even Tiger, who rarely laughed out loud, wore a broad smile.

Stuart cleared his throat. "I guess they've been expecting this," he said in Peigi's ear.

She joined in the laughter. "Could be."

Eric raised his hands again, and some quietness settled. "Stuart Reid and Peigi, who have become the dearest friends to Shiftertown that we could hope for ... Under the Mother Goddess ... *I proclaim you as mates.*"

He shouted the last, and the Shifters erupted into cheering, snarling, howling, the humans among them making no less noise.

Stuart found himself hauled aloft, and Peigi too, on the shoulders of Cormac, Graham, Eric, and anyone who joined in. The cubs danced and hollered, and soon Peigi and Stuart's six cubs were carried around as well. Peigi laughed as she caught little Kevin and held him safely against her.

Then the party truly got started.

The Shifters had never done much in the way of hugging with Stuart, always uncertain of him as a creature of Faerie, but that changed tonight. Probably lots of alcohol helped, but Stuart found himself hauled into embrace after embrace, from male Shifters and females alike, even Graham.

"You did good," Graham thundered into his ear as he squashed Stuart in a hug. "For a fucked-up, creepy dark Fae shit."

"So did you," Stuart said, thumping Graham on the back. "For an asshole Lupine."

Graham bellowed laughter and released Stuart to swing Peigi off her feet.

As was tradition, the mated couple danced along with the Shifters, until the Shifters were in a riotous enough condition that the couple could slip away, unnoticed, and finally find some time alone.

Peigi and Stuart ended up in the kitchen of their house, no lights burning, Shiftertown ferociously loud outside. Music blared, Shifters danced, or chased each other, or caught mating frenzy and ducked into the shadows. Nell had taken charge of their cubs, she sending Stuart a knowing smile.

The first ten minutes they spent alone were devoted to kissing. Fierce, passionate kisses that had Stuart's hands inside Peigi's jacket, molding to the curves of her breasts.

Peigi responded by dragging open his pants and closing her hand around his hard cock.

Stuart wasn't certain of the details after that. Clothes left their body and fell to the floor, marking their path down the hall to the bedroom.

The Shifter ladies had enjoyed themselves in here too. Rose petals were everywhere, as well as garlands hanging from the bed, walls—anywhere they could be hung. For luck, Stuart recognized. And fertility. Everyone wanted cubs to come from this night.

Peigi's mate frenzy boiled high, and Stuart's matched it. They were naked as fast as they could be, falling on the bed together in laughter.

Stuart slid inside her, groaning with it, no more mirth.

He gazed down at the mate of his heart, at her glorious eyes and tender smile, and gave himself over to her. He drove into her, her body meeting his, their breaths mingling, cries echoing.

Peigi, my mate, my heart.

I love you.

Their frenzy wound up to the highest peak, Stuart burning with the brightest pleasure of his life, then dropped them together, sweating, breathless, laughing again.

Loving.

Always.

Mates.

———

PEIGI WOKE AT DAWN, TANGLED IN BLANKETS AND STUART. She rubbed her eyes, groaned, and closed them again.

A kiss touched her mouth. "Morning, love," Stuart said gently.

"Don't sound so chipper," Peigi mumbled. She dragged her eyes open again. "I'm *sore*."

"Good." Stuart's smile made his eyes sparkle. "So am I. I wonder why?"

"Wild sex. At a guess." Peigi chuckled, deciding soreness was a small price to pay for a night of wonderful passion. "Want coffee?"

"Eventually." Stuart pressed a kiss to her breast. "After I get enough of looking at you."

"You've always been so sweet to me."

His brows went up. "Really? The scary, kick-ass *dokk alfar* who can teleport and make iron into metal rain is *sweet*?"

"Yeah. You are." Peigi rumpled his hair. "I've always known you had a big heart."

Stuart dropped a kiss to the corner of her mouth. "Not nearly as big as yours, love. Nowhere near."

"I'll debate that." Peigi met his kiss and indulged herself in the taste of him.

When they finished, Stuart lay down against her, his arm across her abdomen. The quietness of the early morning soothed her. Bands of first sunlight leaked through the half-closed blinds, showing her that the gray rain had gone for good, and desert blue sky had returned.

It was quiet outside, which meant Shifters were sleeping off whatever they'd done last night—dancing, imbibing, mating. Mating frenzy was catching.

"Stuart," Peigi said after a long, comfortable time. "About the mate bond."

"Mmm." Stuart burrowed against her. "What about it?"

"I formed it for you a while ago." Some Shifters worried about achieving it with their mates, but Peigi had never been concerned, always knowing for certain what was in her heart for Stuart. "When I first moved here, and you were there for me. Surprised me, but there it was."

Stuart raised himself on his elbows to stare down at her. "Really?" He seemed more interested than surprised.

"Yes." Peigi touched his face. "Why do you think I was willing to sacrifice my blood so you could open a gate?" She touched her chest. "I felt it—the mate bond. The gift of the Goddess."

Mate bonds could form whether Shifters were mated or not. It had nothing to do with the mating ceremony—which was a social tradition—and everything to do with the bonding of love and a mystical union.

"I'm glad." Stuart's voice went soft. He stroked his thumb across her shoulder. "Because I formed it for you. Around about the same time."

Peigi's eyes widened. "You did?"

"Yep. For a Shifter. Imagine my shock."

"Are you sure?"

Stuart's grin warmed his eyes. "Very sure. *Dokk alfar* form mate bonds. It's something of Fae that got transferred to Shifters. I was stuck in this world, alone, and then you walked into my life. You looked at me, and boom." He pressed his fist to his heart. "Mate bond. Why do you think I kept volunteering to stay with you?"

Peigi's jaw went slack. "You never told me."

"You never told *me*."

"I was afraid you'd run. At least, as it was, I could be with you. But I think we both knew."

"Possibly," he said, his smile unwavering.

"I love you, Stuart."

"I love *you*, Pegs." Stuart's eyes warmed as he slid his arm around her. "Mate of my heart."

It was a long time before they got around to coffee.

———

When Stuart led Peigi out of the bedroom much later, both of them finally dressed—which had taken a while—her heart was full.

Her gorgeous mate walked beside her down the hall, the two of them laughing like cubs, and she loved him. She shared the mate bond with him, and they had six beautiful cubs in their lives. And if the Goddess was good to them, more would come.

Peigi had the feeling they would. And, as Stuart had said, they could try every day and every which way to make certain of it.

By Stuart's expression as he halted to kiss her—again—he too had found peace. His life, which had been close to a living hell for fifty years, was now eased. He'd found home.

As Stuart and Peigi walked into the kitchen, they were confronted by a line of cubs, Noelle standing slightly in front of the others, a piece of notebook paper in her hands.

"I already signed that," Stuart said.

The coffee pot was percolating—one of the cubs must have figured out how to work it. Or maybe Nell had come over and started it. The first cup would be interesting.

"This is a different contract," Noelle said with an official air. "This is an agreement we came up with last night, at Nell's house. She didn't help with this one—we did it ourselves."

"Ourselves," Kevin repeated proudly.

Noelle cleared her throat and read. "We, the cubs of Peigi and Stuart, are petitioning you to be allowed to stop calling you Peigi and Stuart." She peeled her gaze from the page, her eyes filled with nervousness. "We want to call you Mom and Dad."

"Oh." Peigi couldn't speak, couldn't breathe. Stuart was likewise still.

"We all signed it." Noelle held up the page, showing six signatures, some more scraggly and awkward than the others. "We're in agreement."

Donny watched them worriedly. "Okay, Peigi and Stuart? I mean, Mom and Dad?"

Peigi sank to her knees, her eyes filling with tears. "Of course you can," she said, her voice barely working. "Stuart?"

His hand was on her shoulder, he leaning down to them. His voice was low, gentle, the hard warrior becoming the warmhearted man Peigi had always known he was. "I wouldn't have it any other way."

"Yay!" Kevin cried.

Noelle flung aside the paper and burst into tears. Peigi opened her arms, and Stuart knelt next to her, the two of them gathering in the cubs as they rushed them.

Peigi's heart sang, the mate bond in accompaniment, as she held her cubs, kissing, hugging, laughing, crying, Stuart beside her, her life complete.

THANK YOU FOR READING! I WAS THRILLED TO WRITE PEIGI and Reid's book at last.

To stay up-to-date on upcoming Shifters Unbound novels, join my newsletter at:

http://eepurl.com/47kLL

or visit my website:

http://www.jenniferashley.com

ALSO BY JENNIFER ASHLEY

ABOUT THE AUTHOR

New York Times bestselling and award-winning author Jennifer Ashley has written more than 100 published novels and novellas in romance, urban fantasy, mystery, and historical fiction under the names Jennifer Ashley, Allyson James, and Ashley Gardner. Jennifer's books have been translated into more than a dozen languages and have earned starred reviews in *Publisher's Weekly* and *Booklist*. When she isn't writing, Jennifer enjoys playing music (guitar, piano, flute), reading, hiking, and building dollhouse miniatures.

More about Jennifer's books can be found at
http://www.jenniferashley.com

To keep up to date on her new releases, join her newsletter here:
http://eepurl.com/47kLL

Made in the USA
Las Vegas, NV
13 November 2021

34382033R00156